'WHAT SO CURRAN?

'My love! – Linda – He sprang towards her. She backed, blazing with the contempt of a wild thing caught unawares.

'Go away,' she said. 'Don't dare touch me. I despise – *hate* you, Ben Curran –'

'What is the matter with you? What do you mean?'

'You never came.' Like ice the words cut him. 'Even when I wrote you never answered.

'It was a nice game for you, wasn't it, two women at once?' Her lip curled momentarily. 'What sort of man are you, Ben Curran? Or aren't you one at all? Are you just a greedy creature out for fame and gold ready to trick any poor innocent stupid enough to believe in you –'

She broke off, shivering. 'Go away. Get out of my sight.'

# Heronsmere

**MARY WILLIAMS**

SPHERE BOOKS LIMITED
London and Sydney

First published in Great Britain by
William Kimber & Co. Ltd 1983
Copyright © 1983 by Mary Williams
Published by Sphere Books Ltd 1986
30–32 Gray's Inn Road, London WC1X 8JL

Printed and bound in Great Britain by
Cox & Wyman Ltd, Reading

# Contents

To the memory of dearest Bill

# Introduction

No house stands there any more. The wide expanse of wooded moor now thrives untrammelled by trespassing feet where once the stately mansion reigned.

Heronsmere is gone. But bird and fox, badger and other wild creatures have returned to their natural habitat.

Sanctuary.

In the spring thorn and may blossom foam by the spreading copse of wind-blown trees.

Nature has claimed its own.

The orderly paths and terraces of the flower gardens have now crumbled, leaving only a few stones as relics where streams ripple through curling bracken to the valley.

At the cottage near the rim of the hill the warden lives, keeping watch that no shot is fired or wild flowers plundered from their beds. On stormy days the booming of waves and salt tang of brine is carried on the freshening air. Sometimes, through a quiet night, an owl calls from an ancient summer-house — the only man-made relic of a bygone era. At all times of the year gulls dip and rise again — white wings silvered against the light.

The ghosts of past passion and tragedy have long since been exorcised, although occasional visitors to the preserve may have imagined the bent shadow of a woman watching from the trees — one hand enclosed round a stick. This could have been of course merely a trick of light and shade — a momentary illusion cast by the movement of branches in the whispering wind. The impression, whatever the cause, has never been frightening; a little sad, perhaps, like a film of cloud passing the face of the moon. But with each new morning the sadness is gone, replaced by fulfilment of the earth's natural heritage, bred from earliest times before the first Celts trod the wide acres of ancient Cornwall.

# Part One

BEN

# *1*

## 1815

When he was old enough to notice the shining deep blue-black quality of Cornish cliffs washed cold and clear from sea or rain, he saw profiles of elemental giants reaching to the sullen sky. On spring mornings as great waves crashed, taking loads of sand with their ebb tide, he visioned monolithic elemental shapes in the boulders left behind. The ever-changing pattern of the shore — of dark weed, rocks, secret pools and silvered bone of fish, bird, and animal carcases torn from the ocean bed — presented to him a whole new pattern of life, somehow to be salvaged and given new strange birth.

He was a miner's son; the youngest of five, and in appearance and character quite unlike the rest — tall and sturdy, with tousled fair hair, wide jaw, and eyes more Nordic than Celt — clear, ice-blue eyes, lacking the fiery gleam of his brothers'. Through him — bred of a certain Danish forbear, who'd been wrecked off the coast near St Ives generations ago, a whole new twist to the family character was to be re-established. The Currans had been in mining for centuries, working their lives out first as streamers, then tunnelling along dark levels for precious copper or tin, but as tut workers only, and dying mostly in their forties, the servants of crafty shareholders and adventurers, earning at best an average wage of £2 a month.

Ben Curran was not set in such a mould.

He meant to be master of life, and of himself.

He started first with a small pocket-knife which he

sharpened to a fierce edge on a stone. Wood was his early
medium. He was only six then, so not yet due to be employed
with other children at the surface of Red Bell mine. In the
meantime, until his seventh birthday, he helped his hard-
worked mother about the cottage which was thatched and
had been built by his grandfather and helpmates during one
night, which had made it, according to law, forever the
family's own. The walls were of cob, the roof of thatching
reed. There were only two rooms, an upper and lower storey.
The latter was divided into two, and shared by his parents
and the five sons. In summer the air was stuffy, and in the
winter cold. But the hearth below was large, with a chimney
seat, a trivet to hold the kettle and baking iron, and sufficient
room for bellows and a fork to stir the glowing turf fire.

Outside the shack was a fenced-in patch of ground where
potatoes and greens were grown to feed the family, and house
a goat in a small stye. The cess-pit was only ten yards away,
towards the coast, and when the wind blew from the sea the
smell could be nauseating. The family were used to it, the
menfolk, too tired after long shifts down the mine to notice.

But Ben, with his quick mind and cold far-seeing eyes,
although a mere child was already searching for another
different and more edifying environment. The sight of his
mother's tired face — lined and irritable — depressed him.
Her constant sighs and grumblings when his father and
brothers were absent, sent him scurrying from his numerous
tasks up the moors to the hill top where the air was sweet,
tangy with the scent of heather, sea and brine. On one side,
in the distance, smoke belched from Red Bell where the
pumping rod rose and fell like a giant's arm against the sky.

Occasionally he'd watch the Bal maidens tramping wearily
home from their long day 'bucking' and dressing ore. Sometimes they sang, but not often. The sight of them cast a
shadow over his lusty young spirit. He would never be like
them — never. And as though the devil was after him in such
moments, he'd turn and run wildly in the other direction to a
spot overlooking a lush valley where the great house stood.
Sir Geoffrey Penherrion's home, the gracious Heronsmere.

Sir Geoffrey was the largest shareholder in Red Bell. Ben envied him, not because of his wealth, but because he could have beautiful things about him, and collections of precious treasures from abroad. He knew this was so; he'd heard it from the lips of an old woman who had once worked there as a servant, and had recently died.

Fine carved things of ivory, she'd said, statues studded with pearls and jewels. Well, one day Ben meant to have such things. Not jewels perhaps — but treasures. And though he couldn't buy them he'd make them himself.

So he collected wood and stone, anything that might be of use to him when he was older, and stored them in his own wooden box near the hearth.

His mother was amused in her grim way; but so long as he did for her what she asked, she didn't complain.

And in secret, Ben began to cut and carve.

He started with a piece of old apple-wood, from which the simplified but curiously natural shape of a mouse eventually emerged. The image stimulated him to do others in different poses and positions, either crouched with head alert, listening, or half sitting up on haunches, tiny hands holding a nut. After the mouse he tried a small rabbit, but being under life-size it lacked character. So, disgusted, he laid his tool aside for a few days and when there was time searched the moors for new ideas and fresh wood to dry. It was then, one quiet spring afternoon that he heard the bird singing. He looked up sharply, and there it was — a blackbird piping from the branch of a wind-blown stunted tree newly feathered with frail green buds. Delight stirred Ben's blood. He ran home with the fresh breeze singing in his ears, and for several days recalling the perfect lines from delicate beak to throat and breast — the shining contours of glistening wings and tail, he chipped and worked and polished. The result was sufficiently pleasing for him to show his father and elder brother Nat.

They were tired and grimed from the long day down Red Bell, and his father spoke more sharply than he'd intended. 'A bird all right. Clear 'nuff to see that,' he said. 'But time's

comin' when you'll be seein' few of 'em. Best start learnin' to
use y'r hammer, boy. More sense f'r the future there.'

Disappointment, like a cold stone, filled Ben's whole
being.

In two months he was due to start at Red Bell. Working for
his mother — the brief freedom he'd had following an hour's
primary lessons at the Church School — would be over. He'd
be just one of the crowd destined for servitude in darkness
and dust, damp, and the stagnation of the hungry mine. And
he couldn't — he wouldn't do it. Wild thoughts stirred him.
Perhaps he'd run away to sea. Perhaps — but then he'd be
discovered, he realised, beaten perhaps, and sent back for
another belting by his father. James Curran was not a cruel
man. He had seldom used a hand against any of his sons, but
at rare times discipline had to be enforced because families
like his had only one chance of livelihood — tin.

*Tin!*

How young Ben had grown to hate the sound of the word.

Shortly following the episode of the bird, he wandered
down a dangerous rocky path to Hook's Cove, a secret haunt
of wild creatures; seals, gulls, and shags standing beautifully
poised on jutting rocks with their slender necks and beaks
lifted high above the waves. The sand in the narrow inlet was
dotted with glistening boulders encrusted with limpets and
barnacles. Small pools remained when the tide receded,
filled with tiny darting fish. Caught between the stones were
thick lumps of green and black weed, entangled often by
lumps of driftwood.

Here the young boy collected curious specimens of teak
and mahogany torn from bygone wrecks. There were, as
well, strangely shaped, withered, dripping roots of plant-
growth long dead, that held a curious semblance of prehistoric and imaginary creatures in miniature. Ben's mind
seethed with excitement as he viewed them from every angle,
envisaging their future use. Here, a macabre elemental
creature, bent and symbolic of the cave's secrets — an old
troll simply carved; there, a sleek fish rising from the waves,
or a mermaid with flying hair. Silvered bones, whiter than

ivory, reminded him of minute gleaming castles that could one day, possibly, be built to a larger scale. The gleaming pearl-quality of deserted shells held the lustre of gems — gems equalling the richness of those hoarded in Heronsmere.

Stones, too, had their fascination — perhaps the strongest and most practical of all — because he knew that when he was older and stronger, and had somehow managed to obtain tools, he would chip and hammer — not for tin or copper as was expected — but at shining dark granite and marble, creating his own fantastic monolithic designs, creatures already half evolved on the sea-shore.

That afternoon, still in a rebellious mood following the unsympathetic reaction of his father the evening before, and badly needing understanding from someone whose imagination reached further than shafts, adits, dank levels, shifts, the miserable ceaseless toil of hammering and sweating in dangerous conditions underground, he scrambled back up the path bordering a narrow rocky ravine, and made his way half a mile across the moor in the Penjust direction.

There, in a half hidden fold of the moor a crabbed old lady, Martha Crane, reputed to be a witch, lived with her young granddaughter Elfrida. The stone cottage, though small, was furnished in a different manner than other dwellings of that type, with antique furniture, brass, and shining objects of coral and glass arranged on carefully dusted shelves. The old lady, the widow of a seaman, had never lost pride in her appearance, and from the time she had taken in her daughter's child, a mere baby when the mother died, she had seen to it that the little girl was neatly, and sometimes extravagantly dressed. None knew who the father had been, nor exactly from what source Mistress Crane's income came. It was true enough that Martha was a competent spinner, and never lacking a market for her craft; it was also not denied that she was in some way under Sir Geoffrey's protection. Cottages for miners were scarce, but he had never allowed the old woman to be evicted. Some said she had laid an enchantment upon him but none voiced the suggestion openly, and everyone who saw her little girl was awed by her beauty. She had exquisite features, large, slightly tilted eyes of bluish grey sometimes changing to green, and thick shining hair of so pale a gold it was almost white.

Martha was strict, seldom allowing the child any contact with natives or inhabitants of the village Zelah, a mile away. But it was stated on good authority that at certain times of the moon — or on 'feast days' or other periods of celebration, the young girl was attired as richly as a princess, with fine lace trimming her petticoats and blue satin gown. At such times she wore velvet slippers showing silver buckles. Cobwebbed lace filmed her golden curls, and her slender dimpled arms glowed pearl-pink through net mittens. Unless wearing a white apron she was seldom allowed to feed the two white goats that provided milk for the strange couple. But birds and wild animals came to her hand. Such idiosyncrasies merely emphasised a reputation for the two being in league with strange powers, though none could prove it. The most suspicious of country people in the vicinity whispered that the fine lace and material woven at the cottage was done at night by the devil himself.

Others, of a more practical nature, laughed the suggestion to scorn, referring slyly to the Squire's purse-bag that could so easily afford provision of thread for spinning and weaving, giving credit, as well, to old Martha's skill and hard work in making worthy use of it.

The Currans had forbidden Ben ever to visit the cottage. But for some time he had done so at rare intervals. Although she was only a child, Elfrida's beauty entranced him.

On this certain occasion, the impulse to see her was overwhelming. He sped, lightly as a young fox through the curled ferns and heather like a prisoner released from tormenting confinement. The sweet air of young summer fanned his face. His spirits bounded. The goats, half startled, raised their heads sharply as he approached. The next moment Elfrida appeared at the door. She was wearing a yellow dress with a white frilled apron. For a second or two she did not appear a child at all — but as some beauteous creature from

an old legend told to him at school. The silver-gold hair was a
halo round her small face. One day, he thought, he'd make
an image of her so she could always be his — a possession, like
the tiny porcelain figures on her grandmother's mantelpiece
so treasured by old Martha. The idea was awesome. He
paused abruptly, and stood facing her as she came towards
him down the pebbled path. During that brief interim of
time, both, despite their youth, sensed dimly that their
futures were already somehow secretly entwined.

Then the spell was broken. Mistress Martha's aged face
under a lace cap, poked round the door.

'If you'm come to visit, boy,' she called sharply, 'then do et
in a proper fashion an' come in. An' you, Elfrida — doan' you
dare mess up that dress with they long ferns.'

Elfrida smiled, lifted her chin, and offered her hand with a
curiously adult gesture to Ben.

'Are you going to have tea with us?' she asked politely. Her
voice was clear, her tones precise for a country girl.

The young boy nodded. Martha Crane's teas were good.
He'd eaten there once before, and was already anticipating
the delicious cream, and sweetmeats baked on her own
hearth.

For a few minutes, when he'd entered the cosy living room,
he was comparatively tongue tied — not only by the
ornaments and brightly polished copper, or by the numerous
strange curios and foreign shells shining in the fading sunlight, but by the company of old Martha herself. Over her
black velvet gown she wore a white satin embroidered apron
tied at the waist. Her bodice was half-covered by inumerable
strings of many coloured glass beads, and the lace cap tied
under her lean pointed chin, by white ribbons.

She must be very old, Ben thought — as old as God — or
the Devil. Her nose almost met her chin, and she bore an
uncanny resemblance to a piece of drift-wood he'd collected
that week, except for her finery of course. He'd never seen
such clothes before. But he knew she was less frightening
than she appeared; and when she repeated Elfrida's invitation, he smiled and said, 'Thank you, ma'am.'

The meal was lavishly tempting — surprisingly so for peasant folk of the vicinity — with heavy cake, fruit tart and a liberal amount of 'clouted' cream.

After this incident young Ben was a frequent visitor to the forbidden premises. Once or twice he brought specimens of carving, including simplified versions of a fox and badger. He showed also a strange troll-like creature made from driftwood that caused Martha to exclaim, 'Where d'ye get th' ideas from, boy? Books?'

And Ben shook his head. 'We don't have books, ma'am — not at home.'

'So it's all there, in that young head of yours is et?' She ruffled his fair curls with her bony fingers. 'Then you see you go on with et,' the old lady told him. 'There's talent in thee, an' talent's not to be buried in hell-holes like Red Bell. Next time the Fair comes — Camborne or Penjust way, take them along boy, and I warrant thee'll get more for them than you do think.'

Mistress Crane's advice set Ben's ambitions alight.

A fair! he'd never thought of that; never dreamed of selling things he'd made, or even imagined anyone except old Martha and Elfrida would like them.

For the next few days he was quiet and more subdued than usual as he helped his mother at the cottage. In his spare time he stopped rambling about the countryside or searching the coves and beaches, and worked tirelessly in the small shed built by his father at the back of the dwelling where the goat nibbled and foraged about the sparse moorland furze. He carved the animal recumbent, and also standing with her neck arched upwards for shoots from a stunted wind-blown tree. Pink thrift grew thick between the boulders sloping downwards towards the sea. Cream clouds floated across a paper-pale sun-washed sky. Already the glint of early bluebells shimmered through the tender green fronds of curling young bracken.

It was as though a whole exciting new world held him spellbound. He worked with such energy, that sweat drenched his shirt and bare brown legs. Already the shadow of Red Bell

had faded. If he could sell his own creations he need no
longer fear a future down the dark mine. One day perhaps
fine ladies would have his carvings on their shelves and chests
– ladies like Lady Penherrion of Heronsmere. And later on,
when he was quite grown up, he would make something big
– something grander and finer even, than the great
boulders of the cliffs and moor – giant figures hammered
and carved from granite. His father wouldn't be cross then.
He'd make money, lots of it, so his mother wouldn't have to
work so hard. And how pleased Elfrida would be. Like a fairy
dancing, a dainty creature of the elements, she invaded his
thoughts at odd moments, even through his concentration.
When he was a man perhaps they'd get married and live in a
hall as splendid as Heronsmere, where she could trail about
in pretty clothes all day and have servants to look after her.

Yes. One day, somehow, he was sure he and Elfrida would
be together.

So he worked on until his young muscles ached, and the
wooddust half blinded him. He wrapped his treasures in his
piece of old cloth and went back to the cottage.

'Where've you bin, Ben?' his mother asked, too weary to
notice his bundle. 'Wanderin' I s'pose, as usual? An' with all I
have to do, and your brothers and dad likely to be in any
moment—'

'Sorry,' Ben muttered.

'Well then, hurry up an' help me get them plates on the
table.'

Ben hid his treasures, and for the rest of the late afternoon
and evening devoted himself zealously to tasks about the
cottage.

The following week Penjust Fair opened.

Without saying anything to his mother Ben slipped away
when he'd collected wood for her, attended the turf fire,
carried swill to the pig, and taken washing out for her to hang
on the line. The pig pail was heavy for his youthful limbs, but
ambition and excitement fired him, and he had no conscience at all in escaping parental control. With him he had
his bundle of treasures, and a stout stick to clear the brambles

and undergrowth across the moor. He followed a narrow
tangled route used by sheep and shepherds that led straight
to Penjust, cutting off the bends in the high lane above,
and a jutting headland of rocky cliff. The area was not
without dangers — there were dark overgrown pits of
deserted mine shafts to avoid, and pools of sucking black
bog at certain points where the track was lost. But in going
that way instead of by road he saved a mile and a half of
walking, making the distance only three miles instead of
almost five.

When he reached the small town the square and streets
were already busy with early crowds.

Stalls displayed wares of every description, including
clothing, boots, handwoven cloth and lace, saddlery, quack
medicines, and a variety of pots and pans. There was a
special booth for refreshments, where the gingerbread was a
main attraction. A waxwork theatre had been erected at one
corner, and a portion of the main street had been fenced off
for farmers selling and buying cattle. A small group of girls
and women stood nearby waiting to be hired, and a dwarf
was performing acrobatics to the jeers and applause of a
gathering crowd. Clutching his precious parcel close, Ben
pushed his way through the medley of boots and rustling
skirts. Once a small dog darted from under a female cloak
and nipped his ankle. He gave a yell; the owner, who was
stout and belligerent-looking with a complexion as ruddy as
her crimson attire — probably the wife of a well-to-do farmer
— shrieked and kicked the little boy's behind with the toe of
her hard boot. Ben fell, scrambled up again and pushed
ahead. At last, tired and grimed, he reached a haberdashery
at the corner of a cobbled alley that was quieter than the
main thoroughfare.

He went into the store. An elderly man wearing a faded
dark green coat over a yellow waistcoat and cream stock, was
examining a small snuff box through a magnifying glass. He
looked up sharply as Ben entered. Staring at him the little
boy noticed that the shop keeper had very beady bright eyes
under thick bristly white eyebrows.

'Well, boy?' he said, 'well? What is it? Can't you see I'm busy?'

Ben reached up and heaved the bag on to the counter. 'Things,' he said. 'My things — I've made 'em, mister, an' Mistress Crane she said they were good.'

The old man frowned.

'And who's Mistress Crane? Never heard of her I haven't, nor where she bides, or comes from.'

Ben did his best to explain, while the frown on the man's face gradually lifted to an expression of surprise.

'Mean to say you've walked all that way?'

Ben nodded. 'Soon I'll be goin' down the mine an' that'll be much wuss. If you could sell my things, mister, p'raps I wouldn' have to. See?'

The old eyes narrowed for a moment, then the rather cracked shrill voice said with a hint of irritability in it, 'Very well then, I'll tek a look. But sellin' things isn't easy, boy, unless it's food, and stuff them Cheapjacks fool folks with.' His fingers fumbled with the string that Ben had tied so laboriously round the bundle; the next minute several of the simple animal shapes were laid one by one on the counter, including a mouse, otter, badger, bird, and the curious interpretation of a witch-like creature carved from drift-wood.

Ben waited anxiously as the old man's eyes travelled from one to the other, giving nothing away, allowing no quiver of expression to betray his opinion.

The pause to the little boy, seemed interminable. He could hardly bear to breathe. 'I can do better things than these — bigger,' he said at last, 'if you liked 'em I could, honest, mister.'

'Could you indeed?'

'Yes,' Ben answered. 'An' if you *don't* like them, I'll — I'll find someone—' Doubt suddenly engulfed him, intensified by hunger and exhaustion.

'Who said I didn't like them?' The old voice was suddenly sharp. 'I like them very much, boy. They're good. Very good for such a little 'un. But sellin' them — that's a different matter—'

Ben swallowed hard, and was about to reach for the otter when there was a tinkle behind him from the door, a click of the latch, followed by a rustle of skirts and light footsteps accompanied by the tapping of a stick.

Ben jerked round. Coming towards them was a lady with a delicate white-gloved hand resting on a silver knobbed stick. She wore a tall crowned hat trimmed with a profusion of bows and feathers. Her skirts were frilled under a deep blue velvet cape. Light filtering through a side window of the store showed that she was young, and gentle-looking. Dark wings of hair framed a pale face. Her grey eyes were luminous and rather sad, although the lips were smiling. From one glance at her, Ben was awed. She was obviously very rich. Not beautiful, like Elfrida, and of course she wouldn't be able to dance, because the poor young lady was lame.

He was still staring when the haberdasher, bowing, exclaimed in exceedingly polite tones. 'Good morning, m' lady — a great honour to be sure. An' what can I be doin' for you, m'lady—?' Remembering Ben suddenly he wagged a gnarled finger at the little boy. 'Away with you now, child. An' best take your things with ye.'

The little boy was about to reach for his bag and animals when a sweet voice said quietly but firmly, 'No, no. I would like to have a look at them first.' She smiled down on Ben. 'Did you really carve these figurines, child?'

Ben nodded.

The lady picked up the mouse and otter, and her interest deepened. 'But they're — they're quite delightful,' she exclaimed. 'Simple, but clever. I like them.'

Ben's eyes widened in astonishment. A gasp of excitement swelled his young lungs. 'You do? Honest?'

As she bent further towards him he had a clear look at her face and discovered that although at first she'd appeared just nice but rather plain, she wasn't plain at all. Kindness and appreciation gave her a warmth and radiance that impelled him to say in a burst of gratitude, 'You can have one if you like.' He looked quickly at his selection, chose the otter and held it out in his grubby hand.

'This one lives near us—' he said breathlessly. 'Or a seal — if you'd rather have a seal—'

'I would like several,' the clear voice said. 'And of course I will pay you for them — if they are for sale; are they?'

Before he could reply the haberdasher interrupted, 'They're certainly for sale, ma'am — m'lady. This young man's goin' to mek many more for me, aren't you, boy?'

'Ben,' the child asserted. 'My name's Ben.'

'Hm. Yes. O'course it is. I know y'r name all right.'

Ben glowered momentarily. 'You didn't until now — not until I told you,' he said stubbornly.

'Well,' the young lady said brightly, 'there's no need to argue. You're called Ben. And where do you live? What's your other name?'

Ben did his best to explain, and the brief conversation ended by the elegant visitor saying, 'I think I know where you mean, and it's not so very far from my own home. I'm Marion, Sir Geoffrey Penherrion's daughter.'

'You mean — from that — that big place?'

She nodded, and took his hand, with her other still holding the otter. 'That makes us neighbours. And I'm very glad we've met, because I know many people who I'm sure will like your carvings and want to buy them. Even Mr Tregale—' Her eyes turned fleetingly to the shopkeeper. 'You'll be able to give a fair price for our young — sculptor's — work, won't you, Abel?'

Abel Tregale's head bobbed ingratiatingly, white whiskers quivering above his stock, his cheeks flushed rosy pink. 'Of course, ma'am — of course, I said so if you remember, m'lady. S'long as you like them I'm sure they're good—' He broke off, rubbing his hands together appreciatively.

'And what do you expect for these?' the quiet voice continued. 'More important still, what are you prepared to pay our young friend?'

After a short discussion between the two adults who were to set the pattern for Ben's future, the sum was fixed — a sum that left Ben at first too numbed by excitement and delight to

speak. Then, suddenly, after a considerable pause he exclaimed, 'So I won't have to go down Red Bell. I'll—' he
broke off, so lost in his dream, that Lady Marion thought at
first something was wrong.

'What's the matter?' she enquired. 'Was that troubling
you? The mine?'

He nodded, then contrarily shook his head.

'I just want to make things — these things,' pointing to
his bundle of carvings, 'and big, much much bigger.
Wood, and stone, and — and — there's stuff in Hooks'
Cove you wouldn' b'lieve. P'raps you'd come with me,
ma'am — one day. There's a path leading down, all rocky,
but I could show you—' Something he could not understand, a shadow, crossed her face, making him suddenly
silent.

'I'm sure you'll carve splendid things, Ben,' the gentle
voice said, 'and when you do — when you're old enough I'll
be one of the first to see. But at present you'll have to work
very hard, and I'll do all I can to help. Unfortunately—' she
glanced wryly at her stick, 'I don't think I'll be able to see your
cove, Ben, because of this wretched lame leg of mine. Unless
of course—' with a forced attempt at humour, 'I grow wings.
You may even be able to make me a pair. What do you
think?'

Ben did not know what to think. His young head was whirl-
ing. The sound of the Fair from outside, the chatter and
shouting, rattling of carts, laughter, and music intermingled
with occasional cursing and applause for the acrobats, rang
through his brain like the ceaseless refrain in some strange
dream. Everything, briefly, seemed to fade into a confused
blur before his eyes. The colour left his cheeks. He tried to
speak, but no words came. Then he heard the young lady
saying, 'Come along, Ben, you must have something to eat.
You look very tired. We'll find a coffee house and then you
can tell me more about yourself.'

The deal with the shopkeeper was settled. Lady Marion
bought all the carvings, and put several gold coins into her
reticule, saying, 'These are yours, Ben. I'll take care of them

for you until you get home. My man will drive you there when we've both had refreshment.'

Her cool slim hand enclosed the boy's. They went into the street where the coachman was already waiting to accompany her Ladyship to the Penherrion chaise. Quite soon they were deposited at the Green Lion, Penjust's most select hostelry. There, in a private room, Ben gradually relaxed. His eyes brightened; with the grime cleaned from his face and hands, and his hair combed from his wide forehead, he gave a fleeting momentary impression of the handsome man he might be one day. A wave of mixed emotions flooded Marion Penherrion's whole being. Although she was only eighteen she knew she had little hopes of marriage. Her lame foot which had been twisted at birth was a considerable impediment, and she had no pretensions to beauty. Some old man might be induced — or 'bribed' by her father, to offer his hand at some future date, but the thought was offensive to her, and she knew she would refuse. Therefore she would bear no child of her own. Perhaps, then, the matter of adoption might be accepted eventually by Sir Geoffrey. If so she would delight in encouraging young Ben's talent in every possible way. The very idea might appear, at first, outrageous. But Geoffrey Penherrion desperately wanted an heir. His one son, Ralph, had been a disastrous disappointment. After a wild period at Oxford, during which time he had been 'sent down' twice for outrageous behaviour including cheating at cards, he had died in a hunting accident following a drinking session the night before.

The shock had driven his wife Lady Henrietta to her bed, and her demise had followed a year later. Sir Geoffrey had not fretted for her unduly. Their union had been one of convenience rather than passion, and after the birth of Marion, the marriage bed had been a sterile affair. Thanks to her dowry, however, and the liberal fortune left behind, Heronsmore and the estate flourished. Penherrion was one of the richest men in all Cornwall, and his two mines, 'Red Bell' and 'Wheal Mary' lacked neither manpower, nor the wherewithal to construct and expand wherever tin or copper beckoned.

Still, except for his one girl — and a lame one at that — he had no legitimate heir to follow. And Sir Geoffrey was proud of his family. No man, after all, was immortal. It fretted him that when he was gone, there would be no Penherrion dynasty to perpetuate his name.

Perhaps — at this point Marion managed to curb such wild thoughts, putting her mind to more feasible and practical objectives. In Ben's creations she recognised a certain genius, which meant at least, that she would be able to show them to her friends, and hopefully get him orders. In this way, therefore — through a chance meeting, Ben's future was set, and the dreaded future planned for him at Red Bell averted.

From that day he never missed visiting any available fair, where his talent, combined with his good looks, earned him considerably more than was possible from surface working at the mine.

When he was thirteen he became apprenticed to a monumental mason near Truro, and his future career as a sculptor first took root. By then he was already five feet nine inches tall, broad shouldered, and startlingly handsome; his blue eyes had the far-seeing quality of his Danish forbears; his hair, from the Cornish sun and winds had become bleached to brightest gold. Although his skin was bronzed the fine hairs on hands and arms glistened almost white in the sunlight, holding a sheen that equalled the stones and wood he polished.

To his family he appeared a curiosity, almost an alien, although they were all grateful for the money he managed to bring home at regular intervals. His father James was awed, and because of it went out of his way to withhold praise. Deep down it seemed wrong to him that a mere boy could wheedle gold from rich folk — and shopkeepers too — just for picking bits of riff-raff from the sea shore and making images from them. Real animals were more to his liking, except snails and white rabbits that could mean ill-luck to a miner. Ben's brothers were secretly envious. Only his mother showed gratitude, never ceasing to wonder, those days, that she could have borne such a clever young giant of a son, and Ben's regret in leaving the clob cottage was only for her. His work, Elfrida, and his mother were all that really mattered to him. In that order.

Elfrida.

Her grandmother had died that year, early in 1821, and the girl, a year older than Ben, lived alone at the cottage, on the moor. She continued with her spinning and weaving, and whenever Ben saw her he became increasingly aware of her beauty, whether she was dressed in her best clothes or working gown and apron.

He called to see her on the afternoon before his departure for Truro. The autumn sunlight streaked slantwise across the moor, licking the gorse and brown crisp bracken to a patterned vista of gold and shadow.

She was busy about the small vegetable patch when he appeared. Her silver-pale hair hung loose about her shoulders over the shawl and blue cotton gown. She had a bucket on one arm, and from the weeds protruding from it and a spade stuck into the earth nearby, Ben knew she had been digging. It wasn't right, he thought with sudden indignation, for any girl so young and delicately made to have to work that way. Yet when she looked up, her face was radiant. Slender she might be, but during the last years childishness had changed to young developing maturity. Physically she appeared straight and strong as a young sapling tree.

Strange sensations stirred through Ben. A lump of longing rose in his throat. His affection for her had always been strong. But now he was leaving, knowing he might not see her again, for quite a long time, he wanted her suddenly not as a boy needing companionship, but as a permanent part of his existence. His whole body seemed to have hardened. For a moment he could not move. Then, after swallowing hard, he said bluntly, 'I'm off, Elfrida.'

'Off?' Her blue-green eyes widened. The petal lips opened slightly. He wanted to kiss her suddenly, not as he'd kissed her

once or twice before, but with his mouth pressing hers hard,
drawing her sweetness deep into his very being. Yet he did
not move.

'To Truro,' he said. 'Master Saul Jacob's. I told you didn'
I? I'm going to work there. So you'll not be seein' me for − I
dunno how long, Elfrida.'

'Oh. I see.' She smiled brightly. 'Well − I know you'll be a
fine mason, Ben.'

'I'll be more'n that, one day,' Ben told her, tearing his gaze
from hers. 'An' that's a promise.'

'I don't need promises. And you don't need to give me any.
What you do, you'll do for yourself. That's what my grandma
said, and she was right. You'll be yourself always, Ben.
You're that kind.'

Her apparent nonchalance briefly angered him.

'So that's all you care. Just hullo and goodbye. Haven't I
mattered at all to you then?'

'Of course you've mattered. We've bin friends, haven't we?'

'Some time we'll be more'n that,' he asserted. 'You just
wait. I'll be back. And there'll be gold in my pocket. For you
and me, Elfrida.'

At first he thought she was going to laugh, but only a smile
touched her lips − shy, tentative, and quite without guile.

'I'll be here, Ben,' she remarked gently.

''Cos we're sweethearts?'

She stiffened. 'No. If we were you wouldn't be leaving.'

'One day though?' he persisted.

'Perhaps.'

He frowned, stifling an impulse to shake or slap her, make
contact somehow. She looked away suddenly. 'Please go,
Ben. Goodbyes are so horrid.'

The commonplace remark brought him back to earth suddenly.

'Goodbye, Elfrida.'

She turned. He was smiling again, the old boyish smile she
knew so well. She went forward and touched his hand lightly.
'I will miss you, Ben. But when you come back I'll bake you a
cake − your favourite. The one Grandma used to make.'

A minute later the farewells were over, and he was on his way back home across the moor.

The next morning, Lady Marion, on the pretext of having shopping to do, gave him a lift to Truro in the family chaise.

# 2

For the next five years Ben Curran worked hard for his master, Saul Jacobs, learning assiduously how to use his tools — to make measurements correctly, estimate the texture and potentials of stone and granite, and envisage designs which he meant to develop one day. Most of Saul's commissions were for plaques and tombstones, so one of Ben's primary tasks was to gain correct knowledge of the alphabet, ancient and modern lettering, and then how to cut. He found such work limiting and boring, but he never lost sight of his goal, and when he was sixteen, he helped Saul, who was getting old, with some of the simpler sculptured figures used in memoriam.

The Jacobs' house was a square grey granite building, set back from the road on the outskirts of a small village Gwynck, two miles out of Truro. Saul's great-grandfather had started the family business, and converted the place — originally a farm — into both domestic and business premises. The yard, where a large shed and outbuildings were used for working premises stood at one side, which meant good publicity and created interest from strangers and visitors to the district.

Saul, although not so highly creative as his father and grandfather before him, was a keen business man, and precise at his craft; like young Ben his apprentice he had a sensitive appreciation of the qualities and potentials of all types of stone. He was never out of employment. The business now was well known through Cornwall and further up country. However, one thing he had to face as the years passed — his sense of originality was beginning to fade. Ideas did not come so easily. Day by day he began to depend on young Ben's imagination, at the same time curbing many impractical flights of fancy. At such times the boy managed to stifle his irritation, knowing it would not always be like that. Saul was nearly sixty. A time would come — if Ben was prepared to stay that long — when most of the responsibility would fall on him. In the meantime he was earning a sufficient wage to help his family considerably, and take a little pleasure himself when he felt like it.

He was a good wrestler, and earned a name for himself in local contests. When he won he was treated in the village hostelry to a pint of mead by the landlord, and occasionally in a nearby kiddleywink of more dubious reputation. For spring and autumn fairs of the district he was generally able to provide small sculptures or wooden carvings of animals worked at in his spare time.

Women liked him, and he learned early how to have what he wanted of them, although he gave his heart to none. At the back of his mind the image of Elfrida lurked. For weeks he would forget her, then suddenly, resurrected by a chance word, phrase, the glimpse of buttercups in a field perhaps, or sweet heather-scent blown on a wayward wind, she'd be there — an illusory figure, but vividly real. Beautiful in her remote wilderness, enchanting as some haunting dream. On the rare visits to his home he made a point of calling on her. Yet the words of endearment on his lips never came. She would stare at him as though waiting for something — her clear eyes searching his face. But the dignity of her, the façade of calm hiding her wild sweet self, somehow unnerved him. In a strange way he was afraid. Not of Elfrida the girl or his desire of her, but of committing himself. Once he was pledged to Elfrida he felt that he would be bound for ever. And he was wary for the future. Although in her company frustrated longing could so easily have turned to lust, all natural instincts were stifled under a façade of friendly indifference. Talk between them became practical, almost mundane. After describing his work, his immediate future projects, and relating a few anecdotes concerning village life, he would be away again, hurrying across the moor with all possible speed in an effort to erase her completely from memory.

On such rare visits to the locality he generally paid a call at Heronsmore to inform Lady Marion of his progress. Although she was not yet thirty she already regarded her as a middle-aged woman who was content to sponsor him in every possible way because of his work. It was through her that his first introduction to Saul Jacobs had been made, and he was grateful. Apart from that, the interior of the great house was itself an inspiration. Not the architecture which through the years had become an edifice combining different periods, but the luxurious atmosphere of wealth; of rich soft carpets, tapestries, wide mosaic-tiled halls, looming galleries hung with ancient portraits of bygone ancestors — and most of all the sculptures and treasures from many lands, including ivory figurines and larger carvings in pure white marble.

Marble entranced him. One day waiting in the wide entrance hall for the butler to inform Marion of his arrival, he wandered to a recess where a life-size half-clad figure of a woman glistened from the bluish light of a stained glass window. Her pale breasts were bare, her skirt fallen from one hip over the navel to her ankles. She had one rounded arm lifted above the nipples to a shoulder. The folds of the tumbled material over her thighs and stomach somehow suggested a snake's coils enfolding her. Yet she was enticingly beautiful. Even the hair rippling from her face down her back held rhythm and sent a shuddering feeling down Ben's spine. A hand tentatively slid over the white shining surface of a thigh.

Marble.

Strange emotions seized him. He was still staring, his bright blue eyes entranced, when he heard someone saying behind him, 'You like the statue, Ben?'

He turned quickly, and saw Lady Marion staring up at him.

'Yes,' he said. 'I never saw it properly before.'

Marion, who was wearing grey, shrugged.

'It only catches the light properly at certain times of the day. When my mother was alive she considered it rather untasteful. So my father had it moved there. It once stood at the foot of the stairs.'

'Why didn't she like it then?' Ben asked. 'It's marble.'

'Yes. And quite valuable.'

'What's it called?' His face flamed suddenly. Through his enthusiasm he realised he must sound ill-mannered, even gauche. 'Sorry,' he said, 'I should've said "Lady Marion". I mean — it was just the light shining on it—' he broke off.

She reached a hand out; he took it awkwardly.

'I understand. And you really needn't trouble to be polite. I appreciate your enthusiasm. It is a lovely statue, and its name is "Lamia".'

'Oh.'

'From a poem by John Keats', Marion told him. 'But I don't suppose you've read it.'

'No. I've not much time for reading. And anyway I s'pose it doesn't really need a name. But—'

'Yes?'

'If I'd carved that,' Ben told her thoughtfully, 'I wouldn't have had the draperies. I'd have had her naked and smooth with an arm out and a bird on it—'

What impelled the thought in him Ben had no idea. It was so frequently the way those days. The sight of something created by someone else — or a glimpse, a trick of light on a tree's branch or undergrowth led instantly to another picture in his mind — something set alight by the enthusiasm of his own inner vision.

'I expect that's because you've been working on memorial work,' Marion told him. 'The bird, I mean — as a symbol.'

Ben shook his head. 'Oh no. I don't think in symbols — nor memorials or tombstones,' he confessed. 'It's life I'm aiming for—'

'I understand.'

But did she? It was hard to put herself in his place. She could only view him objectively with a deepening sense of admiration — his tall broad young form, proud stature and brilliant burning blue eyes set on things far apart from her own sphere and background. If he was her son — or even lover — beneath her gentle restrained exterior feelings stirred that made her draw away, astonished and ashamed of her own weakness.

'Come along, Ben,' she said in colder, more aloof tones. 'I'm a little tired. There's a book on sculpture in the library you may like to see.'

He followed her obediently into the shelf-lined room which had three walls entirely lined by shelves of calf-bound volumes. Lady Marion directed him to a recess where a fire burned welcomingly. 'Do sit down,' she said, 'I'll get it for you.'

The book was a large one bound in vellum, containing a carefully illustrated selection of great sculptured masterpieces of the world with a full bibliography.

Ben glanced at it, and was instantly bored.

'I don't read much,' he said. 'I haven't time. And—'

'Yes, Ben?'

'I'm afraid that sort of thing doesn't really help me,' he confessed. 'I'm not clever enough in one way, and I like to work out my own designs. Master Jacobs calls me an original.'

'I'm sure you are.' Her voice told him nothing. 'But the more knowledge you have the easier you'll find it to be accepted.'

'Accepted?'

'To be able to talk on your own subject with influential people,' she explained. 'People who can help you with your career.'

He frowned, and for a second appeared far older than his years — so handsome, dogged, and in command of himself that her heart lurched. Oh, how she loved him, or so easily could.

She took the book away with a sigh, then smiled and said lightly, 'Tell me what you've been doing, all that's happening at Master Jacobs' these days.'

There was not much to tell, and when he left it was with a feeling of relief.

Marion, a static figure, stood watching him as he strode down the path towards the drive; then, as he disappeared behind a clump of trees bordering the moor, she turned and went slowly back into the house. Oh, she thought to be as strong as he was — lusty and young, able to race across the moors without a sign of impediment or limp! For a few moments envy stirred to brief bitterness. She had sensed his longing to be off — free of any commitment or sense of duty. She recognised without a shred of self-illusion that there was little now she could do for him. His mind was independently set on the course he'd chosen. Well, she'd known it would happen one day. What she had not accepted was how important he'd become to her. As she turned to go back to the library she met her father at the door. He followed her in. He was a handsome man still, but slightly portly, with hot tempered eyes faintly reddened through past indulgencies, and frustration with the present.

'So your young rustic's gone,' he said, with a querulous edge to his voice. 'Didn't stay long this time.' He paused, gave her an ironic glance and continued, 'A good thing too. He's a man now — almost, and not your kind. Steer clear, Marion. If you want to do good works concentrate on the Parish. The Church is always involved in some charity or other. Another thing—'

'Yes?'

Although her manner was so controlled, her voice almost cold, he continued bluntly, 'You'll get talked about. And you've a position to keep up. To have people sniggering would annoy me intensely. I know your heart's in the right place, but Ben Curran's not concerned about you — never has been except for what you could give from your pocket. To him you're — well, getting on, girl. And I know for a fact he's at the Crane place when he gets the chance. What goes on there I don't know, nor does anyone else, now the old woman's gone. But the girl's a strange one. A beauty too. I don't want you mixed up with her type.'

'Why should I be? I seldom see Elfrida. And to suggest I've any kind of — of liking for Ben in the way you mean is an insult—'

Her face had whitened. With her lower lip trembling and her clear eyes strained, she looked almost plain. Why couldn't she fuss herself up a bit, her father thought. Those greys and browns she wore made her colourless and insignificant somehow. Orange now, or red, would show her black hair off, and with a touch of salve on her lips and earrings or some kind of jewellery she wouldn't be bad looking. As it was, he was growing daily more doubtful of finding her a suitable husband. Any possible suitor he produced was either ignored by her or put off by her prim airs. Once again his mind turned resentfully to the past, and the son who'd so disastrously let him down. To other things also — a wild sweet autumn evening years ago when frustrated by his chill wife and their sterile bed, he'd lain with Susannah Crane, forgetful of everything but the luscious fresh body so freely given — the molten sheen of dusky gold hair and red lips soft and warm under his, so willing and tender she'd been, and he with the life flooding from him like a stream suddenly released. On the whole, he thought, looking back, he'd managed to extricate himself exceedingly well from that evening's madness. She'd known of course, that nothing could come of it — legally. She'd even told him as much, because in her own way she was proud.

'Don't worry, Squire,' she'd said with a kind of amused contempt in her voice, 'I'll not be saying anything. I knew what I was doin', I can look after myself.'

She'd stood up then, gathered her skirts over her shining white thighs, as he said politely, 'I'm sure you can. I've always admired your independence, Susannah, and I've wondered why you're not married before this—'

'Marriage?' She'd lifted her chin up, and laughed, and at times he still recalled the lovely rhythmic motion of her chin and throat, the outline of the firm white breasts before she pulled her shawl round her shoulders. 'When I see what marriage does to some folk I'm not all that mad for it.'

At the time he'd not envisaged or considered the possibility of there being a child. Later, when he'd heard she was pregnant, he'd made a bargain with Martha. Susannah had died shortly after Elfrida's birth, and Sir Geoffrey, anxious at all costs to keep the infant's paternity secret, had doubled the sum ensuring the old lady's silence. If anyone guessed the truth nothing was suggested openly. Susannah, after all, had been a wild one, with a dubious name among the local inhabitants.

Over one thing however, Mistress Crane had been stubborn. She would not leave her home under any circumstances whatever. If any effort was made to evict her, she would cause such a scandal Sir Geoffrey's name would become mud through the district and beyond.

So at the cottage she'd stayed, too near to Heronsmere for Sir Geoffrey to be completely comfortable, but sufficiently far away over the moor for him to avoid contact except on rare occasions, when he'd merely lifted his hat, given a cursory 'good day' — more of a grunt, and passed on.

At rare intervals he'd glimpsed the girl — a fairy-like figure with her pale hair flowing loose over the fancy clothes Martha insisted on her wearing. He'd cursed the fates then, for giving him a wasted son and a crippled daughter, while bestowing such grace and loveliness on his unacknowledged bastard.

Resentment made him almost dislike her. But he'd kept his promise, and after Martha's death had increased her allowance which was delivered by messenger every month, from solicitors in Penzance.

Elfrida had had no direct knowledge of her benefactor's identify. Any questions she'd put to her grandmother when she'd asked had been sharply dealt with and subdued.

'That's my business,' the old lady had told her. 'And if you start poking your nose into things that don't concern you there'll be trouble. You just thank your stars, girl, you doan' have to go out working scrubbin' floors. A lady you can be, s'long as you doan' put on airs thinking you're as good as the squire and his highborn wife.'

The squire! Elfrida had frequently ruminated about him — wondered why such gifts of food and presents should be sent to the cottage from Heronsmere at Christmas and other festive occasions. She had formed her own theory about him, which could be true or not, but she'd never revealed her suspicions to Martha, having learned that secrecy concerning any possible Penharrion relationship was part of the bargain. If the pact were broken in any way disastrous results might follow. So Elfrida had held her tongue. It had not been difficult. She had an inherent passion for the moor, freedom, and all wild things. Following Martha's death she had felt a sense of 'aloneness' for a time, but was never lonely. She had the goats to look after that she milked with her own hand. There was the small garden, and the spinning wheel for any spare time.

On occasion when the impulse stirred her, she would spend most of the day wandering about the coast, collecting shells, or gathering the wild spinach that thrived on the western headland. In the spring the ground above flamed bright with gorse, alternating with patches of purple bell-heather. Gulls flew white and silvered against the sun, and on summer days larks sang. As she threaded her way between rocks and furze, careful always to avoid bog or dangerous deserted mine-shafts, she would hum old songs lowly and sweetly in another tongue — the old Cornish language her grandmother had taught her. Sleek seals would slither over boulders by the sea's edge to meet her, and she would think then, 'They're my friends. I don't need people, except Ben perhaps. Yes. I would like to see Ben more.'

She seldom went to the village, because as she'd grown older women had whispered and seemed to avoid her. She knew why. Martha's reputation as a witch had tainted her granddaughter in the eyes of decent God-fearing folk. Pretty she might be — but odd, and one apart. There was her mother too — Susannah who'd been a loose wench, if ever there was one — too free with the men by half, and who'd borne the child out of wedlock. Sons were warned to steer clear of 'that theer Elfrida'. Most obeyed. The ones who didn't, following Martha's death, had met with such a fiery rebuff that they'd left before getting a foot in the door, startled by the contemptuous brilliance of her strange eyes, the vituperative young voice, and erect challenging slim figure. Her beauty, combined with the wild words on her lips had quelled, and almost frightened them.

'It was as though she'd put a spell on me,' one youth said to another, 'stuck there rigid as a beanpole I was, an' such a tiny bit of a thing like her. I could have swep' her off her feet an' had her easy where I wanted, if she hadn' bin so scarey. But you jus' wait. One day I'll lay that wench good an' proper, sure's my name's Jem Varney.'

But he knew in his heart he never would. There was something strange about Elfrida Crane, and he'd no intention of getting too deeply involved with a witch.

'That theer Ben Curran goes visitin' her,' one of his pals said tauntingly.

'Him?' The word held a sneer. 'Two of a kind I reckon. Thinks he's a bit better'n the rest of us with his chippin' an cuttin', an' la-di-da swagger. My ma says he was bred wrong. Must've bin.'

'Don't you go sayin' things like that in his old man's hearin',' his friend warned. 'Dad says he's a hot temper, an' if it got about you'd scandalised his missis there'd be trouble. Everyone down the mine's a bit afeared o' James Curran.'

'It don't stop me thinkin', anyways. Where'd Ben get that hair? You tell me that. A real yeller mop. An' those light eyes of his. The Currans is all dark – except him.'

'The girls seem to like him.'

'Girls!' Jem laughed scornfully. 'I could have any I wanted if I gev a mind to et. There's more in life than women—'

If Ben had an idea of what was thought of him, he didn't care. From his very earliest years he'd recognised he was 'different'. So was Elfrida, for that matter. This was another bond they had in common.

Meanwhile back at Master Jacobs, he kept his emotions firmly under control dispelling ruthlessly any lingering thoughts of the solitary girl.

Saul's wife, Ellen, was an observant shrewd woman with an eye to the future. Saul, she knew, was beginning to depend more and more upon his young apprentice. His ideas were limited. The day was not far off when he would be incapable of running the business himself. To take on an unknown partner would be risky. Ben, with encouragement, a proper wage, and more comfortable quarters could surely be persuaded to stay on when his apprenticeship ended. So she made a room in the house ready for him, and persuaded him to leave the poky bedroom over the working premises.

'He will do well,' she told her daughter Maria, meaningfully. 'We must try and keep him satisfied.'

Maria, Saul's only child, had been afforded a better education than most young women of her class, and now, at twenty two, gave painting and singing lessons to children of more prosperous parents in the vicinity. These included the vicar's two girls, Ellen and Margaret, and the plain but aspiring daughter of the village grocer. What Maria earned was negligible, but her prestige gained enormously, and the best parlour where the sessions were held became a sanctum of high respect in Gwynk. Prestige, however, as Ellen was beginning to learn, did not appear to attract lovers; at her age Maria was almost on the shelf. It was true, her mother often thought reflectively, the girl was not exactly a beauty. She was too thin, rather sharp-featured, and inclined to be colourless, with her pale skin, fair eyelashes and brows. Her hair was of that particular light ginger shade needing a lively face to brighten it. And Maria's vitality all seemed submerged by her teaching. Her figure was too erect and forbidding. Her smile almost automatic and brittle. Yet with a bit of titivating and more vanity over clothes, Ellen could visualise her daughter quite differently — even as pretty.

So she set to work, determined to change her offspring's image. She got a lift with a neighbouring farmer to Penzance one day, where she purchased silks of various shades, and gave more than her husband would have approved, for a gown of sea-green velvet trimmed with yellow satin ribbons. In a coffee house — the most select in the town, she picked up a fashion magazine from a nearby table, and under a veneer of casual interest, eyed the pages avidly. Open work cotton mittens she discovered, were in vogue, and flower posies were not only worn tucked in at belts but in the hair, so when she'd had coffee she made her way to a haberdashery and bought a number of frivolous items to enhance any feminine allure Maria might possess.

Saul was at first outraged then glum, when he learned of

his wife's extravagance. 'I don't know what came over you,' he told Ellen resentfully. 'I've slaved all these years to give the girl good schooling, an' here she is earning not enough by this fancy needlework stuff an' singin' to keep her in food alone. Why did you do it, wife? 'Tisn't as though she's a beauty likely to wed a rich man — or anyone else for that matter.'

Ellen's face flamed. A sense of guilt made her belligerent and on the defensive. 'Shame on you to speak like that of your own daughter. She could be striking if she wanted. Now no more lecturin', Saul. If you must know, I've plans for her.'

The exact nature of her plans she couldn't quite define herself. But she knew the importance of proving Maria's capacity to interest a young man, and Ben's presence in the house gave a chance to test it. Not that he was eligible as any serious suitor — for one thing he was too young, though he didn't look it — secondly his background was against him. On the other hand, his talent and looks were outstanding. A flattering word from him to her daughter might inspire Maria's thoughts into more romantic channels than mere teaching, and admiration from one young man might draw others to notice her. Oh dear, to think that with so much else on her mind, she, Ellen, had to plan and manouvre so deviously. But there it was! Unless something was done, Maria, poor girl, was likely to end up as a narrow minded spinster trilling tunes and embroidering daisies until her fingers and her voice failed, and that would be an ignominious state for Saul Jacobs' daughter.

The next day Ellen's campaign began.

Maria was bewildered.

'What's all this for?' she demanded, when the stays, starched new underwear, and green velvet were held up before her. 'I don't need clothes.'

'Oh yes you do, dear,' her mother affirmed politely. 'You may be clever at scales and singing, but only children hear you. There's another kind of cleverness you don't have that's important.'

'What?'

'Looks! femininity. Or isn't that important to you? Haven't you any thoughts of getting married one day?'

'If I had what difference would it make? I don't meet any men.'

'You will,' Ellen said with tart confidence. 'Of course we're a little out of the way here. But if you can be made to blossom a bit—'

'Blossom!' Maria looked almost cat-like as she spat the word out. 'How ridiculous.'

'And don't you talk to me like that, young lady, or you'll be sorry. I'm still your mother and mistress of this house. So you'll do as I say this minute, understand? I've paid more than I can afford for these clothes. What's more I'm behind with the baking. Sally will have to do more than she's hired for, this week, which will mean an afternoon off for her later, and I have the vicar's wife coming for tea on Saturday. The reverend gentleman's seeing your father about some monument or other. I could do with two servants instead of that one girl. This house is large—'

'Oh I know, I know,' Maria said resignedly. 'You're always telling me.'

'Hm. Well — try and remember it, and to please me, for goodness sake show a little vanity.'

The lacing-up, the fitting, the loosening and recoiling of the ginger hair on top of Maria's small head, followed by a spray of artificial flowers at the corsage of the velvet dress, and a touch of lip salve, were at last completed. Staring at herself in the mirror, Maria was quite impressed, so was her mother. The difference was remarkable. Instead of the prim teacher a proud-looking young woman stood with chin up-lifted above the throat.

'Hm! quite good,' Ellen admitted. 'But you need this round your neck. It's too thin. You must feed yourself up.' She handed her daughter a tulle scarf, continuing, 'And you're too pale. Your cheeks need brightening.' She fetched a geranium flower from a pot on the landing, and told Maria to crush it on the rather high cheekbones.

'Make up?' Maria gasped. 'But you've never approved. You said—'

'What I once said is done with. If that painted hussy who

worked at the inn could catch a rich husband, there's no reason why you shouldn't. Be careful though. Gently, and not too obvious. Then I've some rice powder—'

Dinner that night was made a special occasion, attended by Ben who was at first taken aback, then intrigued by the starchy Miss Jacobs all made up 'like a sprat to catch a mackerel' as his friends would have put it. Until then he'd hardly considered Saul's daughter in a feminine light. During the few days he'd lodged in the house any lingering glance he'd thrown had been at Sally the maid-of-all-work, who was a farmer's daughter, plump and fresh-looking, with full breasts almost bursting the buttons of her pink print bodice, and an overt gleam in her round glassy-blue eyes. Not a beauty, but enticing in a lusty way, with a swing of her full hips suggesting she'd be worth bedding. When in a few idle moments his mind had strayed from work and ambition to other matters, it was of Sally he'd thought. In no way seriously of course, because he now held a superior position in Master Jacobs' household, but as a foil to any invading longings for Elfrida.

The sight of Maria Jacobs in all her finery quite diverted his attention to another direction.

And she was aware of it.

After the meal work was abandoned for the day, rather to Saul's disgruntlement, since he preferred both he and Ben to continue for an hour either considering designs and plans, or labouring physically in the yard. But Ellen was adamant. 'Tonight is a celebration,' she said, 'a welcome for Ben into our home. Why don't you show him some of your paintings, Maria?'

'I'd like to see some,' Ben remarked. He was curious; titillated by wondering what kind of art this rather strait-laced but elegant looking young lady — one he'd never properly noticed before — dabbled in.

Ellen nodded agreeably. 'I shall leave you two together. I'm sorry — you'll forgive me, Ben, I know. But I really must give a little attention to what Sally is doing.'

She left, closing the door quietly, leaving Ben and Maria on their own. He glanced round the room shrewdly, noting the shining brass, the freshly polished gleaming mahogany furniture, the potted ferns, and carefully displayed spray of artificial flowers on the round table. The carved chest — under the oak framed portrait of William Jacobs, founder of the business — was of solid teak. He liked that. Teak was durable. Seamen used it for their own chests. He'd seen more than one, with drawers inside containing carvings of flowers, birds and fruit which must have taken more than one ocean voyage to complete, and could imagine how such creative toil had helped men whose thoughts and minds must frequently have pined for their loved ones.

Maria's light voice suddenly broke the silence. 'I don't know why Mama imagines you'd be at all interested in my small efforts,' she said with a hint of apology that could have been genuine or false. 'I don't go in for grand, large designs like you. Mine are all small.'

'I'd like to see them all the same,' he told her. After telling him to sit down by the fire she produced an album from a bureau drawer, and opened it, then placed it on his knees. There was the smell of lavender about her as she moved, and looking up he saw her usually pale complexion had deepened, making the geranium tint quite unnecessary. He tore his gaze from hers, noting, as he glanced down the brilliance of the antique opal brooch pinned on the velvet bodice between throat and breasts. Unconsciously the knowledge stirred in him that the old man — Saul — must be quite prosperous, even rich. Funny it was, that the master's wife was so keen to interest him in his daughter. And it surprised him he'd not noticed her eyes before. They were curiously light between the fair lashes — changing from greenish-pale blue, to dark grey glistening with shadowed black and gold — like quartz that could be polished to show luminous sea-pool patterns. He glanced down awkwardly.

'Do you like those?' she asked, with a slim white finger indicating a page of butterflies.

The designs were intricately painted in water-colour, so minutely depicted he could imagine that at any second they might rise and flutter from the paper.

'Did you do them?'

'Of course.'

'But how? Catch them did you — from the moors and pin them down—?' His voice already held condemnation.

'Certainly not. We have an illustrated book on butterflies upstairs. I got the details from that. I wouldn't kill anything beautiful, ugh!' She shuddered. 'I detest cruelty. Even flies! — it's not nice having to kill them. But butterflies! — they're so lovely—' she sighed. 'They were almost the first thing I ever noticed as a tiny girl. The little blue ones, you know, from the moor. And the daisies in the grass.' She turned a page. 'Here they are — changed into patterns for my pupils to copy. I have a whole daisy sampler upstairs that I did myself. It won a prize at school.'

'That's clever of you,' he said. She was sharp, and it was obvious to her that in spite of his praise and recognition of her skill at drawing and with the brush, any praise he gave was mostly mere politeness.

She shut the book with a snap.

'I'm sure you've seen enough of my little efforts. They must appear rather — ineffectual to you, Ben. But then a woman couldn't possibly aspire to creating anything that would please you.' The word 'aspire' pleased and complimented him. 'I've heard that Lady Marion Penherrion has great faith in your work,' she continued. 'So have I. I think you'll make a name for yourself one day — not just like my father as a stone and monumental mason — but as a — a sculptor.'

'That's what I intend,' he told her. 'Whether I will or not's another matter.'

'I'm sure you'll achieve anything you really want to,' she said. 'You're that kind of person. Oh, how I hope I'll see that day.'

'Why shouldn't you?'

'I don't know. I — well—' her voice lightened. 'You never know in life, do you? Things can happen so easily to change things. I'm twenty two after all. One day I — I don't suppose I shall spend my whole life teaching children how to use a brush or sing at school concerts. I haven't even much of a

voice myself—' She broke off, and he was amazed at such
show of humility. Before she'd appeared to him so sure of
herself — a rather starchy and remote young woman who
considered herself slightly above other people.

'Your voice sounds pleasing to me,' he told her, rather
abruptly, because the situation seemed to be taking rather
too personal a line. 'I've heard you from the back sometimes.
But of course no one wants to go on at the same thing for
ever—'

'Except you,' she said softly.

He glanced at her again more directly. The determined set
to his chin fascinated her; there was something intimidating
in the cool appraising glint of his ice-blue eyes that for a few
seconds held her spellbound, changing him suddenly from a
mere youth to maturity.

'Yes,' he said, 'you could say that. I know where I'm going.'

'I don't. Not for myself, I mean.'

'You'll get married,' he said, 'like other women. A pretty
one like you. Sure to.'

He hadn't meant to embarrass her. But she blushed.
'Marriage isn't the only thing,' she said. 'But it's nice of you to
call me pretty.'

'In white I reckon you'd look real beautiful,' he said,
reverting for a few seconds to his native Cornish burr.

'White?'

'There's a statue at Lady Marion's,' he told her, 'carved in
marble, white marble. You could look every bit as good as
her, if you—'

'Yes, Ben?' she queried.

'If you had less on,' he said, 'simple, to fall in drapes.
That's what I like — shiny curves from the waist—'

Her heart quickened.

'If you mean what I think you do, I'm quite shocked,' she
told him.

'No you're not.' There was a glimmer of white teeth. The
sun slanting through the window lit his hair to sudden brilliant gold, catching his handsome features from a sideways
angle, so the well formed arrogant features were accentuated.

She could even define the fine gold hairs filming his chin and on the backs of his strong young hands. Something in her melted, but she retorted quickly, 'You shouldn't contradict in that way.'

'Why? It's true isn't it? You're not shocked, Miss Maria, because you understand. You're clever. You know what I'm talking about. From those patterns — those sketches of flowers and things, I c'n see you've a knowledge of design. If you broadened your ideas a bit I reckon you could help me quite a lot—'

Her lips parted in surprise.

'Me? Help you?'

'Not in the actual work of course. And I've plenty of ideas myself for the future. But on the way I've got to fit them in a bit with what folk want. You know — what's acceptable, I mean.'

She shook her head. 'I think you exaggerate. I don't see many people. I should have thought Sir Geoffrey's daughter — Lady Marion — would be more use there.'

'She only knows top folk. She's a nice lady, and her home's crammed with beautiful stuff. But she doesn't go out much anyway, or meet people, because of being an invalid.'

'Invalid? But I thought it was just one foot.'

'That's more'n enough,' he said, thinking, 'yes, more than enough to keep her from climbing down to Hook's Cove, or scrambling through the heather, and racing across the moor when the wind's so clear and sharp and smelling of bracken you want to sing and leap with the joy of things. But Elfrida can do all that, and more. Elfrida's the most beautiful thing in the world to me, and the most important — except for my work—'

Something of his sudden wild change of thought must have affected her.

'Well, Ben,' she said brightly, 'I'll give you any advice I can, I promise you. I naturally know a little of Parish affairs, and the tastes of religious people.'

'Yes.' He forced his mind determinedly from Elfrida. 'That's what I was thinking. It's this monument I have in mind at the moment—'

'Monument?'

'A cross, I should say. Granite. They're wanting one for the churchyard. Quite big, about eight feet, with a good deal of carving in it to commemorate some saint or other—'

'St Laurec, I expect.'

'Maybe. Well your — Master Jacobs — thinks he'll get the job, providing I can shoulder the whole business. I've been pondering on something primitive, or legendary if you like — a sort of story not just Christian but from pagan times. That would give a chance for deep cutting patterns of trees and wild life in the background. Even Pan peering. But simplified you see, and strong, to catch the light and shade—' He paused watching a frown crease etch a faint line between the eyes. After the short silence she said, 'If I were you I'd leave out the Pan. Pan's wicked, isn't he? And most people round here wouldn't understand the historical idea. I mean birds — or even legendary animals — prehistoric creatures — they could be worked in without anyone criticising or recognising what they were — but for a Church you don't want to suggest the devil.'

He stared at her with open admiration. 'You're right, Miss Maria—'

'Miss?' She gave a short high-pitched laugh, and moved to glance idly at a book on a small table. 'Can't you call me Maria? We've known each other quite a long time now.'

'But — your father? Master Jacobs? And your mama! Guess they wouldn't like that.'

She gave an uncharacteristic toss of her head.

'Oh, I don't think you need worry about them. They think highly of you.'

So 'Maria' and 'Ben' it became from that moment.

The following week a huge slab of granite was brought by cart to the yard, and Ben began to measure and make the first marking for the primitive design he'd worked out. Saul was content to leave the whole project to 'young Curran', as he now called him, and at the same time employed another lad, Willie Care, to assist with some of the heavier manual labour. Willie was strong, lusty and agreeable, with no ideas of his own, but quite content to follow instructions. At first Ben mildly despised him — his lack of ambition and crude ways which were those of a yokel. But in time Willie's robust sense of fun and laughter became a steadying influence at odd periods when Ben, the perfectionist, quite failed to produce the high quality of work he'd envisaged.

Maria also was encouraging and in the autumn of 1826 when Ben was eighteen, the cross was finished, delivered to the Church, and installed in a commanding place overlooking the road. A service of Thanksgiving was held, attended by Saul, Ellen, Maria, Ben and his assistant, after which Willie departed to get hilariously drunk at the village inn. Ben would have joined him in the ordinary way. But the occasion was no ordinary one. The Monument marked Ben's genuine elevation to the status of an up-and-coming monumental mason and sculptor, although no one remotely guessed the ambitions and wild ideas surging through his brain.

Time passed. Ben's powers increased, but Saul's were quickly failing. The time came when he suffered a severe stroke which paralysed the whole of his right side, and kept him completely speechless and bedridden. Ben had regrets, and was distressed by his master's plight, recognising how good to him Master Jacobs had been. But it soon became obvious that in future he would have to shoulder responsibility for the business of 'Jacobs' Monumental and Stone Masons', if it was to survive at all.

'It must,' Ellen insisted when she'd recovered from the shock of her first grief. 'Although he can't speak I know he wants you to carry on, Ben. He's great faith in you, and we must work out the financial side between us — with the help of Mr Grotes of course — our solicitor—' her lip quivered. 'You didn't intend leaving, did you?'

'Of course not,' Ben answered stoutly, although he knew full well, he would not be content to remain at Jacobs' yard for ever. 'That would be a bad thing after all he's done for me.'

'And not helpful to you either,' Ellen pointed out shrewdly.

'There's a good career waiting for you here, Ben — and other things—' with a glance at her daughter who looked white-faced and strained in a sombre black dress that somehow seemed to herald death.

Just for a second Ben was stirred by compassion — a quality that was rare in him, except for animals and wild hurt creatures of the moor.

'I'll stay,' he said, 'don't you fret, mistress — we'll get over this somehow.'

And they did, with Willie's manual help, and Maria's unfailing assistance and any advice she could give in the matter of design.

Saul died the following February. During the preceding months Ben had made only one visit home to see his parents. Due to the financial help he'd been able to spare, the clob cottage had been brightened and put into better order. They had sufficient to eat, and a new cesspit had been made further away from the door. 'The future doan' look too good though,' his father James told him. 'Red Bell's tin production's slippin. The squire doan' seem to bother so much these days either. He had a fall some months back from a horse. An' he edn' bin the same man since. Some think he's gone funny like—' he touched his head significantly.

'And Lady Marion?'

James shrugged. 'You should know. Don't you visit now?'

'I've not had time.'

'Well, lad, maybe you should. They say she's often sick an' needin' company.'

Ben grudgingly accepted his father's criticism, although he did nothing about it. Instead, when he left his family that afternoon he cut straight across the moor to Elfrida's cottage. It was warm for the time of year, already heralding the close approach of spring. Gorse flamed gold from brown undergrowth, spattered with budding young green. By boulders and in sheltered places celandines opened their pale yellow cups. Even occasional primroses clustered in lush hollows, and from the distance the sea glittered, calm and shining as a sheet of pure iridescent glass.

The air, fresh and heady with the mingled scent of heather and damp springy earth quickened Ben's blood like wine. The whole world seemed to be before him — his for the making and taking. No ugliness marred the prospect before him, no ugly talk of wars or disaster to come. There were always rumours of course — but Ben didn't bother much with newspapers, and now William the Fourth reigned as King — 'Sailor Billy' — placidity seemed to envelope the country. Miners still had to work hard of course, many were taking off to America. But with the Whigs in control of English politics and many reform bills going through it did appear to most folk that the lot of working folk was gradually to improve. Anyway, such far off mundane problems were far from Ben's mind as he swung towards Elfrida's cottage. He whistled merrily, swinging a thorn stick about the brambles and constricting bushes cramping the narrow track. 'Elfrida, Elfrida', his heart sang.

When he reached her gate she was hanging something out on a line in the small front garden. The tips of shoes shewed under her blue working dress. She could have been a creature from some fairy tale or legend, with her hair glittering as soft and pale almost as the few solitary clouds drifting white across the sky. Against her slender thighs the material blew back gently in a faintly rising breeze, outlining her tantalising form and accentuating the tiny waist.

'Elfrida,' he called. She turned suddenly, involuntarily wiping a hand on her apron and untying it. It fell to a bush and hung there, fluttering for a few moments like a white bird, then she hurried towards him. He took her hands, and without realising it, was pulling her against him. 'Oh Elfrida,' he said breathlessly, 'how I've missed you.'

'And me too — me too,' she answered, 'you've been a long time away, Ben—' She broke off, staring up at him, dazzled by the handsome strength of him — the tall sturdy form, and piercing brightness of his eyes. For a few moments they clung together smiling, enveloped by a new strange ecstasy. Then the smile died into silence. The look between them deepened into something stronger — something mysterious and unknowable, yet holding all the knowledge of man's most urgent need for woman and hers for him.

He found his lips first on her mouth, then cheek and neck, travelling to her shoulder and down her slender rounded arm which was still damp and glistening from her washing.

'Let us go somewhere, Elfrida—' he murmured against her ear.

'Where?'

His hand travelled to her waist, lingering there, above the soft curves of buttocks and thighs. Her whole body was trembling, and against her quickening heart she could feel the thudding of his own.

'Anywhere. Here—'

'The cove?' Her voice was a whisper.

'Later—' he said − 'later.'

'But—'

She struggled only slightly as he lifted her up, then her arms were round his neck and he was carrying her round the side of the cottage to the back, from where the moorland sloped towards the cliffs and sea. By a tall standing stone, some ancient menhir of the past, he laid her down in the shadowed privacy of a nest of twisted sloes. The bracken was soft and sweet smelling about them. There was no wind there. Very gently, controlling the violence of his emotions he unbuttoned her bodice and skirt, removing all constricting clothes from the pale column of her body.

His gaze for some seconds was transfixed by the living perfection of form and features − lips, eyes, and shadowed hair tumbled about the shoulders − the exquisite rosy-tipped breasts thrusting towards him like mysterious pink buds of flowers from green fern fronds. Hardly daring to breathe his palms cupped them, then a hand slid tentatively, almost with reverence over the shining satin smooth beauty of her thighs. She gave a great quiver and sighed. Her stomach quivered under his touch, and suddenly restraint left him, and he was in and of her − pulsing and taking, hurting yet thrilling her, so there was nothing any more but the leaping primitive journey to complete mating − a torrent of unutterable joy that ended on moans of exquisite fulfilment. For minutes they still lay entwined, until the vortex of darkness gradually lifted.

He eased himself, and gently withdrew. When his sense could register, he saw the quiver of her lashes like tired butterflies against her cheeks. Then she opened her eyes.

He kissed her gently.

'Was it good, my darling?' he asked presently.

'Yes, oh yes.' There was a pause before she continued, 'I love you, Ben.'

'And I you.'

This was true. Yet later at her cottage, after his senses and body had quietened, a niggle of discomfort rose in him, and when Elfrida asked, 'Are you off to Heronsmere?' he replied: 'I don't reckon so. Not today. I've got to get home for the horse. I rode from Truro cross-country.'

'It wouldn't take you long,' she suggested. 'I've heard the squire's in a strange state — hardly ever talks now, and Lady Marion's not well.'

He was puzzled. Sickness always mildly offended him.

'Why are you so anxious to see her?' he enquired. 'I should've thought after — after what's happened you wouldn't be sending me off to another woman.'

Elfrida smiled, touched his cheek, and reached up to kiss him.

'It's because of that,' she told him, 'partly. Because of what we've had, and have. Because everything's so wonderful. I can't bear to think of that poor lady crippled and left alone with someone wrong in the head.'

'He really is, then?'

She nodded. 'I think so. And Ben — you do owe her something. It was she gave you a start.'

'Not altogether. I began carving when I was a kid you know that very well. And with or without her I'd have got where I am.'

'I know. But still—'

Unable to resist Elfrida's pleading, and not wishing to appear to her in a poor light, he agreed reluctantly, and presently took a short cut from the cottage to Heronsmere. He arrived at the back door, and was waved in by the cook who was having some kind of an argument on the steps with the gardener.

'Come to see m'lady, I s'pose?' she queried, irritably. She was a crabbed-looking elderly woman, wearing a full length apron over a blue dress, with her grey hair pushed under a mob cap.

'You go wait in the kitchen,' she said, 'and I'll get word to Lady Marion. It's best she'd hear from me than that new stuck-up butler we've got. Everything's changed here now. Everythin'.'

Ben nodded and entered the house. The kitchens were large, having four inner doors leading to dairy, butler's pantry, a flagged narrow corridor that eventually joined the hall, and another in the floor from which stone steps led down to the cellars. A wood fire was burning in the large grate. On a shining deal table were numerous cooking utensils. The smell of baking came from the oven.

A girl was polishing cruets on a tray near the stone sink as Ben went in. She was young and comely, and obviously no regular kitchen maid. Ben turned his flashing smile on her, and she blushed. At that moment the cook appeared.

'Go an' ask if Lady Marion'll see this young man', she said shortly. 'Ben Curran, that's his name, an' doan' make a shout about it either. The master's had a turn not more'n half an hour back, an' we doan' want a scene.'

The girl rubbed her hands on a cloth, gave a little pat to her white cap from which odd curls of reddish hair escaped, and walked smartly through the far door into the hall. She returned two minutes later saying that Lady Marion would be pleased to see Mr Ben.

'She's in the conservatory, Mister Curran,' the girl said, 'it's warm there, an' she's not bin feelin' well today, so if you come with me—'

'I know the way,' Ben interrupted sharply. The girl would have protested, but Cook shook her head with a negative wave of a hand. 'Let him be. He shud be used to this place by now.'

'Thank you, Mrs Deane,' Ben said flashing a warm glance

at her that turned into an appreciative smile as his rested once more on the girl. She'd make a good model, he thought, stouter than the marble statue in the great hall, but beneath the starchy dress the full lines of her figure would be firm and young and well-shaped.

The pause was only brief. He moved suddenly and strode down the corridor towards a large reception room which led into the conservatory.

Marion was standing there by some exotic flowering plant, one hand resting on her stick. She was wearing purple, which didn't suit her. Her skin looked sallow and more drawn than when he'd seen her last. Her eyes looked enormous, and unnaturally bright, as though she might have used belladonna. Although tulle had been draped to soften the haggard lines of her neck, the taut muscles and sinews were still visible. She was breathing quickly, and the warmth of her smile somehow discomforted him.

She went towards him with one arm outstretched. 'Oh, Ben,' she said, 'how good to see you. It's been so long — but I expect you've been busy—?'

'Yes, very busy.'

'Sit down and do tell me all about it — your work, successes, your life in Truro, what commissions you've got—' The words poured out breathlessly with the excitement of a young girl on the brink of some new and wonderful experience. Yet nothing else just then was youthful about her. The years between them were suddenly cruelly obvious — a gap that for the first time made him feel awkward and ill-at-ease. She was too effusive, too intense in her welcome. All grace in her seemed to have crumbled since their last encounter, into premature age — an observation made more acute through his passionate, so recent interlude with Elfrida.

He did his best to present a factual picture of his days in Master Jacobs' home, trying not to exaggerate the importance of his newly elevated position, although at odd moments he spoke a trifle wildly, unable to disregard the avid enthusiasm on her homely face, and wishing heartily that he'd obeyed his own instincts not to call that day.

The atmosphere of the conservatory became stifling to him. He loosened his stock automatically which she instantly noticed.

'Is it too hot for you, Ben?' she enquired. 'I'm so sorry. I've not been well you see, so I need the warmth. But we could go to the library—'

'Oh no, Lady Marion—'

'Lady?' the little pout she gave did not become her.

'Marion then,' he said. 'I can't stay long. I've left my horse at home, and I've got to ride back to Truro tonight. It's been nice seeing you though.' He paused, adding a second later, 'I'm sorry your father, Sir Geoffrey's, not well.'

The light in her eyes chilled. Her under-lip tightened.

'He had a fall, you know.'

'Yes. I'd heard.'

'In time he may recover. But it will be slow, and nothing's certain. He's become difficult at times — then at others sometimes for a whole day, he says nothing at all.' She drew a hand across her eyes wearily.

'It must be very hard for you,' he commented, trying to sound sympathetic.

'If I could get out more it would be so much easier. But my foot prevents walking, and very few friends call now — in fact hardly anyone—' She broke off, taking an impulsive step towards him. 'Oh Ben — if you only knew how you help me — how wonderful it is to have you here — please—' Instinctively he backed away. She appeared not to notice, but followed him and took his two hands in hers, staring up at him with such hungry ardour he shrank inwardly, ashamed for her, and for himself in feeling such instant repulsion. To have a high-born lady pleading in that way — it wasn't decent, he thought wildly. He'd respected her before. She'd been a symbol of all that was gracious in life. But their worlds were different; and compared with him she was old — old!

'I must really be going,' he heard himself saying automatically, desperately trying to extricate himself from the embarrassing situation.

'Not yet — not yet—' Her hands clutched at him fiercely.

'Dearest Ben — I know I'm not beautiful, I can't expect you to — to admire me in that way. But you like me, don't you — and I can still help you in some ways. I'm not so very old either — ten years or twelve between us, it's nothing Ben. Please, please don't reject me. I need you so much. There's been something between us always. Even when you were a little boy you stole something, Ben — my heart. You couldn't guess it of course, but you were so beautiful and fair — and — and kind of different. I think I loved you from the very beginning. And now you're a man—'

She broke off as Ben tore himself away. 'Don't say it,' he said sharply. 'You're upset and sad, because of your father. For your own sake don't shame yourself by saying things that aren't true—'

'But they are. Oh, Ben, don't go—'

He turned quickly on his heel.

'I must. I'm sorry our friendship has to end like this, and I shall always be grateful for the encouragement you gave me when I was a kid. But it ends there. What you feel — what you think you feel — just isn't true. Goodbye.'

He took a few quick steps to the outer door leading into the grounds, and tried the handle. It must have been locked, it wouldn't move. Turning abruptly he went back to the inner entrance, hoping to escape unimpeded to the reception room. Lady Marion limped after him, pleading and imploring hysterically. As he crossed the room a large figure confronted him suddenly from the shadows. From a puffed florid countenance bulging eyes held an ironic gleam. He was breathing stertoriously, and as Ben tried to pass he gave a senile grin and pointed towards the conservatory.

'Gad!' he said, 'What a pretty sight. What a fool to be sure. What a snivelling monster I bred to inherit—'

Ben glanced back, and saw Marion on the floor, where she'd tripped, both hands clasped to her thin breast, tears streaming from her red-rimmed eyes. For a moment pity for her replaced disgust. He turned to assist her to her feet, but was pulled back by a sudden wrench at his coat collar.

'Get out — you young oaf,' Sir Geoffrey shouted, heavy jaw

thrust forward over his stock. 'Damme, man! Grab your
chance before the fruit of my loins has her claws on you. Take
a good look at the poor wretch—' Ben jerked himself away
and was about to strike the man when Marion's shrill cry
broke the tension. 'No. Don't. Do what he says. Can't you see?
He's — look at him.'

She'd got up by then. Ben automatically obeyed her, and
to his amazement saw that the bucolic countenance — Sir
Geoffrey's whole manner — had abruptly changed. All
colour had drained from his puffed cheeks and lips; he stood
rigidly erect, staring with contempt at Ben. 'I believe you
have been upsetting my daughter, sir. Kindly remove yourself before I have to call for assistance. Lady Marion is not
strong. I will not allow intruders to harass her—'

'He hasn't harassed me, father,' Marion said. 'This is Ben
Curran, my — my protégé, if you remember. I invited him
here for an account of his work and progress—'

All life seemed to have drained from her. Her voice sounded
sad and infinitely weary. Resignation enveloped her like a
shroud.

'Hm! Very well.'

Penherrion did not move, but waited by his daughter as
Ben after a brief pause, passed on towards the hall door.
They were still watching, standing side by side static as two
effigies, when he made his way quickly over the flagstones.

Once outside he hurried, half running, to the drive.

The encounter had numbed him. Even memory of Elfrida
was briefly obscured by the macabre impact of the meeting.

As he made his way up the hill to the Curran cottage the
light gradually deepened, enveloping the landscape by
sinister twilight. At intervals ancient standing stones pro-
truded dark and forbidding from the tangled undergrowth.
The wind was increasing to a persistent whine, carrying from
the distance the hollow sound of Red Bell's pumping engine.
From out at sea a ship's syren moaned. This was his own land
— the earth he'd been bred to, but suddenly Ben had an
overwhelming urge to be astride his horse and away, on the
journey back to Truro.

It would be a dark ride with only a few stars and a thin crescent moon showing intermittently through a rising belt of cloud. The thought of Master Jacobs' comfortable home and a good meal waiting with the brisk attractive presence of Maria to greet him increased his energy, and he covered the distance to his home in a minimum of time.

Never again, he told himself determinedly, would he be induced to call at Heronsmere. In future his visits to the locality would be very few indeed.

At that point he did not stop to consider Elfrida, neither did it occur to him that his living seed had already taken root in her womb.

Ben felt not only physically but mentally and emotionally drained, when he reached Gwynck that night. Rain had started during his journey, and his clothes dripped as he went into the Jacobs' after unsaddling and stabling his horse.

An oil lamp shone from the kitchen. He took off his coat before entering, shook it, then slung it over his arm, went in, and hung it on a peg just inside the door. He sat on a bench and was about to remove his boots when Maria emerged from the back hall. She walked quietly and was wearing a white wrap over her night-shift. She put a finger to her lips.

'Sh — we mustn't make a noise, Ben. Mama's had a long day. Father was taken worse after you left—'

'I'm sorry. If I'd known I wouldn't have gone.'

'You couldn't have known,' she said. 'Now sit down by the fire and take those boots off. I've broth on the range, and there's a hot brick in your bed. The warming pan's ready too.' He obeyed her, grateful for her concern and practical thought. Although it was late, past one o'clock, she moved quietly with brisk efficiency, and when some of the chill had left him he noted her slender figure had rounded out a little since he'd first known her, and that when the lamplight caught her hair the gingerish fairness became a deeper auburn. The ripple of fine silky waves falling to her shoulders made her appear much younger than her twenty-four years. Fine tendrils feathered her forehead. She looked almost pretty.

'You shouldn't have waited up so long,' he said. 'You'll be tired in the morning.'

'It's morning already. And I don't need much sleep. Anyway, I was worried.'

'About me?'

'Naturally. You're one of the family now; well, in a way, aren't you? And anything can happen on the roads these days — cut-throats, highwaymen.'

'They'd not get much out of me. I'd not be worth tackling.'

'They wouldn't know.' There was a pause after which she added flatteringly, 'You look outstanding on horseback, Ben.'

He grinned, and turned a work-ridden hand upwards.

'Me? With these?'

'No. Your hair — your — your stance. Your height and strength, and the way you ride. But I expect many women have told you that?'

He shook his head. 'If they have I've not listened. There's no time in my life for women.'

Her thin brows lifted above her shadowed eyes. 'None? Don't tell me that with your looks you've had no experience?'

The question, quite out of character with her usually prim exterior, took him aback. He didn't speak for a moment, then he said cautiously, 'I have my pleasures when I feel like it. I'm not a monk.'

And suddenly, with a pang, the memory of Elfrida blotted everything else from his mind. The impact was only brief. Almost instantly he was back in the present, warmed by the broth and a tot of brandy.

'I didn't mean to pry,' he heard Maria saying almost apologetically. 'These few hours have been rather a strain with my father lying so ill. I went to Gwynck earlier to try and get the apothecary. He didn't answer the door; out I suppose. But there was no point in waiting. It didn't seem right leaving Mama alone. The girl's at her home for the night —' her voice wavered, 'so if I sound frivolous you must forgive me. I was trying to get my mind into another direction—'

Ben inwardly cursed himself for his thoughtlessness.

He nodded. 'You've had a bad time lately. Wish I could do more to help.'

'That's impossible. You've done so much already. Without you I don't know we'd have got through at all. The business I mean — and — and everything.'

The implication of the last remark went by unheeded.

Presently, he was on his way up to his room where sleep overcame him immediately he was in bed.

He woke later than usual, dressed hurriedly, and went down for breakfast. The rain had increased, lashing against the windows and walls of the house on a rising wind. He thought of his brothers and father tramping across the soggy moor to the mine, and recalled days in his childhood when ships had been dashed on the rocks defenceless against the gales fury. This was the kind of morning when such tragedy might occur, followed by ugly plundering for cargo. Apart from the crew, natives at such times could become regardless of human life, fighting among themselves while sailors — seamen drowned. Even women could scream and fight each other when their families needed food and a little comfort to ease their hard lives. As a tiny boy he'd heard his mother tell of a nasty scene between bal maidens and other young women of the district for a box of figs discovered by chance in a hiding place under the cliffs. His eyes had boggled at her description of half naked female figures clawing and striking until the blood ran. The wreck had been of a merchantman on its way to Bristol, and of the crew only two had survived.

The following evening folk had gathered again from all parts of the district to search the shore. Occasionally a few small items of value had been discovered and cunningly hidden from the Military — the eyes of authority could not be everywhere, and hungry bellies defied conscience. James Curran himself had once retrieved a medallion which he'd sold to a dealer in Penzance. After that, Ben recalled, there'd been better food in the cottage for quite a time, and James had brought a young pig back from market to be housed in a wooden shed at the back of the cottage until its time came for more useful purposes.

Ugh! how Ben had hated the poor creature's dying screams. By then the pig had become his pet, and for a few moments following the killing, he'd wanted to kill everyone else as well, especially his father. The terrible feelings had lasted only a moment of course. After that he'd run away for the day, and hidden grief-stricken in his own retreat by Hook's Cove.

But he'd never forgotten the experience. And it had taught him something — that for survival man often had to do things that were odious and foreign to his better nature. It was about that time that the urge to create beauty from corruption and decay — salvage life from death — the struggle and inequality of the two worlds — of the rich and the poor — had fired his imagination like the seed of a tree determined to spring straight and strong from the hard earth. And he'd never wavered.

Neither would he now. And no compunction concerning Lady Marion's pitiful attempt to ensnare him would be allowed to interfere with his course. She had not deliberately wished to, he realised, when facing the incident objectively. She was tired, sick, lonely, and desperately in need of affection. But he had none to give of the kind she wanted. The idea was ludicrous. Perhaps he should have noted the way the 'wind was blowing' — as they said, earlier. But he'd never guessed. She was so much older — lame, rich, plain and a cripple. He wouldn't think of her or look on her again; no, he wouldn't. When he wanted a girl he'd find one to cool his passions until he could somehow contrive to have Elfrida always near. In the meantime Maria Jacobs was entirely satisfactory as a companion and ally in his work. And how she'd blossomed lately. Who'd have thought a few years ago — even one — that she could have turned from the prim young teacher into such an attractive creature? Not sensually, but smart to look at, intelligent, and always polite now, treating him as an equal — the up-and-coming partner of 'Jacobs, monumental and stone masons?'

Poor old Saul. Ben was genuinely grieved by his sorry state. From Maria's expression as he went into the parlour for breakfast that morning, he knew he was worse.

Maria nodded to his enquiry. There was the glimmer of tears in her eyes.

'I got up early and fetched the apothecary. There'll be a doctor coming later, but I don't think there's much hope.'

'Oh. I'm — I don't know what to say.'

'Say nothing. I'm trying to keep calm for Mama's sake. She's upstairs with him now. I can't drag her away from the bedside, although it would be better for him — and her. What use is praying and moaning when a man's dying?'

How brave she was, Ben thought admiringly. No hysterics or feminine vapours — no sobbing or wailing like he'd heard from women who'd lost their men down the mine. In spite of her rather frail form this daughter of Jacobs' had strength.

He ate his breakfast in almost complete silence, then went out to the yard to join Willie with the work on hand.

That same day, towards evening, Saul Jacobs died, and by an ironic coincidence, a letter was delivered the next day which was to alter the whole course of Ben's life.

## 3

Weeks before Saul's illness, Ben had noticed an advertise-
ment in a daily paper. This asked for designs and tenders
from monumental masons, for a statue to be erected at
Brexley's new pier head. The pier had been constructed as a
harbour of refuge at the western side of the fishing resort,
and the building was almost completed when the notice
caught Ben's eye. For two days his imagination had played
with the idea of submitting a suggestion. He had made
innumerable sketches, considered the use of stone, granite,
and marble carefully, dismissing the latter regretfully, realising the expense entailed and its unsuitability to the granite
structure of the pier itself. At last a possible pattern had
emerged. His imagination had been fired, and when the final
drawing was on paper it showed the simplified arched figure
of a woman with both arms extended outwards and forwards
to the sea, as though embracing all mariners to safety.

The lines of the carving were rhythmical — skirts blown
back as though from a great wind in perfect unison with the
swirling hair. The profile was tilted upwards, chin bravely
thrust towards the Atlantic. Both arms were extended ahead,
and on one wrist was a bird.

This he had stated in his letter to the town authorities was
merely symbolic of peace and refuge, and could be included
or not, as they required. He had envisaged it to be within the
height of ten feet, excluding the plinth, and in a particular
sturdy type of granite having a greenish tone which could be
polished to a brilliant surface. He had also added that having
tested the stone there was no question of its not withstanding
the fiercest of weather. He had priced the work tentatively at
a sum which seemed immense to him, but lower he knew,

than was generally paid for such work. Due to Saul's illness, Elfrida, dealing with extra orders at Jacobs', and consultations with Maria, the matter had been pushed to the back of his mind.

When he read the communication therefore, he was momentarily stunned by shock, then elated. The letter stated that his design — among others — had been favourably received, and as it included several features more original than most — his presence at Brexley's Town Hall was requested on a certain date and time.

The signature was of an important town dignitary. That it might be a joke did not occur to Ben. He had sufficient self-confidence to know it was true, and that the following week, in spite of the recent sad event, he would have to take temporary leave from Jacobs' yard.

Maria was outwardly encouraging when she heard although the thought of being alone in the house with her fretting mother dampened her spirits.

'It's a big thing for you — for us' she said. 'My father wouldn've been proud.'

'It mayn't come off,' he said. 'I guess there are lots of us with appointments.'

'Perhaps. But I don't think so. How long will you have to be away?'

'Only a night. They're paying for expenses if I go. At some lodging house probably.'

But when eventually Ben arrived at Brexley for his meeting with the contractor and architect responsible for the new pier, he discovered that his 'lodgings' for the following night were to be at a reputable coaching house which catered chiefly for the most select of guests, yet was homely enough to be welcoming and put him at his ease.

The meeting was scheduled for the following morning in Council chambers, and although no eyebrows were raised or too-effusive smiles given, the male breasts of the three dignitaries present were surprised — even mildly shocked by the arresting appearance of the young man who gave a momentary impression of some sea-going Nordic hero from

legend, rather than an ambitious young stone-mason wanting a well-paid job. The light from the window in the rather
gloomy official room turned his fair hair to an aureole of
gold. He stood proud and straight, almost arrogantly before
them, his cold clear eyes unswervingly upon their faces — two
of them stout and ruddy, the other yellowish and lean. He
answered questions decisively, though his stomach churned
with nerves.

'They won't like my idea,' he thought, 'they're not my
kind. No imagination. What they want's an effigy of the King
or something.' Towards the end of the interview, during a
pause in which he felt a queer sense of foreboding, he
suddenly said, 'If you don't like my idea, I've others.'

'Oh?'

'Plenty,' he retorted, touching his mop of hair. 'Inside here
sirs. I'm not short of suggestions. If you didn't want a
woman's figure it could be something else.'

'Such as?'

'You could have a sea-horse — a giant thing — even a kind
of mermaid. Then there's the anchor idea. But you wouldn't
get the design there. For the sea you should have the feeling
of waves breaking, an' flying things like birds, or a woman's
hair—'

He broke off there, disturbed by a tumult of emotions that
revived suddenly the memory of Elfrida's pale waving tresses
blown back on a Cornish wind — of her perfect profile out-
lined against the clear sky above the moors.

He pulled himself together abruptly and heard a man's
voice saying. 'No, I don't think so. Your original suggestion
was the one that interested us. Well, Mr Curran, before any
decision's made you'd better come along to the site. Know
Brexley, do you?'

Ben shook his head. 'I've not travelled. But I know stone,
and wood, and how to chip and carve and construct.'

The hint of a smile touched the lean sardonic countenance. 'Hm. You've a good opinion of yourself, young man.'

'Fair, sir. Confidence. If I hadn't that I wouldn't be here.'

Instead of jeopardising Ben's chances of obtaining the

important commission, his assertion appeared to revitalise the interview, with the result that half an hour later he was being conducted to the site.

The new pier stretched like a gigantic arm from the western side of the town, providing considerable refuge from the wild Atlantic for ships driven by cruel gales and weather towards the rugged coast. Half a mile away, to the east, the natural harbour for fishing boats remained intact — overlooked by the 'old town' — a conglomeration of twisting cobbled streets and higgledly-piggledly cottages which every year was drawing more visitors to the area.

Ben felt a sudden revival of elation. The coloured sails — the atmosphere — the foreign, almost Breton-like quality of the vista made him say suddenly, 'I like it. New things welcoming the old. No break — no messing about with the character of the place by some brash monument. This new part — the pier, should be symbolic if you know what I mean — beyond time, not panderin' to fashion or any new fangled cult. You want a feeling of waves and wind and — and—'

'Yes, Mr Curran?'

Dispelling a sudden trespassing vision of Elfrida, Ben added ambiguously, 'Creation, movement. Something that'll go on forever—'

'I like your enthusiasm, young man. But nothing does endure forever you know. Quite likely in a century or more some clever-dick of a Johnny may want the whole thing changed again. That is if we accept your design of course.'

Ben lifted his fine head a little higher. His jaw had a dogged thrust when he said, 'Not mine, they won't. I don't intend to be forgotten. What I make I aim to remain.'

From the fleeting gleam of admiration in the other man's eyes, Ben knew his show of self confidence had made an impression. He'd hoped, when he first set off for the interview that the matter would be settled on the spot. So he was vaguely disappointed when he was told at the end of the discussion that he would be hearing of the official decision in a few days.

'Well?' Maria demanded as soon as he arrived back at

Jacobs following the wearying journey from Brexley to Gwynck, 'How did it go? Did you get it Ben? Did you?' In spite of the reddened lids of her eyes which were still strained from grieving for her father, there was such enthusiasm in her voice — such expectancy, he was briefly touched. During the last week she had lost weight, but extreme thinness had accentuated the fine bones of her face, which combined with the wispy gingerish hair gave her a waif-like appearance.

He smiled and patted her shoulders. 'Don't know yet, Maria. But I think they liked me — or my design, anyway.'

'Come into the kitchen then, and tell me all about it,' she said. 'I've kept something hot for you.'

He followed her into the room, and when they were both seated by the fire following a tasty meal which Ben ate with relish, he did his best to put her in the picture, describing Brexley, the hotel, the people he'd met, mimicking the voices and expressions of the sombre lugubrious character, and the more rotund owl-like appearance of the other two officials with such adroit whimsicality, that in spite of her sadness she smiled.

'That's good,' he told her. 'To have the gloom off your face for a minute makes you look — well, almost a girl, Maria.'

She instantly stiffened. 'I didn't know I ever seemed so old to you.'

'You didn't, and you're not,' he interjected quickly. 'What I meant was — no one could expect you not to feel down, after what you've gone through — losing your father, and having the responsibility of everything — your mama so upset and depending on you, and the business. Of course while I'm here I'll deal with that as well as I can, and Willie's sturdy and dependable. But—'

'While you're here?' Her voice was shrill with shock. 'What do you mean? You're not thinking of leaving? You can't. Tell me, it's not that is it? You belong to Jacobs' now. My father said so. Time after time those were his very words. "Ben will carry on when I've gone," he said. "While he's at the Yard you'll have nothing to worry about."' There was a pause, her voice was softer when she continued, 'You do believe me, don't you?'

He hesitated before answering. Then he replied cautiously, 'Yes, I believe you, Maria.'

'And you'll stay?'

He turned away, trying to avoid the over-anxious demand in her slightly protuberant eyes. At that moment she did not look young at all — merely haggard and hungry for something he couldn't give her.

'Well then?' she persisted. 'Say it then. Say you'll be here — always.' Her hand gripped his arm. He gently eased it away.

'Always is a long word, Maria, and so's belonging. And no one can look ahead too far. I wouldn't leave you in the lurch, you know that. Jacobs had done a lot for me. Why do you have to go doubting things—?'

'Because I want to be sure. You're all I've got now — except for Mama.'

He got up and walked to the window uncomfortably. 'Come on now! a young lady like you's got all life ahead. One day you'll meet some good man who'll marry you, and be a fine husband. You'll have children and a nice home and all this sadness'll be forgotten—'

'Thank you!' she said, startling him by the sharp comment. 'Who do you think you are, Ben Curran, to think and suggest I need a good man? Or a husband for that matter?'

He shrugged, and ambled back towards the fire. 'It's what most women want.'

'I'm not "most women".' Her tones were acid. 'There are other things in life. I've got my — my teaching, and I thought I'd been some use to you—'

'Of course you have,' he told her, relieved to find the subject on safer ground. 'Without your help I wouldn't have—' He broke off, knowing that what he'd been about to say was quite untrue. The fact was, that he'd have achieved his object with or without any minor advice or feminine suggestions from Maria Jacobs. The yard and Saul's practical assistance and background had set him on his feet, it was true, but he wasn't going to give any exaggerated impression of indebtedness to Maria.

In the pause that followed Maria regained some composure,

knowing it had been dangerous to betray her inner feelings so heedlessly.

'I've been rather stupid, carrying on like this,' she said, rubbing one eye with a shred of handkerchief. 'Forget it, Ben. I'm just tired. And never fear I want to tie you down. That would be most unfair. It means a great deal to me just having you here when you're so needed—' She smiled, and appeared a different woman. Thank heaven, he thought, in the reaction of relief. Women were the devil and no mistake. There was no making out any of their real feelings, such complicated creatures as they were, and always on the look-out, seemingly, for something he hadn't got to give. Even that poor lame Marion! As for Elfrida! let her long for him a bit, he decided, with the ruthless decision of a man dedicated to his work. She'd be there — waiting — when he had the time and opportunity for making the journey. At the moment he'd got enough on his hands without risking the danger of further emotional involvement. She knew where she stood now — she was his. They both knew it. He trusted her completely. And if he found, when the time came, he'd been wrong, he'd tame her in the good old-fashioned way so she never looked at another man again. He grinned to himself, and with a sudden surge of vitality and renewed enthusiasm went out into the yard to contemplate and discuss his plans for the monument with Willie.

One of the conditions imposed for the commission was the time limit of six months. A short enough period for such a work, but Ben was sure he could do it, with the maximum energy, and no moment for slacking. He had to wait for a fortnight until the immense slab of the special granite needed was delivered, and during that time Maria was careful to keep her feelings — externally — on an even keel. When he was tired and exhausted through amending plans, working out further costing, and arranging for space in the yard — for new trestles to be delivered and other equipment, Maria was always available with quiet encouragement and some vintage or other to restore his equilibrium. Willie meanwhile dealt with lesser orders and being of a placid nature made no grumble at having to work overtime.

Ben wrote a brief letter to Elfrida at that period, assuring her of his love, and explaining why he could not leave Gwynck at such a time.

'But on the first opportunity love, I'll be up and over to you—' he ended. 'Be patient now — I'm on to big things, and one day they'll be yours as well.

Always your own.<br>Ben.'

Life might have worked out very differently for him if Elfrida had ever got his letter. But she didn't. It was left on the hall-table with other correspondence, his own and the family's — to be posted by Ellen that morning.

Seeing the envelope, and recognising the name — for Elfrida the lovely daughter of the old witch Martha Crane, was already becoming a notoriety — Saul's widow very carefully and methodically tore it up.

Maria caught her in the act.

'Whatever are you doing, Mama?' she enquired, appearing in the hall from the parlour.

'Sh!' Ellen put a finger warningly to her lips. 'Come here, Maria.'

She led her daughter back into the room, went to the fireplace and put a match to the torn pieces of paper.

'This—' she said in a low voice, 'was from Ben to that girl he knows — Martha Crane's wild grandchild. She'll do him no good, Maria. It's best they've no truck with each other — for him, and for you—'

Maria stared, shocked.

'But you can't — it isn't right—'

Ellen smiled grimly. 'I already have, my girl. Ben deserves the best he can get in life. He belongs to Jacobs now. You could say that in a way Jacobs is already his. And one day so will you be.'

From that time through various devious means any contact between Elfrida and Ben was effectively intercepted. At times the haunting memory of her returned so vividly he almost threw down his tools to make a wild ride to see her.

Then commonsense returned. There wasn't a moment to
spare. The monument demanded more strength, initiative
and ceaseless hard work even than he'd anticipated. Every
second was needed to get it finished to schedule. When she
did not reply to a second note from him asking for news, he
determinedly put her to the back of his mind. Only brief
notes to his parents ever reached their destination. A communication from Lady Marion met the same fate as Ben's to
Elfrida, although Ellen read it first.

It was a pathetic note.

Dearest Ben, Why do I never hear from you? I am sick, and
so very lonely. Papa has to stay in his room now, he is so very
strange and wild-mannered. Will you not at least pay me a
short visit and tell me how your carving goes? I still have
your wonderful little animals on my mantelshelf. You used
to think so much of me. I don't expect love any more,
although I think at one time you did care for me a little.

   Please forgive me if my words sound so sad and out of
place. And please come.

   Yours ever.
      Marion.

'The poor creature,' Ellen thought with mingled feelings of
contempt and pity. What point would there have been in
risking Ben's distress at having to refuse her pleas? And if he
didn't? Heaven alone knew what the results might be. People
like the Penherrions had power, and she, Ellen Jacobs, did
not intend Maria's chances of becoming Ben's wife to be
jeopardised because of any highly-born possessive lady
thinking he owed her something. Any guilt Ellen felt was
smothered ruthlessly. Elfrida and Lady Marion belonged to a
past that was over for Ben, and in the meantime it was up to
her to see that her daughter made the most of her chances.

   Once the intrigue had started, Maria tried to forget her
mother's duplicity, arguing to herself that there was nothing
else she could do. However calculating and devious Ellen's
actions might be — the word 'dishonesty' was not permitted
— the idea of betraying Ellen was quite out of the question.

So Maria acted with decorum, never forcing her company on Ben when he wished to be alone, but was always at hand when he needed her, assisting in book-work, and dealing with orders which she handed over to Willie. She was careful with her appearance too, and Ben never guessed that the becoming faint flush on her cheeks was not entirely due to nature. She bought two new dresses — one of a peach shade, one of a bluish green that emphasised the shade of her eyes. When Ben noticed her at all he was impressed by her new dignity. She symbolised the future of Jacobs. Emotionally he was not involved, but there were moments when he visualised her as an attractive and competent business partner.

In late summer the towering sculpture was completed, polished, and before despatch to Brexley stood imposingly in Jacobs' Yard for two days until the carriers arrived to dispatch it, with plinth, on its journey to Brexley.

Ben, unwilling to trust his precious work alone with strangers, accompanied the driver. He looked magnificent wearing a new bottle green jacket bought for the occasion, white stock, and with his tall silk hat resting on his knees.

'You should have gone by train,' Ellen had said critically before they started, 'or at least have worn something simpler for the journey. Those fine twill breeches will get all dusted on the way.'

Ben had smiled. 'There'll be plenty of dust where I'm going,' he'd said. 'Gold dust, ma'am.'

His teeth had flashed in a brilliant smile. Although he lifted a hand to the two women watching him from the gate, the ice-blue eyes hardly saw them, but were on another vision — far away — a vision encompassing grander and even finer works than this, which would one day earn him fame in posterity through the world.

The journey was tedious and slow, entailing a night en route at a hostelry where Ben insisted on having a room overlooking the inn yard. He slept very little, and many times got up, glancing out of the window to ensure himself there was no prying or poking by intruders at his masterpiece under its cover.

When at length he reached Brexley the following after-noon he almost wished he'd taken Ellen's advice and travelled by train. But an hour later, fortified by a good meal and wash at the hotel, a liberal amount of whisky, and the assurance of his own reflection in the mirror, weariness disappeared as if by magic. Elation soared in him — a sensation that never entirely deserted him during his three days at Brexley. He received an official welcome at the town hall the next day. Later came the unveiling of the statue at the end of the pier. When at last the speeches and murmurs of approval had abated, his own self-vanity turned to awe.

So proud and lovely and far-seeing she looked — his dark green shining goddess of granite with her flying hair, tilted breasts, and chin turned to the waves. The afternoon was mostly grey, but when the sun momentarily broke through the clouds it seemed to him, fleetingly, that she really lived, a queen of the elements of rain and wind and sparkling sun — of light and shade, tears and laughter.

Elfrida!

Emotion shook him. She seemed everywhere. Just for a short time he imagined his palm pulsed through contact with her flesh. He waited for the whisper of her voice in his ear, the touch of her soft lips against his cheek. Then abruptly he came to himself, felt a further congratulatory pat of an official hand on his shoulder, heard mechanically stilted words of approval from guests anxious to make his acquaintance.

So this was success!

He lifted his head proudly, fully aware of feminine eyes turned on him from every direction. He savoured the acclaim — a golden haired young giant of a man with the world, metaphorically speaking, at his feet.

Excitement, following the wining and toasting, gave him heady dreams that night, filled with all the glamour of success. A rich man's dreams! yes, he would be rich one day. Other sculptors would follow him around and try to steal his ideas. Women would fete and court him. And all the time there would be that secret glow in his heart for just one — Elfrida of the moor, for whom he'd build a home of shining marble, and have her richly attired and beautiful for only himself.

At times he tossed and turned in the bed restlessly — reaching over the sheets for a touch of her arm or breast. Then once more his mind would succumb to unconsciousness and its deep wild wandering.

In the morning however the elation had died to a dull headache. His throat felt dry, and the exhilaration had turned a little sour.

But when, at the end of the day he arrived back at Gwynck good humour revived. Maria's stare of astonishment as he flung his bag of gold on the parlour table enhanced his self-esteem to such an extent he suddenly grasped her by her shoulders and planted a firm kiss on her cheek.

She blushed, gasped and put a slender hand to the cameo brooch where her thin throat pulsed.

'Oh Ben!' she exclaimed. 'To think it's really true. You're a success. Oh — I'm so proud of you.'

The way she spoke, almost naively — she, the cool composed Maria Jacobs — might have irritated him at any other time. But just then he accepted the praise as his due. Ellen also was gratified, but in a more businesslike way. 'We shall have to charge more now, Ben,' she stated presently, as they finished a late meal. 'We'll have to see a solicitor to get you made a proper legal partner of the firm—'

'Partner?' The word came out sharply; she seemed so cock-sure.

'Of course, Ben, equal sharing with Maria and myself. What I thought was—' On and on her voice ran, giving him no opportunity to agree or demur. As far as Ellen was concerned all plans were made and ready for formal signing. There was a moment when he was on the point of interrupting, of telling her he'd have to think about things. But he wisely held his tongue. With Maria gazing at him so admiringly and her mother so obviously anxious to get him 'ensnared' — that's what it certainly appeared — he knew the power really lay with him. When they got down to 'brass-tacks' he'd have a few of his own ideas to offer.

Next morning, after a meeting with Willie in the yard, he had his horse saddled for a ride to see his family and Elfrida.

Maria remonstrated at first. 'Can't you go another day?' she asked when he pointed out how long it was since he'd seen his parents. 'There'll be people calling today to offer congratulations, and Mama's already got some wine up from the cellar — home-made elderflower.'

'That's true,' Ellen affirmed. 'One day can't make that much difference.'

'I'm going this morning,' Ben affirmed with a stubborn set to his chin. 'Let the folks wait. Sorry. I've got duties at home you know. Maria knows that, don't you, Maria?'

Maria grudgingly nodded her head.

So by ten o'clock Ben was riding cross-country towards the North Coast. The air was fresh and heady with pungent autumn scents of misted damp undergrowth, tumbled brown leaves and fallen blackberries mingled with the faint blown tang of brine from the distant sea — spindrift. As he headed from twisting narrow lanes to the open country the easy canter of horse and rider turned to a wild gallop. Mine stacks emerged against the silvered grey of hills; gulls wheeled over the small stone-walled fields, and at intervals ancient menhirs rose from the past, standing sentinel-like from the tall withering bracken. Occasionally in sheltered places a few late foxgloves still bloomed languidly. But soon they would be gone. Winter lay ahead — a period of crisp frosts, wild rain and gales interspersed with calm fog-wrapt periods when only a whisper of wind broke the silence. The waves would be quiet then, lapping gently at the pale shore. Hook's Cove would be shrouded in mystery, with a thousand shimmering shells and pebbles glowing iridescently from rain and sea.

Gradually all memories and images from the past resolved into just one form — that of Elfrida. His pulses quickened with the strong leaping of his heart. He'd meant to call at his home first, but at the dividing of the moorland track, he decided impulsively to take the turn leading to Elfrida's cottage. From a hundred yards away, he saw, to his surprise, there was no smoke coming from the chimney. Neither was there any movement or flash of white where the goats were generally tethered. No cloth or apron hung from the line where washing was so often pegged, and the door appeared shut.

He reined his horse for a few seconds, then jerked the animal to a canter. At the gate he halted again and sat with his hand on his mount's bridle, staring. A sense of fear and desolation rose in him. All life seemed to have departed. The blinds were drawn against the muslin window curtains. The garden was neglected and over-grown with brambles.

'Elfrida—' he called automatically, then cupping his hands, '—Elfrida — it's me—'

There was no reply.

The promise of a glitter of pale sunlight behind the mist slipped away again into enveloping grey. He dismounted, tethered the mare quickly to a stump of dead tree, pushed the gate open, and as he did so it creaked and fell to one side from its hinges.

He ran up the path, and tried the door knob several times. It didn't move. He banged his first frenziedly against it, all the time shouting her name. In a fit of fear and anger he kicked the wood and splintered it sufficiently to see that all was dark and deserted inside. At the back of the cottage the animal sheds also were empty and bereft of life.

He was about to force his way through the broken door when a man's gruff voice startled him.

'No good lookin' theer, young Curran. There edn' anyone at Martha's any more.'

Ben swung round. Dan, an old shepherd he'd known since childhood, stood bent and wizened with locks as grey and thin as cottongrass straggling over his shoulders. His face was brown and gnarled, his eyes seemed to probe Ben's with a furtive malicious triumph.

'Where is she then? Where's Elfrida?' Ben asked, steeling himself not to grip the ancient shoulders and shake him till the answer came rattling from the toothless jaws. The old face thrust itself an inch or two nearer. Then he cocked a thumb towards the valley. 'Squire's place, that's where.

She'm with 'er ladyship all fine an' sly an' full o' wickedness. They say down to Gwynck, they two of 'em do roast toads o' night, an' dance over chamber-pots when moon be full. You kip away young Ben unless you do wish th' Devil isself to get 'ee—'

With a curse Ben pushed the unpleasant character aside, untethered his horse, and the next moment was riding madly, regardless of bog, stones, or hidden shaft, down the slope towards Heronsmere.

He led the horse by its bridle down a side drive, handed it to a stable boy who stood gaping nearby, then made his way to the front. Facing the terrace the door stood slightly ajar. He ran up the steps and tugged the bell pull several times. A crone of a woman in a mob cap, muttering to herself, emerged from the shadows moving grudgingly towards him. The rattle of distant cutlery from the kitchen broke the complete silence except for the slow shuffling of the servants' footsteps. Ben was about to speak when a splash of brightness lit to pale silvery gold from a narrow Gothic window brought a brief glow to the scene. A figure in a full blue gown pushed the old woman aside, and hurried towards him. Her face was pale, no smile touched her lovely lips — there was no welcome in her eyes.

'Elfrida,' he said, '—Oh Elfrida—' He moved to enter, to take her into his arms crushing her sweetness hard against him, drowning his senses in the soft mass of silken hair, the flower-like heather-scent of lips, cheek, and yielding soft flesh.

But her stance chilled him. She stood remote and cold, with eyes narrowed, and mouth tight and condemning. She had put on a little weight, he noticed; in other ways, too, she appeared subtly different — more voluptuous, but still infinitely desirable.

'What do you want?' she asked in a voice he'd never heard before. She turned briefly to dismiss the old woman, while he struggled for words, to understand. It had been a long time of course, he told himself. Six months. More. She was angry with him — she'd missed him. It was just a mood — when she faced him again he was smiling.

'My love! — Elfrida—' He sprang towards her. She backed, blazing with the contempt of a wild thing caught unawares.

'Go away,' she said. 'Don't dare touch me. I despise — *hate* you, Ben Curran—'

'What the hell's the matter with you? What do you mean?'

'You never came.' Like ice the words cut him. 'Even when I wrote you never answered. And Lady Marion—'

'Well? What about her?'

'You know very well. After all you'd been to her, leading her on, letting her think you cared — you couldn't spare a second even when she was so ill.'

'But I didn't know—'

'Of course you knew. She wrote to you, just as I did — but no answer came. Maybe in time I could let myself forgive what you did to me — it was a nice game for you, wasn't it, two women at once?—' Her lip curled momentarily, he had no way of knowing the pain it cost her recalling those wild passionate moments on the moor. 'But *Marion!* after her generosity to you, and her father so mad and sick! What sort of man are you, Ben Curran? Or aren't you one at all? Are you just a greedy creature out for fame and gold ready to trick any poor innocent stupid enough to believe in you—' She broke off, shivering. 'Go away. Get out of my sight.'

'No.' The word came out flatly, like the crack of a pistol shot. He took her by the shoulders and felt her body stiffen as he forced her against him. Anger flooded him. She struggled wildly to keep her lips from his. But his mouth was on hers, his hands and arms ruthlessly about her body as she fought and scratched, finally releasing herself. One hand went to a cheek. Her face was a bitter mask. Suddenly the fire in him drained, leaving him wretched and bewildered from the conflict.

'I shall be back,' he said with an effort. 'Obviously I've got things wrong somewhere. And this talk of letters — when did you write?'

She turned away. 'Don't pretend, and don't try and get round me again. You know very well. You're nothing to me, Ben Curran. Just go please, and leave us at peace.'

'Us? *Us?*'

He saw then, another figure coming towards him down the hall; she had a limp and was wearing black.

At the foot of the stairs she paused, watching them and saying nothing. Her face in the poor light appeared drawn and greyish, quite without expression, except for the eyes which burned with a curious dead-pan kind of triumph. There was a pause in which slow understanding began to stir Ben's bewilderment. That last interview when he'd had to repulse her! — surely, surely the once gracious lady could not have resorted to such devious jealous deceit? Unable to think of any suitable greeting he adjusted his stock, turned on his heel, and walked quickly down the steps to the drive.

He turned once. The two women were standing together watching. The one so fair and desirable, the other formidable as some stone effigy forever in command. A sense of fatalism encompassed him. It was as though a wall had been built which he would never now be able to penetrate.

He did not, after all, call on his family that day, but rode straight back to Gwynck.

Maria, self-possessed, with only a crinkle of anxiety between her brows, was waiting for him.

Her admiration and esteem for him was suddenly very important — an anchor of normality which subdued his irrational ardour to commonsense.

Later that evening he recklessly asked her to marry him, a proposal which Maria Jacobs gratefully and warmly accepted.

# 4

Because of practical issues Ben was content for the time being to start his wedded life with Maria at the Jacobs' home. Two rooms — a parlour and bedroom were re-decorated and made ready for early November, following their marriage. Ellen was pleased, and inwardly congratulated herself for the successful outcome of her planning. The wedding was a quiet affair at Gwynck Church, with a reception later at the house. Although Ben's parents and his eldest brother attended, Ellen contrived somehow to keep them in the background without appearing deliberately inhospitable or rude. Ben, slightly surprised and bewildered by the culmination of events, was too busy in his new role of husband to notice any deviousness on his mother-in-law's part. Although he'd gone into things with his eyes wide open, truth at odd moments threatened to divert his thoughts with discomforting persistence. He managed always to dispel it, shutting his mind like a door snapping on the past.

Maria, now, was his wife, bringing further security to his future. Saul had left her well-off, and from thereon Ben would share not only the marriage bed, but the successful business as well. In this he would have the greater power. Her place, as a woman, would be in the home, and to provide him with children — strong sons preferably, who could carry on a famous tradition after him. Yes; it was all settled now. The fame would come. Everything he'd planned for was on the way. Everything except — Elfrida. For one second during the festive proceedings, her image suddenly swamped him. Maria was about to cut the cake. Her face, pale and narrow under its curled mass of fine ginger hair, seemed to disintegrate, leaving another's beneath the entwined crown of orange blossom – the lovely, ethereal, condemning countenance of the girl he'd held so wildly in passion – Elfrida! oh Elfrida!

His hands gripped the edge of the table. Sweat trickled down his forehead. Something must have shewn, for from close by as in a dream he heard someone saying, 'Are you all right? – I say, p'raps a tot of brandy—'

Angry at his own unexpected weakness Ben pulled himself together.

'Brandy? – I've had too much as it is. God though! it's hot in here.' He struggled with the stock at his neck, wishing heartily for the whole thing to be over – the congratulations and stupid jokes, and Maria's cow's eyes doting on him so obviously. But of course that wasn't a fair description. They were good eyes, he told himself as he recovered, a little pale and protruding, but changing colour in certain lights, like quartz. And her figure in the white frilly dress with the fitting bodice, was better than he'd imagined – quite full breasts above the small waist. Promising, he thought, tearing his mind to the present. It never occurred to him there could be padding under the silk or hoop-like contraptions accentuating the hips.

Through reason of business being brisk at the yard, a honeymoon had been deferred until January. So the wedding night was to be spent under Jacobs' roof. The bedroom had been repapered in a maroon shade entwined with a paler pink rose design. The furniture, made by Saul's father was of mahogany on Chippendale lines. The bed, wide and canopied, had a patchworked quilt on it, beneath an eiderdown the same shade as the walls. Ewer and basin stood on a marble topped wash-stand. Rugs covered a large portion of the oil-clothed floor.

Ellen had placed a large receptacle of pot pourri on the dressing table, and artificial flowers and dried rushes sprayed out from a glass vase on the heavy chest of drawers. The effect was meant to be cosy and inviting, but as a faint waft of camphor and polish drifted to the door on warm air from the fire, Ben felt a sudden cloying wave of misgiving – almost fear. On the threshold he paused, staring past Ellen who was holding the door wide, and smiling beguilingly.

'Come, Ben,' she said coyly, 'your wife is waiting for you to carry her over the threshold.'

Ben jerked himself to attention. He turned his head, looked down, and saw a trembling, hopeful smile on Maria's lips.

'Of course,' he said.

He lifted her up, felt her wriggle slightly, and suddenly grudging desire rose in him. Her whole body was trembling when the door closed, leaving them alone.

He laid her down on the bed, waited a few moments until Ellen's footsteps had receded down the stairs, then returned to his bride. She had eased herself up, and was making a pretence of tidying her hair and straightening the lace at her throat.

He stood looking at her, smiling wryly.

'No need for formalities now, Maria,' he said.

She sat up. 'What do you mean?'

'Oh come now.' He drew her to her feet again, and with a clumsy motion that was partly due to nerves, pulled the dress apart, and let it fall to her feet revealing the layers of petticoats and false cups above the stays.

'Those! what are they?'

She crimsoned.

'You'd no right to see. You should be more — more polite.'

She turned away, fiddling with the contraptions, and reaching at the same time ineffectually for the long white shift laid on the bed. With a touch of mischief he jerked the waistband of the top petticoat, then the second, leaving her body exposed except for her slippers and frilly pantaloons reaching to her ankles. She looked round wildly for a wrap, but was too late. It already lay over Ben's arm. He laughed. She slapped his face. He pushed her on the bed again and drew the stupid garments off. Then, driven by resentment and an urgent desire to be master — to prove from the first where they both stood, he flung off his coat and breeches and was on top of her, ravishing her thin body — forgetful of everything but the *need* to forget — to forget in demonstrating his power over this one woman the dark deep need for another — for Elfrida.

When it was over he said almost apologetically, 'I didn't mean to be rough. But that's what marriage is—'

'Is it?' Her voice was cold, though her eyes were hot, her body burning with pain and humiliation. Had he but known it, his apparent disregard for her feelings would never completely be erased from her mind.

'You'll get used to it,' he said casually. 'You shouldn't have fought me so—'

'And you shouldn't have taken so much for granted. There are things you'll have to learn, too, Ben—'

'Such as?'

'You'll find out.'

In spite of himself he was discomforted. He'd no wish for things to go badly with Maria and himself. Out of bed she would be an asset, and she still possessed considerable power at Jacobs'! So he did his best to comfort her, and later, when he lay exhausted but not at peace by his sleeping wife, he closed his eyes so the looming fire lapped mahogany furniture and feather mattress into an illusion of heathered hills which at last took him to oblivion.

During the weeks and months following the stark realism of that first night, Ben made an effort to make amends, under a show of consideration which was partly due to sexual indifference. Maria, on her part, was careful mostly, to hide any aversion she felt to the physical act, and be — as Ellen put it — a dutiful wife.

The romantic illusions she'd had before marriage — of shared secrets, tenderness, and whispered words of adoration and sentimental avowals from her young husband had been dispelled for ever, as though a seering wind had stiffened her to stoical acceptance of her true position.

As compensation she took every opportunity of behaving decorously in public, of being the perfect hostess when the necessity arose, and interesting herself determinedly in the future of the Yard. Ben was astonished, even admiring, of her increasingly quick business sense and acumen in pointing out the need for adjustment in any new project or commission.

There were times when although he knew she was right, he resented it. His ideas could so easily soar beyond practical issues. On a small scale he toyed with suggestions that were not really sculpture at all — but mobile creations combining a number of materials — clay, shells, wire and driftwood, put together so at a waft of wind they moved, becoming living creatures of earth and air.

This was his game, his relaxation. But Maria was ruthless in condemning it. 'There's no point in it, dear,' she said in the firm quiet way she adopted towards children. 'Your genius must be strong and powerful enough for the world to recognise it. These little things are original and quite — charming — in their way. But they mean nothing, Ben. No one would understand them.'

'No one has to, but me,' Ben said once.

Maria shrugged her shoulders lightly. 'I'm sorry. I shouldn't criticise. But there's that large tombstone for Sir George Carndale's grave—'

'It will be finished to schedule,' Ben said coldly, 'and I very much doubt the old rake would care a damn whether he had an angel or a chamber pot over his head, or a piece of flying metal.'

Maria flushed.

'You sound quite disgusting.'

'I am. I feel it. So might you, if you were kept hacking at granite and stone for dead men's bones all day.'

Stifling another hot retort, Maria said more gently, 'I'm sure something big will turn up again soon, Ben. There have been a lot of gravestones lately. But the Yard's doing so well, and that means security for all of us, doesn't it? Especially for you. Fame — never forget the future.'

As usual Maria proved to be right.

Shortly following that brief conversation, an important

personal contract was completed, for Ben to design and sculpt a figure for some private gardens on the outskirts of Bristol. He had almost forgotten his entry which had been submitted to tender, having heard nothing for a considerable time, and telling himself some better known and more available firm had probably snapped up the opportunity before his drawings had even been properly noticed.

He was naturally elated. Being a lover of nature, from which he visualised imaginative and pagan forms emerging, he waved the letter delightedly, gave a whoop of joy, and flung it on the table before the astonished gaze of Maria and her mother.

'No more memorials or gravestones for a bit,' he announced, with a wide grin radiating his face. 'No more dreary tablets to death and decay. This means life, Maria. A chance to give the devil a bit of a dance, instead of those eternal praying angels—'

'Whatever do you mean, Ben?' his mother-in-law asked with a touch of acid shock in her voice.

When he'd explained Maria looked at first pleased, then gradually, as certain aspects of the project registered a small frown deepened between her eyes.

'You'll have to go up there, I suppose?' she asked dubiously.

'Naturally. For a day or two. What matter? There'll be Willie and the boy to carry on here. Bristol's a long way, and I shall probably have to spend quite a time discussing this and that. Anyway all expenses will be paid. See here—'

He pointed to the document. 'It says so. My God, what a chance. It'll be something seeing Bristol, and to think my work's going to stand there—'

'What about Maria?' Quick and flat, Ellen's interruption broke his flight of fancy.

'Maria? What do you mean?'

'She's not had a honeymoon. A change would do her good. I think it could — should be afforded just this once, don't you?'

Her rather hard eyes held his unswervingly. He forced a placating half smile to his lips. 'I agree with you,' he said calmly. 'But not practical.'

'Why?'

'Because the journey would be tiring for her. The trains and the ferry crossing, you know Maria isn't a good traveller, and when I get there, there won't be any time to go sight-seeing or shopping. It'd worry me thinking of her being bored and exhausted and alone. A holiday's one thing — we'll have one a bit later on, I promise — a business trip quite another. I know Maria agrees with me.'

'How do you know?' Maria enquired tartly. 'I should be in the way. Is that it?'

Ben almost said, 'Yes, you would. You're not ready — your clothes aren't right, or your conversation — nothing's right about you for the people I'll have to meet. I mayn't be a gentleman born, but I've got a way with me. People are interested — curious, and I stand out. But you don't. You're ordinary — prim—' The unspoken thoughts raced through his mind while Maria regarded him closely.

'Well?' she continued after the pause. 'I asked a question, Ben.'

He decided to be honest.

'You wouldn't help, and that's a fact. A man wants to feel free when there's important business to tackle.'

'I see. Very well. But—' she hesitated before continuing with a rising note in her voice, 'Don't think it will be like this every time you go away, Ben. I have rights in Jacobs' too. And you've said in the past my ideas on design were often a great help.'

'Of course they are. For some things specially. But this time I haven't got to be limited and all goody-goody religious, Maria. I can be my own bad self. There'll be a Pan hidden in leaves, and nature lurking slyly — creatures peering through human thighs and feet, faces you don't see all at once, but in certain lights when the sun and shadows catch them—'

'It sounds rather disgusting—' Ellen commented. 'Your fantastic notions seem to deteriorate as soon as a chance comes to create something beautiful. I'm sure Saul would agree with me.'

'No. I reckon he'd understand,' Ben replied firmly. 'It was my — originality, if you like — that interested him. And Nature isn't always beautiful. It's got wickedness in it, and ruthlessness. Like women — some may be goddesses, but it's the imp of mischief in others that gets a man.'

'I see.' A wave of irrational jealousy made Maria brittle. 'Obviously you know a great deal about them.'

Ben swung his arm round her waist, and planted a sound kiss on her lips.

'Course I do, or I wouldn't have chosen you.' The richness of his voice, warmth of breath on her cold cheek, the pressure of his body momentarily hardened against her, made her suddenly vulnerable. She softened, sighed and drew herself away.

'You've an answer for everything. Oh, go ahead then. If you don't want me with you this time, you don't. I wouldn't dream of forcing my company on you.'

The trouble was, that during the following months this was exactly what Maria did.

The garden figure which was to be carved in blackish green basalt, had an easier dead-line in time than the pier head statue. Consequently there were brief opportunities in between for Ben to undertake smaller but important commissions in the West. Maria frequently insisted on accompanying or following him to available places where she endeavoured to keep a strict eye on his activities. It had not escaped her notice that her young husband was drinking socially more than he had done before, and she became well aware that other ambitious men of his profession were generally available to 'pick his brains' and ideas when he was over elated by good wine and acclaim.

Generally he kept up a veneer of politeness with her. Once however when he returned late and decidedly in his cups to the hotel where they were staying on the south coast, his temper exploded at her remonstrances.

'Who do you think you are?' he demanded, pulling his shirt and stock off savagely. 'My jailer? My nurse?'

'I seem to be.' The very calmness of her tones affronted him. 'I'm also your wife.'

'Then act like one,' he said shortly, 'go on — disrobe yourself, my love, my sweet one, my warm and gracious spouse—' His face was hot and red, his blue eyes blazing. He took a step towards her. 'Did you hear what I said?'

She backed involuntarily to the bed, fear mounting in her because she had never seen him like this before. But she sat erectly, with one hand protectingly at the neck of her dress.

'You're drunk,' she said.

'So I am.' He swayed on his heels slightly, as his complexion faded again. Any vengeful idea he'd had of forcing her unwillingly to submission, quickly faded. Poor Maria! he was leading her a dance, and he knew it vaguely. He didn't want to hurt her. It wasn't her fault that she possessed no sexual allure to fire a man. Her body was growing increasingly boring to him. If only she'd keep away from him for a bit he might learn to appreciate her good points again. But to have her forever on his heels trailing after him! Stifling the image — he ambled to the window, let the blind up, and stood looking over the huddled vista of roof tops swathed in a blurred pattern under the night sky.

Mist was rising, through which a thin moon glimmered indistinctly. He stood there, thinking of Cornwall and Heronsmere, of the sea breaking on the dark rocks, and of a young woman poised nymph-like by the jutting crags of Hook's Cove. Her face seemed to sway and encompass the stuffy bedroom. He undid the sash of the window, and pulled it down with a rattle. There was no scent of gorse or heather in the air. Only the damp odour of earth and wet sycamores from the gardens of the square below; — select well-ordered gardens with straight paths and conventional flower borders kept trim and well tidied through all seasons of the year. Seats placed at regular intervals for pedestrians were indiscernible now, but in the morning they would be occupied by elderly residents reading their newspapers, and nursemaids pushing prams erectly, occasionally turning an eye to a red-coated soldier on the look out for feminine company.

There was a band-stand in the middle of the large lawn and during the afternoons a cacophany of stirring marching tunes blasted the air. The jarring notes pounded his head now. He wished fervently he hadn't taken the last two or three brandies at the party. If Maria had been with him, he wouldn't have.

Poor Maria, he thought once more, almost with pity.

He closed the window and went back to the bed. She was lying very still, with dark-rimmed eyes looking enormous in the flickering light. The quilt was pulled tightly to her chin. He eased it down gently, and laid a hand above one breast.

'I'm sorry,' he murmured, 'don't mean to be − unkind—' The words were faintly blurred. 'But a man's job, y'know − I have to mix. It's my work, Maria.'

'I know.' Her voice was equable, cool. 'You always say that. And I realise I'm not fashionable or used to the company you keep these days. But I've got eyes in my head, Ben. And half the time they're playing with you − they're thieves − getting you to talk too much − stealing your thoughts, your ideas—' She sighed, and turned her head away. 'Don't do it, please don't do it, unless I'm there. The wining and dining − it'll destroy you if you go on. And all those women—' She paused.

'Yes?' he enquired sharply. 'What women? Any particular one?'

Determined not to be put off now she'd taken the bull by the horns, Maria faced him again and said defiantly, 'Lady Dainton for one − that haughty creature you so kindly introduced me to at the coffee-house yesterday. Oh I know that was a chance meeting, but I heard her mention "tonight". She was there, wasn't she? And I can just imagine you setting out to charm her, and her coy smiles and false flattery. She's got a bad name Ben, and she's not really interested in your work, don't think it for a minute. She's just a cheap made-up creature, playing up to you so she can let everything out to her stuck up greedy husband later — all your plans, your ambitions — your design secrets — everything. And they're probably laughing at you now, because to them you're just a peasant — something to use—'

Ben's colour returned. His mouth set stubbornly.

'What a clever young madam you are, Maria. As if I didn't know. Do you think — tipsy as I may have been — I was fooled for one minute? As a matter — a — a matter of fact, I found it all quite amusing. If I'd wanted I could be bedding her at this minute instead of listening to your silly talk. Anabella Dainton, as you infer, is quite an accomplished whore, but a high class one for all that, and at one point I rather fancied finding out for myself what lay under all her fancy frills and furbelows. We both knew what each was thinking, and let me tell you this — she was let down badly at the way I slithered out of things—'

'Oh Ben — how — how disgusting. And how you've changed.'

Seconds passed before Ben answered more quietly, 'It's the way of things. A man who can't recognise the ways of the world gets nowhere.' He turned his back on her, divested himself of the rest of his clothes, and when he stood regarding her before getting into bed, he saw that her eyes were closed and her lips set firmly against him. The sight of his body, then, his firm, handsome, arrogant body, was offensive to her! He'd long suspected it, but until then had not really known.

He laughed silently, contemptuously to himself, and slipped into the sheets beside her. He didn't attempt to touch or possess her. But from that moment he decided that faithfulness on his part was a waste of time and quite unnecessary.

During the next few years although Ben secured more and more important commissions, and business prospered, finances somehow failed to keep up with his way of life. He spent more time away from Jacobs than with Maria and her mother, both of whom no longer had any illusions concerning his extravagant manner of existence.

He had rooms of his own in London which were used presumably for business purposes, but as Maria and Ellen both correctly suspected were the frequent centre for more pleasurable pursuits. His recognition as a sculptor had increased, but success was insidiously draining and destroying his values, and the day inevitably arrived when legal debts forced him to face the truth. Unless he economised ruthlessly he could become bankrupt. Maria's share in Jacobs' would remain intact, the yard would not close. But the prospect of returning as a dependent on her was so humiliating he pulled himself together, sold what he had of value, managed to face all his legal obligations, and with a sufficient sum in his pocket to give a semblance of modest prosperity, prepared to return to Cornwall. By a strange coincidence on the day before his departure he received a letter from Maria informing him that Ellen, following a bout of fever had suddenly collapsed and died.

> I don't know if you will get this letter in time to be with me for the funeral [the note said] but your company would be a help. In any case, Ben, there will be business matters to settle afterwards which will demand your presence. The solicitors have everything in hand, and people have been most kind. But I can hardly realise Mama's gone yet. The house seems very empty, and unreal somehow, as though I wasn't really here.
>
> Your devoted wife
> Maria.

Behind the simple statement of facts Ben sensed genuine distress and a deep loneliness. When he faced matters honestly — a characteristic of his nature that at odd times he could not evade — he knew he had been unfair to her in the past. Probably though, if he could live that period over again he would do the same. He had to have colour, the challenge and excitement of conquest, of wild almost unimaginable aims. Maria was confined by an inherent primness and inaptitude for giving anything of herself freely and without restraint.

However, she'd tried to help him in any way possible. Their marriage had not been a failure in every way; security and respect had stemmed from it. There had been many times also when he'd shut family obligations from his mind. His short periodic jaunts to his old home following his wedding could be counted on one hand. It wasn't Maria's fault, of course, that the grime and odour of mine-dust, sick tired faces, and a grudging glance of condemnation in his father's eyes on the rare occasions they'd met, had depressed him. He'd been generous to them, sent gifts from time to time and they'd generally known where to contact him if further practical and financial assistance was necessary. That they had not, could have been because of pride — the belligerent staunch pride of poverty against power, of the poor against success and the rich.

Red Bell, he'd heard, was gradually dying; great wealth would be needed to keep it going by sinking new shafts in the western direction. He'd learned too that the Heronsmere estate was in a sorry state due to old Penherrion's mad gambling on the stock market, and his recurring fits of insanity and wild expenditure on senseless projects. On his last visit to Gwynck he'd heard also that Elfrida still lived there with the ailing Lady Marion and some tinker's brat that they'd taken in.

Doggedly he'd set his thoughts against her, assuring himself that she'd probably have no allure for him now anyway. She must be twenty-seven — a year older than himself. At such an age most women had lost grace and their first fresh beauty. Her fierce temper could have made a shrew of her, her fey fair looks could have turned sour. He did not wish to think of her, so he didn't. Maria, at least, had never openly rejected, or deceived him. In future he'd try a little harder to make up for all the months he'd spent away — for the sensual pleasures he'd indulged in, and the fashionable women and aristocratic whores he'd charmed to his bed then left with amused contempt in his heart. Such goings on had been a diversion while they lasted. But locked firmly in his brain behind all the superficial cavorting had been still one overmastering determination — to make the world his stage, the backcloth for his work and monumental prowess.

Now, on the brink of his return to Maria, he forced ambition — just for the moment — to more modest proportions. He would try and think of her more; be gentler and more considerate. Perhaps if he flattered and coated his sexual dominance with honeyed words and cajoling whispers, she might soften to a more feminine image, and even produce the son he wanted. She was thirty-one, nearing thirty-two — oldish by some standards to bear a first child, but he'd do his damnedest to make it possible. Thin, and rigid-looking as she'd appeared latterly, his London experiences had enhanced his aptitude to bend a woman insidiously to sensual longing. And she must have wanted him once, or she'd not have married him.

Buoyed up once more by his own trend of reasoning, he started off on the long journey to Cornwall in a comparatively cheerful mood.

Once over the Tamar a sense of freedom stirred his veins. For the first time he recognised how bored and frustrated he'd felt latterly by the fogs, pseudo-intelligentsia, dreary skies and social inequalities and competition of the City. For the most part he'd shut his ears to the political scene, but that same year, 1834, six agricultural labourers from Dorset had been prosecuted for taking an oath of loyalty to their trade union, and sentenced to seven years of transportation to Australia and Van Diemens Land. Thirty thousand people had marched in protest on the men's behalf with a Petition to Lord Melbourne for their pardon. It had been refused by the House of Lords.

Ben had rigidly held himself aloof from any sentimentalising. But the unfairness, unwittingly, had eaten into him. There was unfairness everywhere of course. Even in Cornwall, where miners who were lucky enough to be employed at all had to toil for so many long hours underground for such poor pay. But at least they had open skies and moors to greet them when they came 'to grass'.

Thinking of his family brought with it the haunting

picture of Elfrida as he'd known her when she was a young
girl. His mouth took a bitter twist. He should have ravished
her far earlier. Taken and claimed her before her own vanity
had made such a fool of him. Yes, he'd been a fool to worship
that strange wild creature who'd thought more of the crippled
Marion than she did of him. She'd played with him —
yearned all the time after a great house and the power she
could wield there, rather than subject herself completely to a
man's desire — his. And what of the squire? — Sir Geoffrey
who'd lost his wits through the fall? Had he ever touched
Elfrida in lust? Had she played the cocotte and allowed
familiarity? The mere notion sickened him. The blood, for a
fleeting instant, rushed to his head. Then he forced himself
with an effort to cold sanity. What the devil was the matter
with him? For years he'd hardly given her a thought, and
then only in self contempt. 'God dammit,' he told himself
savagely, 'it's Cornwall mocking me.'

And glancing out over the windswept autumn landscape as
they jolted along, he assured himself it was so. The wild hills
— the cromlechs and dolmens standing stark among the
misted boulders and undergrowth — the mine-works dotted
at intervals along the sky-line were no mere relics of the past,
but living history, and in a curious elemental way, a challenge. A time would come, he decided, when he'd place a
monument of his own on some familiar hill top — a symbol of
his prowess, and a proof to future generations that Ben
Curran had once trod the untamed heights.

Gradually emotion in him died into pleasanter calm, and
when he reached Gwynck he was in a comparatively equable
state of mind.

She was waiting for him as he'd known she would be, looking wan and dispirited, but with welcome in her eyes. When
he'd kissed her on the cheek dutifully, she said, 'I'm so glad
you're back, Ben — it's been a strain.'

'Yes, it must've been. Am I too late for—'

She nodded before he could finish. 'She was buried yesterday. I didn't expect you to get here. But to wait any longer
would've been distressing. People were very kind. And Sally

was quite a help. Willie too—' her voice trailed off uncertainly. Then she continued, '—You must be hungry. I've kept a meal hot.'

He smiled.

'As always. You think of me too much, Maria. You'll have to look after yourself now, buck yourself up, and—'

'Yes?'

'Rid yourself of those black clothes.'

Her eyes widened with astonishment. 'The mourning? Oh, but I couldn't. Not for six months at least. What would people say?'

'Heaven knows. Would it matter?'

'In Gwynck? Of course. A little later perhaps − mauve. I suppose that would be permissible, if you find this gown so − so dreary. It's new, you know. I bought it specially—' She moved round displaying the fashionable but starchy cut, her small head held erect on the thin neck.

A touch of compassion rose in him. He put his arm round her waist. 'Do what you think right, Maria. Wear the mauve as soon as you feel like it. Mauve would suit you, I'm sure.'

But would it? Mauve was the colour of heather and of rosy sunset turning to violet over the Cornish moors; mauve, streaked with dying gold − the gold of a lovely woman's hair.

He pulled himself together abruptly. 'I hope your mother didn't suffer?' he heard himself saying automatically.

She shook her head.

'No. It was very sudden. I shall miss her of course, but she wasn't always easy. And there were things I didn't agree with—'

'What things?'

'After you've had your meal,' she answered quietly, 'I'll tell you. There's something been on my mind for a long time. But first just let us sit together.'

Puzzled, he agreed.

Later the secret which had tormented her at intervals during their married life, came out. As they sat by the parlour fire, facing each other, the story was unfolded in cool

quiet tones holding a note of sad inevitability and acceptance.

'I know you've never loved me, Ben,' Maria said, 'not
passionately, as — as you may have done someone else, and I
never, in the beginning, expected you to marry me or think of
me in that way at all. The idea was encouraged by Mama,
and when I really thought about it, I knew there was nothing
in the world I'd like more. You see I was fond of you, even
then, more fond than I'd admitted to myself—'

She paused.

'Well? What's all this about, Maria? I asked you to marry
me, and you accepted. Why go into the pros and cons at this
point?'

Haltingly now, becoming more nervous, and playing with
a shred of handkerchief between her fingers she confessed her
mother's guile, keeping her eyes firmly away from his. At one
point, during which no flicker of expression crossed his face,
she said in an attempt at self-exoneration, 'I was shocked the
first time. I didn't agree with it. It seemed — cheating — to
destroy other people's correspondence and I know it was. But
— she was my mother. And—'

'How many times did this happen?' His voice was hard and
cold as granite.

'I don't know. I never took the letters in. It was left to Sally.
I steered away. And when Mama had anything to post, either
Willie or her — Sally — went. You see — I didn't want to
know or be concerned at all. You must believe that, Ben.'

'Oh, yes, I believe it.' Something final and hopeless in the
last remark made her look at him sharply.

'You blame me I suppose!'

'Only partly. Anyway what I believe's neither here nor
there any more.'

'Do you mean you're not — do you mean you're leaving me
again?'

He shook his head.

'Where'd the sense be in that? What's done is done. I just
wish you'd told me earlier.'

'Before you married me?'

'Yes.'

'It would have made a difference wouldn't it? You'd have gone to her — that — that — Elfrida—' She bit her lip knowing she'd made a dangerous mistake.

Dull crimson suffused Ben's face. He went towards her, sharply, enclosing her frail shoulders in a cruel grip.

'Don't ever speak her name again,' he said from between his teeth. 'How do I know what I'd have done when I don't even know what was in the letters? Neither of us do. So you've got to live with it, as I will. But—' he laughed bitterly '—your scheming mama probably did me a good turn, for all her wickedness. I've got the yard, haven't I? And you — a dutiful wife? What more could any man want?'

She searched his face for a sign, some faint glimpse of warmth, sympathy, and that he understood.

There was none.

When he spoke again, it was comparatively lightly, in strange clipped tones. 'You must give me a son, Maria, then we shall have everything sensible people expect, I'm sure.'

She clutched the neck of her dress with trembling fingers. 'A son?'

'Why not. Presumably you're not beyond conceiving.'

She flushed.

'I'm — I'm thirty-three — nearly.'

'Hardly in your dotage,' he observed drily.

Her lip quivered. She managed to draw herself away and moved towards the window. Dusk was falling. The trees outside already emerging as thin indeterminate shapes in the rising mist. She shivered, and presently felt his hand touch her arm; more gently this time.

'Maria,' he said half apologetically.

She turned her head. The glint of tears was damp on her lashes. Compunction smote him.

'We must try and forget the past,' he said. 'What your mother did wasn't your affair. Come now.'

He drew her to him. For a few moments her thin face rested against his coat. Then, with all resistance and armour suddenly gone from her she was sobbing quietly.

Feeling no ardour or desire, he nevertheless presently led her to bed.

And that evening a child was conceived.

# Part Two

ELFRIDA

# 5

## 1835

From a landing window of an upper floor of Heronsmere Elfrida stared eastwards across the moor. Her figure was rigid, her eyes unblinkingly upon the dark dot of a horseman's figure etched clearly against the cold early spring light. It was only late March and quite soon daylight would fade to dusk, but just for a few moments a last beam of the sinking sun lit everything to stark clarity. Against her wish and all commonsense a mounting excitement filled with anguish and anger seized her. The distant form, though so minute and far away was unmistakable. The fair hair an aura of flame above the glossy black coat of his mount.

Ben.

It was years since she'd seen him, but his stance − his erect posture − something compelling and different about him would betray his presence to her anywhere. Once she would have given anything for a glimpse of him − a word written, or brought by message. She'd waited and waited, so their past anger could be erased and kindled into passion once again. But nothing had come, and she knew now it never would. She had been merely an experience to him − a game. He had played with her as he had with poor Marion, while plotting all the time how best to get his hand on Saul Jacobs' business through marrying the daughter.

Well, he'd achieved what he wanted. And now, she'd heard that his pale delicate wife was expecting a child in the summer. It would be a weakling, probably, she told herself, trying to dispel a sense of bitter triumph at the thought. Not

strong and wayward and wild-at-heart like her own Lynette.
In spite of herself a faint smile touched her lips. Ben had
never known he was a father. For two months before the
baby's birth she had taken to 'travelling' and wandered with a
small tribe of gipsies, from fair to fair, and village to village,
paying her way by broommaking, and taking part in any
mimes or shows they put on. Later she'd returned to Marion
who'd welcomed her with warmth, and spread the tale that
the infant was a foundling they had both adopted. Marion
herself had tried to believe the father was some well-bred
itinerant, since Elfrida refused to name him. Stories had got
about of course, but no more colourful than many others
concerning the two strange women — witches undoubtedly
— who lived with the mad squire on his failing estate Heronsmere.

Now he was dying. The apothecary had predicted that
very morning he would be gone before nightfall, leaving his
daughters — the one highly-born and legitimate — the other
a bastard, alone with the eight-year-old girl in the great
house. Alone, that is, except for an ageing housekeeper Mrs
Ferris, and her granddaughter, a scullery maid, Jake who
helped the man Moses with the vegetable garden and stables,
and a part-time dairy-maid from a nearby farm.

Many of the rooms in the large house were now shut and
locked away from habitation. Treasures had been sold, and
what remained were kept securely in an upstairs room, safe
from prying eyes or plundering. Elfrida, on Marion's behalf,
had seen this was done, even before she'd had proof during
one of Sir Geoffrey's mad outbursts that she, Elfrida, was his
natural daughter. She had not been surprised; from being a
child she had sensed it. But the admitted fact had only made
her more protective of the lame Lady Marion who had had to
steel herself against her father's resentment for so many
anguished years. Neither had it ever occurred to her that
Marion had exaggerated or lied about her relationship to
Ben. He had used them both. And she, Elfrida, having given
herself in such wild abandon and passion to him, had built a
wall of defence and fierce resentment against the fair young

lover of her past; a barrier no softening thought or suggestion of sympathy on his behalf could penetrate. It did not occur to her she could be mistaken.

How strange, she thought that day, peering across the moor, that Ben should appear again, at such a moment, when Sir Geoffrey was about to depart from life.

Unconsciously, Elfrida sighed. Life had not been easy during the last few years. Except for the little girl Lynette who from the first had been a lovely passionate character able to anger one moment, the next to charm anyone to her will, and for the fact that there were times when she herself, Elfrida, was able to escape for an hour's ride across the moor on Diamond, her mare — she doubted she could have remained at Heronsmere. Once or twice, before Lynette's birth she'd been on the point of leaving. But the pitiful Marion's dependence on her — her pleading, and the tears in her mournful eyes, combined with recurring memory of Ben's treachery, had broken her resolve. Sir Geoffrey, who before his accident had secretly hankered to see his strikingly beautiful unacknowledged daughter in his house, had put up no objection.

Company for the one whose limp was an affront to his male pride would minimise contact with her, while also reducing any niggle of conscience he felt.

All the time though, resentment at the loss of his son — the unexpected failing resources of Red Bell, discontent of workers, and knowledge of his own banking deficits, had eaten into him like dry rot sapping his strength.

The fall from his horse — a macabre echo of his son's death, had put the final seal on his fate.

He had wandered the lonely lofty corridors of Heronsmere consumed not only by sickness of the spirit, but by mad fits of increasing physical rage interspersed by acute sadness that drove him quietly to his room where he had brooded for days wishing to meet with no one.

Elfrida shuddered, recalling one recent terrible moment when, all self-control gone, he had made an attack on Marion, waving a pistol in one hand. His face had turned

dullish purple as he muttered, 'Cripple, fool—' somehow
Elfrida had pushed in front of the other woman, while the
housekeeper had rushed Lynette to the kitchen. Elfrida'
effect on Sir Geoffrey, her apparent calmness — combined
with her beauty — had been almost miraculous. In a few
moments he had quietened. The weapon had dropped to the
floor. He had put a hand to his head, blinked and said in a
dazed voice, 'Don' know what got into me. Damn sorry. These
headaches—' His complexion by then had changed to greenish grey. He steadied himself against the table, giving Elfrida
a chance to push Marion before her into the conservatory.
Once safely inside she had locked the door, and presently
seen the heavy bent form of Sir Geoffrey turn and make his
way haltingly towards the hall.

'He should really go to some — some institution or other,'
Elfrida had said to her half-sister. 'We can't go on like this.
One day when I'm not at hand he might hurt you badly, or
even kill you — and then there's Lynette—'

Lady Marion had shaken her head.

'No. Not Papa. He's not often like this. I couldn't do such a
thing to him. You know I couldn't. And he'd never hurt
Lynette. He loves her. I think sometimes she's the only
creature in the world he *does* love.'

Elfrida knew this was true. He had never once spoken
harshly to the child. At times he'd seemed withdrawn,
regarding her with puzzled suspicion. But always in the end
she had won him round by a dazzling smile and unswerving
glance from her thick black lashed eyes which were the
brilliant blue of summer skies. Unlike Elfrida's silver-gold
tresses her hair was as dark and shining as raven's wings,
holding the glint of copper lights when the sun shone. This
fact alone had made the story of her foundling blood acceptable. Frequently, in earlier days Sir Geoffrey had wished she
could be proved of his own kin but had put the suggestion
aside.

Except for her eyes a real little gipsy she was — olive
skinned, hot tempered, wild and proud. The sort he'd have
liked for a son, if fate had been kinder. The thought she

might have the Celtic blood of the Currans in her never remotely occurred to him. He had little contact with the tin miners of the district, and would have been affronted by the suggestion that any of his household had had a relationship with those small dark men — workers of the earth and Cornish ore.

So the months and years had passed, while Heronsmere sank into deeper decline. Now the once respected owner was on the verge of death.

An icy wave of air shuddered through window cracks, sending a shiver of dread through Elfrida's frame.

Death.

How she hated the word. And what would happen afterwards? Was she forever to be bound to the ailing woman who even at that moment prayed by the sick man's bed? Or would she take the other way? — An offer that for a year had been open to her, from the new owner of a country house some miles away — a rich industrialist from the North.

Twelve months ago Henry Ashforth, had arrived in Cornwall, eager — even avaricious to put his stamp further afield than on the cotton mills which had made him a millionaire. He had a fancy for purchasing any failing tin-mine that could possibly prove worth while, wielding a tidy fortune given wealth and enterprise for expansion. Well, he had both, begad, and the thought of 'squiring' his presence over wild Cornish land was a titillating challenge. Though his forbears had been of working stock, their stubborn North Country tenacity combined with a cute shrewdness had achieved, during the past two centuries, considerable power, first through contracting in a small way, then investing where there was promise of profit. Wool and cotton had followed. His name was among those of the largest mill owners in Yorkshire, and was watched by the stock-market in London. A decent education had given him a veneer of respectability. He had friends in the most unlikely circles, for he'd discovered quite early, that although beneath the façade he might not be culturally accepted by snob society, money could buy most things. Including women.

And when he'd first seen Elfridas he'd wanted her. Not that he was dissatisfied by the comely, plump wife who ran his northern home in so adequate a fashion — she provided his roots, and was a comforting bed-fellow, having borne as well a strapping daughter. But a man of his type, handsome in his middle years, still with wild dreams in him and an over-powering zest and vitality for living, wanted more than security. With the years time passed more quickly. This lovely strange bewildering creature could very well make him forget it. Yes. One glance of Elfrida when he'd called to make acquaintance of Sir Geoffrey had set his senses alight, and his mind on a determined course.

The Heronsmere estate was sick, its lands and mine half-derelict. But that needn't be so. His nose told him the ore was still red about the surrounding terrain. Engineers had agreed with him. If he sank capital into reviving Red Bell it could pay off threefold. He'd do it, but at a price. Elfrida. In the beginning of course he'd not faced the issue practically. But since Sir Geoffrey's increasing instability and the obviously miserable plight of his daughter and companion, he had broached the topic suddenly one day to Elfrida, telling her in no uncertain terms that if she chose, he could invest and put the estate on its feet again, ensuring security and comfort for poor sickly Lady Marion.

'Aye,' he'd said, 'there's a future here if you still want it. But it'll take money. I have the brass, and if you have the will for it, it's yours — and your aristocratic — friends between you.' The word 'friend' had held implications that had not escaped her. She'd guessed that he'd heard the rumours of their blood tie.

She'd smiled holding her head high, with her strange lovely eyes turned straight on his shrewd light grey ones. The dying sunlight from a window had lit the silver-gold hair to pale brightest flame. 'What a woman,' he'd thought, 'proud like some untouchable princess.' But already he sensed her soft flesh yielding to his — the feel of her slim limbs entwined with his own. 'I don't quite know what you mean,' she'd said, although she suspected pretty accurately.

'You will,' he'd told her, 'you soon will. Then, as I said, it will be up to you. Think about it, ma'am—'

'Miss Crane.'

He'd grinned disarmingly, made a little bow, with his hand over his heart.

'Miss Crane.'

Weeks later he'd put his proposition bluntly. 'A home from home,' he'd told her, with her treated handsomely as befitting a legal wife.

'Legal?'

'As legal as can be,' he'd answered, 'a tidy allowance, everything put in order, with what improvements are needed at the house, security for life for Lady Marion, and workers taken on for the reopening of Red Bell with higher wages than they've ever known before.'

The picture he'd painted had sounded like a fairytale.

'I think you're forgetting Sir Geoffrey,' she'd reminded him. 'This is his property, not mine. I'm merely companion to Lady Marion.'

'One day you'll be mistress,' he'd replied bluntly. 'And that day not so far off neither. I doubt he'll see the year out, and when the time comes I'll be there.'

After this he'd arrived at Heronsmere on several occasions, and always with some superficial, quite legitimate excuse. Already he'd made limited investment in the mines.

Marion, whose sweetness had turned to grudging cynical acquiescence when she'd seen how the land lay, had remarked to Elfrida once, 'Does it matter what the locals say? They only think the worst of us now. You've a right to a little pleasure, Elfrida. It can't have been easy living in this house with only me and — and my poor father for company. When I first asked you to come to Heronsmere it was for both our sakes. It seemed stupid for you to be so solitary with your grandmother gone, and my needing companionship too—' She had not added, 'I also wanted to keep an eye on you — see you didn't become too involved with Ben;' if she had even touched on the topic, reason might have been swamped by frustrated passion or jealousy. She could so easily have blurted out, "I care for Ben very deeply, and in his young way he cares for me. I don't want him wandering, or diverted too much from my attention, because one day — despite my age and position, it's possible he may be induced to marry me—'

For so long she'd allowed herself to play with the idea, made him even as a youth, her phantom lover — the lover of her dreams. Her later pretence to Elfrida, the assertion that he already had become so, had not registered as the fabrication and cruel lie it was. But fundamentally it had changed her, replaced by the cold determination that whatever happened, Elfrida should never know the truth. After all, Ben was hers, Marion's; she had taken him under her wing and first sponsored him from his early days as a child. Elfrida too was important to her. Her affection and beauty — the obligations of her position at Heronsmere had wielded a strong bond between them — a bond that gave power and compensation to Sir Geoffrey's daughter for the indignities and insults of his dislike — the slur of her lameness. Ben's marriage to Maria had been a bitter blow. But a time would come, Marion had told himself, when power and fame would end it. Then he would return to the great house, and see her again as the gracious young lady she had once been when he'd met her at the haberdasher's on that far distant day of the fair. His blue eyes would be wonderingly upon her own, and Elfrida would appear as but the pretty peasant girl she'd taken into employment. The word 'employment' of course, was never mentioned between the two women — but Elfrida had only to mention she wanted anything, and the means to have it were in her pocket, with more to spare. This was her payment. Even Sir Geoffrey before his accident had been generous in any possible way.

Now all that was over.

There had been for some time little in the household to be generous with. The future appeared to Elfrida that evening in 1835 as bleak and lonely as the wild landscape under the fading spring sky.

With the last glow of pale sun fading beyond the horizon, the figure of the horseman moved and rode eastwards, a minute later becoming lost beyond the rein of high moors.

The air had suddenly become cold. Elfrida drew her hand away from sill and glass, and found it was quite numb. She turned, lifted her skirts above her ankles, and made her way to Sir Geoffrey's room on the second floor. With her hand on the knob of the door she looked in. A small oil lamp glowed by the draped curtains of the great bed, throwing an eerie gleam about the woman kneeling by the sick man. Marion glanced up briefly, and Elfrida glimpsed the glimmer of tears on the drawn cheeks. How strange, she thought, for a daughter who'd been treated so badly still to have feeling for the one who'd sired her. No vestige of colour remained any longer on Sir Geoffrey's face. In the uncertain light he appeared an effigy — cheeks sunken below the greenish hallowed sockets of the closed eyes. Only the heavy breathing denoted that he still lived.

Elfrida made the motion of asking if there was anything she could do. Marion's head moved in negation, and when she glanced down once more on the dying man, Elfrida tiptoed back to the door, and left.

It was not until the early hours of the next day however that Sir Geoffrey Penherrion drew his last breath. As though in accordance with death, fine rain was falling, wrapping Heronsmere into its dark grey shroud. Elfrida had expected Marion to be distraught, but now the end had come, it appeared, superficially, that all emotion had been drained from her. She waited for a few moments staring at him, drew the sheet over his head, and with a curiously wooden motion limped out of the room.

Elfrida, who had been standing nearby, followed

She did her best to comfort the older woman, but Marion simply said, 'It's for the best. I'm glad.'

So am I, Elfrida thought, oh God, so am I. She wanted to open the windows and entrances despite the weather, letting the wind and rain in, wanted to feel the fresh sweet air on her cheeks, and to ride — ride from the lonely corridors and rooms across the moors to freedom. But when she opened the front door Marion cried, 'Shut it — it's cold. What are you doing?'

Dumbly, Elfrida obeyed. She stayed about the house half an hour — an hour, doing what she could to be of assistance, but Marion appeared completely in command of the situation, and made it clear she wished for no help.

At last, in a fit of frustration and wild rebellion Elfrida went to the stables, had the boy saddle her mare for her, and wearing only a black cloak over her gown set off in the downpour towards the west.

Where she was going she neither knew nor cared. One emotion only churned in her. Escape. She must get away — anyway for a time, from bleak lonely Heronsmere, from tormenting lingering memories of the horseman against the sky — and from the proud cold invalid who for so long seemed to have dominated her life. Even Lynette. When Ben had deserted her she hadn't wanted the child. But she had borne her nevertheless, and ever since, her strong-willed vitality had been a challenge and a disrupting influence. She loved her passionately because she was also Ben's child. But for that same reason her love frequently turned to irritation and dislike.

When she reached the western ridge she reined by a twisted elder and stared down the slope. The rain had eased slightly, and the first pale gleam of rising sun pierced the sullen clouds; glinting over the huddled shapes of vanes in the valley below. Smoke filtered wanly from a group of clustered trees, and presently the dot of a woman's figure darted across a small clearing to a tent. Elfrida recalled times in the past when, as a young girl she had escaped her grandmother's vigilance, and spent hours with the mysterious people who though not of her kin had understood her so well, and with whom she'd felt an instinctive bond. They had delighted in her beauty, calling her 'the pale one', and 'little princess'.

Once as a child she had been at a gipsies' wedding and watched the couple jump over a broomstick, then stand with clasped hands to be sprinkled with bread and salt as a tribal elder declared them married. There had been feasting and dancing later, in which Elfrida had joined. Her blood had responded wildly to the Flamenco, to the strange rise and fall of violins, to the colour of twirling skirts and flying hair, of wailing and laughter, and emotional abandon. When, at last she'd forced herself to leave, climbing the path that eventually led to Martha's cottage, it had been like entering another world. As the wild music became but a thin echo of the rising wind, a feeling of guilt mingled with fierce joy and loss had possessed her. The grim standing stones and bleak mine-stacks had loomed condemningly as symbols of her own wickedness. Was she wicked? Were *they*? Her friends? That colourful nomad band? People had always said so, and Elfrida had been strictly forbidden by Martha ever to roam that way when they were in camp.

'In league with the devil, 'tis said,' Martha had told her grandchild grimly. 'So doan' you dare speak with them, child, or I'll give you such a beatin' you'll never forget.'

Well, that evening Martha had been true to her word, and for several days Elfrida had felt the sting.

''Tis for your own good,' the old woman had said afterwards. 'There's much of your ma in you. She was a one for visitin' they dark ones — an' look where it got her. Put the spell on her they did, so she went an' laid with an upstart—' The revelation of paternity had died into unintelligible muttering. Elfrida, smarting badly, had still waited avidly for information. But none had come. Much later she had discovered the truth for herself, and as things had turned out, she'd far rather have been sired by one of the Romanies than by the luckless wretch Sir Geoffrey Penherrion.

Still, he was dead now. And his dark destiny had not been entirely his fault. She must try and look back remembering his kindness in Martha's day and later, following the old woman's death, when so many welcome gifts had arrived at the cottage. He had even greeted her quite warmly, when at Marion's request she had been ensconced at Heronsmere as companion to his daughter — the legal heir whose infirmity so affronted him.

Leaving the cottage had not been easy. But once away with

certain personal treasures, and when the goats had been
settled elsewhere, she had put it from her mind resolutely as
though in doing so she could also erase memories of Ben. She
had made a point during the last years of never walking or
riding that way.

Now, suddenly, she had the wish and will to see it. So she
turned, kicked her mare to a quick canter, and the next
moment was taking the steep incline north-east towards her
old home.

By the time she got there the rain had cleared, leaving a
sprinkled brightness over heather and furze. Light caught
the empty windows, giving their sockets a brief semblance of
life. Glass had gone from one. Behind the other curtains still
hung limply, filmed by dust and holed where the lace had
once been so spotless. Did shadows move from the interior,
accusing her like ancient ghosts brought condemningly to
life? Did a thin spiral of smoke curl briefly towards the sky?
But no! it was only a shred of cloud passing. She shivered.
'Warmth' − her heart cried. 'How I need warmth, and Ben.'
And it was as though just for a second or two she was lying in
the heather again, crushed in an ardent embrace − his body
hot and demanding upon her, with her own pulsing wildly to
his need. Ben! Ben! Truth smote her cruelly. For that brief
passage of time she recognised that he would always be part
of her. What she'd once had would smoulder forever somewhere in the deep recesses of her being. Her whole frame
shook.

Then, in bitter anguish, she cried aloud, 'I hate you, Ben
Curran, for wanting and taking me, and lying and going
away. Hate − hate − *hate*—' The cry was echoed by the
mournful screaming of gulls disturbed. As they rose from the
furze into the air she jerked at the reins, flicked the mare's
flanks, and rode recklessly downwards in the direction of
Heronsmere.

'It's over now, she thought dully, when she reached the
stables. 'The worst is over. If I ever pass that place again there'll
be no tie left at all. Nothing. Except working things out, somehow making a future, and − Ashforth. Henry Ashforth.'

Until that day she hadn't really considered any personal propositions on her behalf. She knew she could never love him, but he had wealth and power. He could make material things available that she'd never had. Her grandmother would turn in her grave at the mere suggestion of such wickedness. But her grandmother was dead, and Elfrida no longer believed the dead could move, or in spiritual damnation. Also her own body was cold and needing a little fire to warm it. Maybe in time if she tried hard she could even feel some affection for him. He was handsome, domineering admittedly, but hard men had been known to be softened by a woman's wiles. As for tongues wagging, and the fact that he had a wife tucked away up North! — tongues wagged hard enough already. Gossip had it that she and Marion were in league with evil powers, and if Henry Ashforth cared to, he could make existence a deal pleasanter for villagers and local inhabitants. Red Bell perhaps could be reopened; there would be employment for many mining families planning to set sail for the Americas. A number had already gone; the rest — most of them — were either half-starved or scraping a living from disastrously small wages. Heronsmere could be made a comfortable place again, with the grounds put in order and well cared for. Marion — her thoughts came to a sudden halt. What Marion did with Heronsmere was really her own affair. She, Elfrida, had no part in it.

As matters turned out however, she was wrong.

Following Sir Geoffrey's funeral which took place three days after his demise it was found that the estate and the rest of his failing fortune had been bequeathed jointly to his daughter Marion Penherrion, and Elfrida Crane, to be administered in equal shares by the trustees in the most agreeable way to all concerned. There was also a codicil leaving a legacy of £3000 to his young friend Lynette who had been a source of comfort to him during the last years of his life. This was to be held in trust until she became of age, and on the condition that henceforth she was to be known as Lynette Penherrion, such a formality to be legally arranged as soon as possible.

Elfrida was aghast when she heard. 'I don't want it — nothing,' she protested. 'Lady Marion is his — his — daughter. I've no right to anything—' She broke off, intimidated by the dead-pan expression on the long lean face of the solicitor. 'It is Sir Geoffrey's—' he coughed, and amended, 'the late Sir Geoffrey's — wish. Exactly how the inheritance is distributed is a matter for future discussion. I must also add that when final debts are settled and any small legacies paid, it is exceedingly unlikely much will remain in the matter of bank assets. The mines I understand are on the brink of closure unless considerable finance is available. You might think the best course is to sell Heronsmere. People from up country are finding Cornwall attractive to visit. With sufficient capital anyone with money to spare and an eye to the future might speculate and find the property a rewarding investment—'

'Stop.' Marion's shrill tones cut the dry-as-dust oration like a knife. 'Heronsmere is my home. I don't intend to sell, neither, I think, will my companion Miss Crane wish to leave. I'm sure also, that my father would have wanted his — our ward — to stay. You say her legacy will be held on trust — by the Bank, I suppose, since the Bank are trustees?'

The solicitor bowed his head.

'That is so.'

'Therefore you will be in touch with them, and legal matters and obligations put into order. After that I presume, you'll contact us, so my — my friend and I can decide what to do.' She paused, adding in a soft voice, 'My father did stress the importance of — what did you say? — "agreeable to all concerned"; that was the phrase he used in reference to the administration, wasn't it?'

'Again, you are right, Lady Marion.'

'Well then—' Marion relaxed against the back of her chair. 'There is really nothing more to be said on the subject at present. But do please bear in mind that we both wish Heronsmere to remain intact. That is so, isn't it, Elfrida?'

Elfrida, feeling trapped, nodded.

'Of course.'

When the practical, dreary interview was over and the

solicitor had departed, Lady Marion went upstairs for a brief rest before taking coffee with Elfrida in the small parlour which was warmer than the larger reception rooms and less expensive to heat. She had aged considerably during the last few years. Her dark hair had turned to iron-grey holding white streaks. The luminous eyes which had once been her greatest asset were now heavy ringed; the skin beneath, sagging slightly towards the network of lines etching the prominent cheekbones. Her skin had lost its faint magnolia tinge, and had become dulled to a parchment shade. She was seldom without her stick now, her stoop had become more pronounced, and the dress she wore of black silk, with the bouffant sleeves of the period, and swathes of black tulle pinned high under her chin by a jet brooch only emphasised her thinness.

Looking at her Elfrida was overcome by a sense of deep pity. The tie of half-acknowledged sisterhood between them, for a few moments was stronger than any other emotion; following it, Elfrida felt gloom enclosing her. How could she leave her? How could she ever be free of one who'd treated her well, given everything, materially, that she wished for, and had even connived with her over her disappearance before the baby was born? There had been no condemnation, no open criticism. And when the time came Lynette had been received kindly at Heronsmere. Why? Ben's bastard. Had Marion ever guessed? Ever for one moment considered the possibility that Ben, who had so ruthlessly used her, had fathered the little girl? Her silence over such an important and relevant question had been quite remarkable. And Elfrida had been grateful for it to be so.

She had not seen a certain knowing, speculative look in her half-sister's eyes when they fell upon the little girl — had not remotely sensed that from the first, Marion's intuition had been stronger than any doubt. The instinctive knowledge had given her power. Something of Ben's remained there, at Heronsmere. While Elfrida stayed, so would his child. And she would make sure that if the time ever arrived when he discovered the link, he would be denied contact. Lynette was

Elfrida's — and hers — Marion's. Never, never, would Ben Curran set foot in her house again. Frustration had so consumed her it had become an obsession. Her lie to Elfrida of Ben's faithlessness no longer seemed pretence, but reality — the picture of his love-making, his passionate prowess and allegiance to her, so vivid that they represented truth. For countless nights she had lain alone in her bed sensing — feeling — his arms round her body, known the physical pain of desire, and closed her eyes, pressing her face against the soft pillows, murmuring 'Ben — Ben, darling—'

At other times she'd felt the pangs of defeat and rejection, and hated him. Afterwards she'd tried to dispel her own bitterness, because to all other things, animals, sick creatures, the old and very young, it was her nature to be gentle and kind. Even to Elfrida, she felt warm and generous, and she never doubted that Elfrida felt the same. So she expected no argument on that afternoon following the funeral when she said, while pouring the coffee:

'Of course you agree with me, don't you, Elfrida, that we must not dream of selling Heronsmere?'

There was a brief pause before the answer came.

'Are you quite sure it wouldn't be best?'

'What do you mean?'

'So much needs doing to the house. The curtains and carpets are worn, the floors have weak places, and there's dry rot in parts. Then the grounds! they used to be so lovely — but one man can't do everything, and the weeds are everywhere.'

'But—'

'Wonders could be done with money, Marion. But it would take so much, and it isn't there. Then the mine! it will have to close if we hang on, which means families will be out of work and have to leave the district. Cottages will fall into decay like — like my grandmother's. Do you want that?'

'Of course not. But—'

'It isn't as if we need such a big place—'

'You mean *you* don't.'

Elfrida flushed.

'I didn't, although it's true of course. But so many empty rooms — so many shadows and memories! Wouldn't you rather make a fresh start?'

'No.' The reply was decisive. 'I wish to live here as my father would have wanted. It's our heritage. Family. Besides you can't be sure any wealthy person would be interested. Do you think Henry Ashforth would care tuppence about the place unless he had his eye on you? Oh, Elfrida, I don't want to sound mean. But — do you dislike him? Have you ever considered his — his proposition? If you could bring yourself to show him a little friendship he'd invest more — and then there'd be no question of our having to leave — perhaps I sound immoral. But if I had the chance—?' She bit her lip and looked away—

'Yes?'

'I'd probably jump at the opportunity. He's very handsome. In a way I envy you, because no man has ever looked at me with passion or love. Once I thought Ben cared. But it was mostly greed.' Her voice was bitter. 'You, though — young, beautiful, with no deformity — nothing for people to shudder at or pity—'

With a rush of compassion Elfrida took a thin hand in hers.

'We're both exaggerating. Talking of deformity — how absurd. As for Mr Ashford — I suppose you're right. Many women would take what's offered and be grateful—'

'I don't suppose he'd be here much,' Marion pointed out, 'just visits now and again, and it isn't as though either of us has a particularly high reputation to keep up, is it?'

Elfrida laughed ironically.

'Not where I'm concerned — Susannah Crane's bastard. But you'll always be the Squire's daughter, and if I wasn't here you'd still have esteem. Sometimes I think I should go—'

'No.' Marion said shrilly. 'If you left me I should die — I swear it—'

'Nonsense.'

'And Lynette. What about Lynette? She's happy at Heronsmere. Oh Elfrida — please—'

Eventually Marion's impassioned pleading on behalf of herself, Lynette, the welfare of the miners, and future of Red Bell and Wheal Mary, overcame Elfrida's objections. She gave in with a curious mixture of reluctance and relief, and when one late afternoon in May, Henry Ashford called at Heronsmere, Elfrida found the meeting far pleasanter than she'd anticipated. The day was fine and windless with sunshine dappling the moors and rim of sea and cliffs beyond. The mingled smell of bracken, heather, and wild thyme was heady in the air. Larks sang, and the silvered wings of gulls were bright against blue unflecked skies. Gorse flamed gold along the hills; primroses and wild violets starred the narrow lanes from clumps of young springing ferns.

The hedgerows, too, were lush, with a foam of may blossom and wild cherry. It was as though Nature itself had contrived to make that particular day auspicious for the occasion.

Ashford had hired a chaise from the station, and as the vehicle drew up at Heronsmere he appeared a smart commanding figure chatting for a minute with the driver before turning and mounting the steps towards the front door. Elfrida's heart quickened. The meeting ahead was perhaps the most crucial of her life. From the drawing room window she dispelled determinedly any lingering doubt on her part. Few women she told herself could have refused his attentions. Everything about him was calculated to excite a woman — his air of fashion and looks, and wealth. Even his height was considerably above average, and his attire suggested the city rather than the environment of his native North Country.

He wore a tall silk top hat, below which his thick black side-burns emphasised the formidably carved features and piercing dark eyes. His double breasted coat was cut away at the front to tails at the back, and worn over a white shirt with a ruffled high collar. Striped trousers, wide at the hips, were fashioned to slim elegance at the ankles, covering the tops of his shoes. Such details, though not absorbed at first glance gave an overall impression of extreme elegance. From his chest and on his fingers, diamonds flashed as the sun caught them. He carried a slender silver knobbed cane. For one ridiculous second Elfrida's heart missed a beat. Why? There was no reason she told herself wildly, no earthly reason at all. All fashionable men had canes — but this one! — she could imagine he'd have no compunction in using it if he thought fit.

The next moment she'd dispelled the thought as mere stupidity, and when he was shown into the room she appeared as composed as any experienced hostess receiving a welcome guest. She was wearing pink muslin, with bouffante sleeves and an artificial rose pinned at the bodice just above the shadowed hollow of her breasts. The gown was draped low on her shoulders, and beneath the spreading full skirts and billowing starched petticoats only the tips of slippers showed. They were high heeled, adding quite two inches to her dainty height. But it was her hair that glorified her — its silver-gold beauty curled at the sides, then drawn in a shining mass to the top of her head, pinned with several tiny roses. She looked exquisite.

'Miss Crane—' he said going towards her with hand extended, hat held at his side. 'This is a pleasure.' The faint North Country accent was hardly discernible. He gripped her palm, and the grasp was strong. Beneath the flesh she felt the warmth of hot blood pulsing.

Her cheeks coloured faintly. 'Do sit down, Mr Ashforth' She indicated a Louis Quinze chair, but he remained facing her, standing. Then he smiled. The flash of teeth was strong above the jutting chin, calculated to please. In those first moments she did not notice the faint rings under the eyes, the slight swelling of his cheeks indicating he might have jowls in a few years, or that he held himself purposefully erectly so the suggestion of future portliness did not show.

'I'll stand if you don't mind,' he told her bluntly, 'until I know there's a basis for discussion. I gather from your letter you've come to some sort of conclusion about our relationship — that is, if I sink what's needed into this decrepit estate?'

She wished there could have been more delicacy in the question — a little gallantry perhaps — it would have made things so much easier.

She nodded slightly.

'Yes, Mr Ashforth.'

'And it is—?'

Her chin went up an inch or two higher; he noted with satisfaction the rounded curve of her slender neck, her air of pride and breeding, the tilted delicately sculptured lips and thick lashed lovely eyes. Already in imagination his strong arms were around her compelling and taking her to his will. A prize, and his possession.

'I agree,' she answered, succeeding in keeping her voice calm, though a pulse fluttered at her throat.

'Good.'

'So it's a bargain.'

'I've said so. Need we talk any more about that — just now? I mean—'

'Aye.' The one word was a command. 'I'm not a man to take chances, Miss Crane. Come here.' He beckoned to her.

She took a step forward, and his lips were suddenly hard and hot on hers, until her head fell back, and they softened. Her senses reeled. Other memories tried to claim her — of another man, and another scene — a patch of moorland sweet with thyme and heather — but Ashforth's face suffocated and overcame her. A moment later she was freed. He laughed softly.

'We'll have good times together, Elf — what is it they call you?'

'Elfrida.'

'Let it be Freda. Aye. That's for me only, from now on. Freda.'

'Just as you like.' She spoke automatically.

'So now for the details.'

She listened in a daze while he explained his intentions both personally and for the estate. The sum he intended for investment concerning the mines seemed to her at first, not only enormous, but incredible. Concerning Heronsmere he was more vague, but he left her in no doubt at all that if everything went well between them he was prepared to sink what would be — to most people — a tidy fortune in renovations,

ebuilding where necessary, and having the house not only
rought up to the former standards of bygone Penherrions,
ut refurnished to her tastes and those of Lady Marion.
Proper staff would be installed, though not on an outrageous
scale, and the grounds put into order with gardeners to keep
hem under control. He ended by saying, 'At present the
roperty's nought but a shambles, and I wouldn't have it as a
gift without the wherewithal to take a gamble. But then it
*will* pay off. I'll see to that. And I've the collateral, haven't I?'
His gaze travelled sensually to the upthrust firmly modelled
young breasts above the slim waist, and downwards towards
the gently swelling thighs beneath the soft pink material.

Taking a deep breath she answered with two fiery spots of
colour mounting her cheeks, 'You don't have to remind me.
I've given my word.'

'Yes. Well — just so long as you keep it, my dear. I'm not
one to be played with, and on my part I'll do my best to see no
fine lady in the land's treated better. In some ways I may be a
hard man, but I can be generous to those who please me, as
Mrs Ashforth would tell you.'

Her eyes tightened perceptibly, the beat of her heart
slowed before she said, 'Your wife?'

'Yes. My wife. She's a good woman, and she'll not be suffering through any commitment I make to you. Most of my days
will be spent up North, but I'll be at Heronsmere frequently.
The house, legally, will still be yours and Lady Marion's, naturally. I'm not aiming to act in any way deviously. but you'll
have to see that rooms are kept always ready for when I want a
breath of Cornish air.' His lips softened with speculative
desire. The hard eyes burned into hers. Once more with an
excitement she'd not anticipated or could control, Elfrida
heard him continue, 'I'd suggest a study — and a bedroom.
The bedroom you can arrange as you like — order what you
want, have the fancy fal-als most women hanker for, and see
the bed's good — canopied, with curtains. Or perhaps—'

In a rush of confusion Elfrida interrupted, 'I'd rather you
chose for your own apartments — our tastes might be different—'

He became suddenly businesslike.

'Very well, if that's what you want I'll see about it. In the meantime, Freda my dear, what about taking a look round now? Bring her Ladyship along too—'

But Marion declined to accompany them which Henry said approvingly was very sensible of her as so much trailing round dusty premises might weary her.

An hour later when the inspection was over and a choice of premises had been made, Ashforth left by the chaise which had been kept waiting by the drive. The arrangement for his return in a fortnight had been made, when legal matters were to be settled by solicitors, and mining problems discussed with expert engineers from the North.

Elfrida was left shaken, bewildered, excited yet with a queer sense of fatalism on her that she sensed now, was irreversible.

Later, when she'd tried to explain the situation to Marion, her half-sister said, with a perplexed frown, 'But if two rooms here are going to be his — legally — won't that mean he owns part of the house?'

Elfrida thought for a moment, sighed, and agreed. 'I suppose so. But only a small part. And he did say for his use — that won't mean he owns them.'

'We must contact Mr Hallet — my father's solicitor I think—' Marion said with uncharacteristic business acumen.

'Yes, of course. And if it turns out that Henry — Mr Ashforth — is entitled to full possession — owns the rooms I mean — we needn't go ahead. We can scrap the whole thing.'

'No.' Marion's voice was decisive. 'I want Heronsmere as it used to be — the Penherrion home and estate, I want the mines working, and good conditions for the men employed. I expect we shall have to give a little in return for all that—'

'We?' The ironic tone registered. Marion's colourless cheeks flushed.

'I'm sorry. I didn't mean to embarrass you — and of course you're giving far more than I should expect — than anyone should — to keep our home. If you've changed your mind,

Elfrida, say so. I'll understand. I hadn't the right, in the first place, to encourage you in any way.'

Elfrida's smile was wry, veiled, and a little fey.

'Don't worry. It really isn't such a sacrifice. In fact — actually I find Henry Ashforth rather an exciting man. Overbearing, but manageable, if you know how to do it.'

With which statement Marion had to be content.

# 6

Henry Ashforth arrived at Heronsmere for a prolonged stay in July of the same year. Elfrida, heady with excitement mingled with apprehension, had seen that the premises he desired were ready for his presence, the bedroom as daintily attractive as she could make it, although when the final touches were added she was confused by a number of questions and doubts that before had not occurred to her. Did he like flowers? Or would he consider them mere feminine extravagance. Would the elegant chair be to his satisfaction? Or should she have had a larger more masculine one put there for his use? But then he would have his study for reading and working in — his time in the bedroom would be minimal — except for sleeping in. Or — would it? A tremor ran through her. There was so much about him she didn't know, in fact hardly anything. His role as a lover, which had been the basis of the whole situation — would he desire much of her? Or after the newness of the experience had worn off was it possible he could become more absorbed in the business projects ahead? There was so much to be done. Heronsmere during the future weeks and months would of a necessity be a hive of activity, of meetings with officials, inspection of the mines, and naturally certain entertaining on her part.

In the past the latter would have been frightening to contemplate, but with extra servants now installed, and a good cook to take charge of the kitchen, she knew any worries in that quarter were quite unnecessary. Then Marion. She now seemed completely detached from the new situation. Four rooms had been set aside for her private use, and she revelled once more to have their former elegance restored.

Sometimes her cool acceptance of events caused Elfrida irritation. She had moments when she wanted to rush away — far far away from the commitments she'd shouldered. At such times she was horrified by her own actions, by the thought of being submissive to any man but Ben — of having a ruthless stranger's arms round her — of lying close against him in intimacy with his great hands claiming what was not hers to give. Oh, her grandmother had been right, she told herself then; there was much of her mother Susannah in her. In giving herself to Henry Ashforth she was sinning against the deepest morality of her being — making a sale of her body for personal gain.

Yet it wasn't quite like that, was it? If it hadn't been for Marion and Lynette, and workless miners wanting jobs — she wouldn't have contemplated taking such a course. And as Marion had so often pointed out — they had nothing to lose in the opinion of natives and villagers. Anyway — she might even wear a ring. During the hours of waiting for Ashforth's arrival she took out an antique carved circlet given to her by Martha before her death. It fitted the third finger of her left hand exactly. But the next moment she hastily took it off and replaced it in its box.

She knew she would never wear it in such pretence. She couldn't — not only because of the lying and hypocrisy, but because of Ben. Whatever he had done — however faithless he had been, no other ring but his would adorn her wedding finger. So forever it would be without. Ashforth *might* and *would* possess her body; but never, never could he claim her heart.

'What are you pondering over now?' Marion asked bluntly, as Elfrida wandered to and fro about the drawing room waiting for Henry's arrival.

'Nothing particularly,' Elfrida answered. 'Why?'

'You look so — serious somehow. Restless, yet set and rather cold. I hope you're not regretting things.'

'Naturally I'm serious,' Elfrida answered rather shortly. 'Wouldn't you be?'

'If I was I'd try not to show it,' Marion told her tartly.

'That look on your face ages you, Elfrida. I'm sure Ashforth will expect a smile and pleasant welcome.'

'When Ashforth, as you call him, arrives I shall appear quite delighted,' Elfrida remarked cuttingly. 'But as he's going to be here quite a lot in the future I'd get out of calling him Ashforth — remember you're not the sole owner any more of Heronsmere.'

A dull flush stained Marion's faded cheeks.

'There's no need to address me in such a manner. Two rooms. And for his use only. That doesn't give him any right of possession.'

Elfrida's temper cooled quickly. Suddenly she felt surprisingly tired.

'Oh I think it does.'

'But the solicitors—'

'The document we signed was a little ambiguous in parts, Marion. But don't worry. When I no longer please him I'm sure Mr Henry Ashforth will take off to other parts.'

'To his wife you mean.'

'I didn't mean anyone in particular, and I don't want his wife mentioned. She's the one snag I'd like to forget.'

'Naturally. Yes. I'm sorry if I've sounded hard. The last thing I want is to upset you.' Marion's voice trailed off uneasily. She reached for her stick and moved unsteadily to the window. Lately, Elfrida thought, her limp had appeared rather worse. She had no way of quite assessing the conflict of Marion's moods — of the guilt that sometimes rose to torment her when she recalled days of childhood — times when Sir Geoffrey had done his best to make up to her for her physical disability. And her grandfather, the proud and noble baronet whose portrait dominated the picture gallery upstairs! her grandfather too — and countless other ancestors staring from their heavy frames! — they would condemn and scorn her, she knew, for daring to encourage a jumped-up calculating mill-owner with the future of Heronsmere for the sake of his millions.

In using Elfrida as bait, she had demeaned herself and the name of Penherrion. But then in other ways her brother had done the same, and her father's madness had put the final disgraceful seal on what had once been a fine heritage. Or was it possible that eventually lost dignity could be restored? Surely, surely it would be so. With the mines restored and security established for workers and their families, bitterness and condemnation would gradually give place to good will and trust again. She would be able to visit estate employees and inhabitants of nearby villages without shame or fear of meeting mistrust. Malicious tongues would stop wagging, and when the time came Ashforth would probably be bored by Heronsmere and be off elsewhere, taking Elfrida with him. It would be better so. In spite of a growing warmth for her half-sister, Marion recognised that Elfrida would never be accepted by society. Moral issues might sometimes be overlooked, but the fact remained that no bastard daughter of wild Susannah Crane could have a proper place in certain circles.

Standing by the window staring out over the neglected grounds, Marion felt extreme loneliness. How different if Ben was here. A pang of bitter longing swept through her; her thin hand shook as she tightened her fingers round the gold knobbed stick. Quite unaware she was observed, she was startled by Elfrida's touch on her shoulder, of her voice saying, 'What's the matter, Marion?'

Marion turned. 'Nothing. I was just thinking and wondering why things have to be like this. In some ways the lives of peasants must be easier—'

'Oh no, you wouldn't say that if you knew the drudgery.'

'You were different though, weren't you? — because of my father.'

'Half of me was. The other part knew a great deal of the other side. Some of the tales my grandmother told — true tales — were sad and terribly sordid. Then, although she was strict, I did mix a bit—'

'With the miners you mean — their children?'

'Sometimes. Not often.'

'Ben? He was one of them of course. You knew him well from the beginning.'

'I thought I did.'

'It was the same with me. He was quite an actor.'

The sun suddenly slid behind a cloud causing a shadow between them. Marion forced herself to her full height, though her back was still rounded at the shoulders.

'Well, I'm going to my room for a rest, Elfrida. There's really no point in my waiting with you to greet Mr Ashforth. I'm sure he'll be gratified to see you alone. We shall meet later naturally.'

'Naturally,' Elfrida echoed.

A minute later Marion had left and was making her way laboriously up the stairs to her own premises.

Without her the drawing room seemed curiously, almost uncannily quiet. No drift of wind stirred the curtains. There was no bird call from outside, no tap of leaf or twig against the window, only the steady rhythmical tick-tock of the ornate French clock on the marble mantelshelf.

Elfrida decided she could stay in no longer waiting for time to pass until Ashforth thought fit to appear. He had said about four, but already the sun was low towards the west. Travelling of course was unpredictable. His late arrival was probably through no fault of his; but the tension and knowledge of what lay ahead became unbearable, and soon after Marion's departure she slipped on a loose cape and went out through a side door leading to the drive and gate which had a path cutting straight to the open moors.

She walked westwards, with a deepening feeling in her of a future prisoner having a last taste of freedom. On her right the glitter of distant sea beyond the cliffs held the radiant motionless quality of deep blue glass. As she passed a thick copse of trees the house was temporarily obscured by intertwined trunks clustered in clumps of elder, briar, and the dank branches of rhododendrons blossoming with crimson flowers. On the edge of the thicket was the ruin of an ancient building that some said had once been a chapel, others that it had been a refuge for smuggling. It had no roof now, and only empty holes of windows stared dark and blank from the tumbled granite walls. It was avoided by the superstitious who

believed it was haunted. At certain times of the day, and in a
fading light this was understandable, and as Elfrida passed
that afternoon she fancied shadows moved by the jagged
doorway. She stopped instinctively, listening, with all her
senses alert. Then, suddenly, there was the crackle of twigs
being broken, followed by the muttering of a harsh throaty
voice, and another, younger, lighter on a higher key.

The bushes parted. An ancient brown face framed by a
black shawl appeared; gnarled hands parted the undergrowth, and staring almost unbelievingly, Elfrida saw the
white-frocked figure of a young girl clutching the crone's
hand.

Lynette.

As the three confronted each other, the child pressed her
body closer against her ancient companions. The old woman
carried a basket on the other arm containing mushrooms.
Her eyes, sunken, shrewd, black as sloes, showed no flicker of
surprise; only watchfulness.

Elfrida's reaction was swift.

'What are you doing here, Lynette? How could you traipse
out alone in that clean frock? I told you to stay indoors until
your − your new uncle arrived. Now look at you—'

Lynette's full underlip drooped sulkily. Her dark eyes held
a hint of defiance.

'Why is he my uncle?' she said. 'I don't like Mr Ashforth.
Why has he got to come?'

'Shush dordi,' the old woman said. 'You go now with your
kin.' Her eyes narrowed as they turned again on Elfrida.
'We've met many times before, girl − a princess you were
then, and will be s'long as you remember the truth and livin'
− of earth and sky, and the coming and going of the seasons
− of the wind's whisper, and the earth's waking; of bird and
beast, and summers and winters when most sleep. Riches
may come to thee, but the real gold is of thy heart, wild one.
And one day − one day will come true blossoming − strong
and sweet as the gorse flaming and the larks' song—' She gave
the child a gentle push, then lifted a hand as though in blessing. 'We shall meet again, Rackli,' she said, and with the

swiftness of a fox turned and disappeared into the shadows of the trees.

Elfrida clasped Lynette's hand, and drew her back along the moorland path towards the house.

'It was wrong of you to go wandering at such a time,' she said, but all trace of scolding had left her voice. 'But I understand. They're friendly folk. Still—' she stared down on the shining chestnut dark curls — 'I do so want you by me when your Uncle Henry arrives. And please — do be nice to him, Lynette.'

The brilliant black lashed blue eyes stared boldly upwards into Elfrida's luminous ever-changing grey-green ones. 'Are you going to marry him or something?' she asked after a perceptible pause.

'No.' The one word was a tight little sound.

'Then why have I to call him Uncle and be nice? Is he going to give you and Aunt Marion a lot of money or something?'

Elfrida was about to deny it when she changed her mind, disconcerted by the little girl's perception.

'He's going to help,' she answered. 'Not only Aunt Marion and me — but the whole estate, our home. Your great Uncle Geoffrey — lost a fortune when he was so ill. There are a lot of debts to be paid, and unless we're able to do it many miners and their families will be out of work with not enough to eat, because Red Bell will have to close. You wouldn't want that, would you, Lynette?'

'Oh no,' the child looked momentarily distressed. 'You mean friends like Billy Pender and Ted?'

'What do you know about them?' Elfrida was curious. Lynette glanced away. 'Not much. Except they're nice, and know where the badgers are. Sometimes—' She broke off hesitantly.

'Yes? Do you mean you go off alone and meet them? But they've had sickness at their cottage, and I don't want you running any risks, or wandering about by yourself on the moor. I can't think what Miss Paul has been doing to allow it.'

Miss Paul was assistant housekeeper and part-time governess to Lynette.

'Oh *her*!' Lynette laughed, 'she's such a funny old thing —
she's always saying, "My eyes can't be everywhere you know,
Miss Lynette. And the next time I find you've disobeyed I'll
have to spank you, indeed I will."' Her tones were so prim
and reminiscent of the good lady that Elfrida found it hard
not to smile.

'Of course she won't,' the little girl continued in confident
matter-of-fact tones.

'Then I'm afraid we'll have to find someone else to take
charge,' Elfrida remarked practically, 'Someone who will,
when necessary.'

'No. You mustn't. Old Paulie's quite a dear in her way,
and she loves me,' Lynette said quickly. 'Please *please* don't
get rid of her. I'll be good, I really will, when Mr Ashforth —
Uncle Henry — comes. I'll be nice to him, as nice as I can be.
But I wish it was someone else going to help pay for things.'

'Why?' Elfrida was suddenly curious.

'I don't know. I — I — he looks at me in such a funny
way—'

'Don't be silly.'

'I'm not. He does. It's his eyes. As if he's trying to see
through me — to know every bit about me — where I come
from — who my father and mother were—' She broke off for
a second, putting her hand to her mouth, then continued
more quietly, 'Who were they, Aunt Elfrida?'

Taken aback, Elfrida paused before saying, 'One day,
when you're much older, you'll find out I'm sure. Is it so
important after all? It's what you are that matters, and you
know your Aunt Marion and I love you very much. You have
a nice home—'

'Does she?' Lynette interrupted quickly.

'What do you mean? Who?'

'Aunt Marion — love me? I don't think so. She goes sort of
stiff and funny when I talk to her. And her hand's always
cold. She doesn't really like me at all — not like a father and
mother would. Not like Uncle Geoffrey. Sometimes he gave
me the top of his egg — once I had a drink from his glass. It
was hot and nice—'

'Well—' Elfrida swallowed. 'If you want to, you can think of me as your mama, and if you like boiled eggs so much—'

'It wasn't the egg so much as the way he used to look at me,' Lynette said quickly. 'And he put his hand on my head. I liked the feel of it − sort of loving and gentle.'

Elfrida's heart lurched. Bringing herself back to the present she said abruptly, 'Come along − we must hurry. Mr Ashforth may have arrived already.'

'Who cares!'

'Lynette! please help me.'

The brilliant blue eyes widened.

'Help, Aunt Elfrida?'

'Please. In a way I'm as nervous as you.'

'Really?'

'Truly.'

The child's face suddenly became radiant.

'All right, I'll be very very nice to this Uncle Henry person. I'll even curtsey if you like!'

Elfrida squeezed one small hand warmly, and laughed softly.

'Oh I don't think you need do that. He won't expect it. Just be yourself.'

Elfrida's fear that Ashforth might already have arrived proved justified.

He had been shown his rooms, and was already taking a look round the conservatory when Elfrida and Lynette reached Heronsmere.

Marion poked her head round the drawing room as they went down the hall. 'I do think you might have been here to receive your − our − guest,' she said petulantly. 'Fancy going out when Mr Ashforth was due—'

'I'd been waiting for hours, and I wondered where Lynette had disappeared to,' Elfrida said, although the latter was not entirely true. 'Miss Paul should have kept an eye on her.'

Marion's lips tightened primly. 'Miss Paul is more concerned with her secret vice these days than with her duties,' she affirmed. 'Every afternoon it's the same. You may not have noticed it, Elfrida, but she drinks.'

'She had a little "tonic" occasionally I know, but I'd hardly call that a vice—'

'Well, it's very inconvenient, especially at a time like this.' Marion fiddled with her reticule and put smelling salts to her nose. As Elfrida and the little girl passed, she said, 'Your friend seems somewhat put out. I hardly think he's in the mood to be bothered with a child. I advise you to tidy yourself, send Lynette to the nursery or kitchen, and try and make peace.'

Lynette did not need to be taken, she just sped away.

Stifling a sharp comment Elfrida hurried upstairs following Lynette and when she appeared at the conservatory door five minutes later only a faint flush on her high cheekbones betrayed her flurried mood. The blue green gown she wore enhanced the changing colour of her eyes — the luminous clear skin, and beauty of the shining pale hair. Her lips were tilted slightly in a half smile. She wore no jewellery, but a single white rose had been pinned hurriedly at her breast.

Henry Ashforth, who was standing with his back to her, examining a hot-house blossom, turned. He looked a little grim, with heavy brows drawn together over the bridge of his nose. For a second there was silence between them, then going forward, with a hand out, Elfrida said softly, 'I'm so sorry not to have been here when you arrived, Mr — Henry. I meant to be, but my — our niece was missing; finding her took longer than I thought. When you meet I'll see she apologises—' Her voice wavered. Ashforth's face relaxed. His hand closed momentarily on hers in a tight grip. Then suddenly, without any preamble, he jerked her close, and his lips were hot on hers.

'No matter,' he said a second later. 'There's plenty of time together ahead. And the child's unimportant.'

Her heart thudded wildly against her ribs in a tumult of emotions — excitement, relief, mingled with an undercurrent of fear. A strong finger tilted her chin upwards.

'What's the matter? No regrets have you? If so be straight about it. The time's past for coy games.'

'Regrets? Of course not.' She forced conviction into her

voice, and smiled brilliantly. 'You must give me a little time though, to get used to—'

'Being my woman?'

She flushed.

'Well — isn't that natural?'

Still with his direct gaze on her he answered bluntly.

'After tonight you'll need no learning. I can promise you that.'

A statement which proved to be true.


Henry Ashforth, despite his humble beginnings, was well versed in his own particular method of love-making, which without sentiment or romantic approach held such overwhelming sensuality and dominant male expertise that although many of any lingering illusions she might have that night crumbled and died — her body responded with an abandon that later surprised her. She knew she could never love him, but her youth, hungry for Ben, took wildly what was offered so that his image might be erased in a dank tide of forgetfulness. All the frustration, defiance, and loneliness of the past years culminated in a bittersweet revenge that deceived even Henry himself; until morning, with periods of sleep between, she allowed him to do as he willed with her — pulsing and giving, feeling only submission as his hardness caressed and ravished her. Her fair hair was a silver pool over the pillows — her body a white flame to his fire.

When it was over and daylight penetrated the curtains, she lay naked and supine, while he withdrew and eased himself over her, staring down. Her eyes were closed. Her rapid breathing gradually steadied to a normal pace.

Presently he said, with his breath still hot against her face, 'Look at me.'

There was no endearment, no word of tenderness or affection. Just a command.

Very slowly the dark lashes lifted. Her blue eyes told him nothing. His mouth came down on hers again, suffocating any resistance. Then he abruptly released himself, swung a leg over the bed, and got up. His look of strength — the sturdy build of the fine naked body filled her suddenly with mild distaste. Exhaustion overcame her. 'Leave me alone,' her heart cried, 'oh leave me alone.' Tears briefly filmed her eyes, but arrogantly gratified, he never noticed.

'Well,' he said, 'quite a promising beginning, don't you think?'

She didn't answer.

He laughed, 'Don't say you're tired?'

'A little, aren't you?'

'Me?' he returned to the bed, pinched her cheek, and squeezed a breast possessively. 'Not on your life, darling. I'm never the one to tire of good things. I've an appetite though. Will breakfast soon be on?'

'When you're ready,' she told him. 'I'm sure someone will be about. Ask for whatever you want.'

'Good.'

He washed, shaved, and dressed with speed, saying little more. When at last the sound of his firm tread had faded down the stairs, Elfrida forced herself to get up. She went over to the dressing-table and stared at herself through the mirror. Although tired she looked very beautiful, but the beauty didn't register — only a dreadful sense of disappointment, of having betrayed herself. To allay it she wilfully turned her mind to Ben, making him the target for all that had happened — debasement of her pride, of giving herself to a man she didn't, could never love. Why? She didn't even like Ashforth. If Ben hadn't let her down leaving her to the forces beyond her control this would never have happened. She would have had no sense of duty to Lady Marion, because she'd never have left the cottage for Heronsmere, never heard of Ben's fast-and-loose games with Sir Geoffrey's crippled daughter. The affairs of the estate would have been none of her concern, and Lynette would have known her real father. Fate had been against her from the very beginning, when she, Elfrida, had been born Susannah Crane's bastard. What she had become and would be in the future was merely the outcome of what had gone before.

And yet — suddenly a wave of truth hit her — she had

experienced a certain physical satisfaction during the night. Becoming Henry Ashforth's mistress hadn't been entirely without pleasure. She'd been quite conscious when she plunged into the affair of what her position would entail. Duty alone hadn't driven her into his arms.

Slowly a sense of proportion returned. What point was there in dwelling on what she'd once had and lost? Especially when so many families needing work would survive? Prosperity would benefit all. Even herself. She would, therefore, make the most of it. Have what clothes she desired, make herself a figure of envy among local inhabitants when she rode in a fine carriage through the village, or down the streets of Truro. Society might condemn her, but eventually all would be impressed. She would no longer be Elfrida the witchling, but 'that theer rich furriner's lady.'

She would wear silks and satins, and ospreys in hats and bonnets. She would hold her chin high, with her hair finely curled and all a-glitter in the sunlight. Maybe Ben would catch a glimpse of her then, and he'd regret the day he spurned her.

Ben.

She bit her lip and turned away from the mirror. She would not think of him. Her commitment now was to Henry.

Presently she forced herself to dress, and when she went downstairs she was surprised to find him talking to Lynette in the hall. The child was looking up at him with a puzzled look in her eyes, her small chin thrust stubbornly out beneath her full underlip.

Elfrida paused at the foot of the stairs.

'So you two are making friends at last,' she said briefly.

Both turned.

'You could say we were becoming better acquainted,' Ashforth remarked. 'She didn't seem too keen on it at first, until I pointed out a few things.'

Elfrida's heart sank.

'Oh? Such as?'

Henry bent and cocked a finger under the child's chin. 'That if a youngster in my care is good and does as she's told there's nought but nice things for her — treats and toys, and even a trip to the circus — but if she's not, and doesn't learn her place I'm quite prepared to teach her, with the back of my hand in the right place. That's what we arranged, isn't it, young lady?'

For a dreadful few seconds there was silence, then Lynette, red-cheeked and stormy-eyed cried, '*No!* it isn't! and it was you who said it, not me. I don't like you — you're not my uncle. I never will — never, *never.*'

She turned and rushed away to the kitchens.

Ashforth would have followed, but Elfrida pulled him back. '*Please.* Not at the very beginning. Children are sensitive. A new routine's starting for her. She's nervous—'

'Nervous? That young firebrand?'

'Underneath, yes. Don't let us have a scene, after — after—'

Diverted, his eyes turned upon her. How very lovely she looked with the early sunlight streaming through a long window across her slim blue-clad form. And this was the beautiful creature he'd ravished and possessed so utterly during the night.

His lips relaxed.

'Very well. This once.' An arm slid momentarily round her waist, then he drew himself away, pulled himself to his full height, tidied his stock and said, 'By the way, I've had what I want to eat. A message came — just before my conflict with that young madam, your niece — wanting me concerning Red Bell soon as possible. So I'm off. Engineers arrived at Truro yesterday, and are getting down to things early. We Northerners don't waste time.'

Trying not to show her relief, Elfrida said, 'Will you go by carriage?'

Ashforth's white teeth gleamed in his face. Smiling, he looked extraordinarily handsome.

'Hell no. There are horses in the stables still, I suppose?'

'Yes. But — the stallion's tricky — he—'

'I'll know how to handle him. There isn't a horse in the land I couldn't break if I had to.'

Half an hour later he was gone.

Elfrida watched as horse and rider cantered from the stables towards the moorland road. The great animal jibbed once then reared. The next moment he was under control, and the pace increased to a gallop.

When they'd finally disappeared Elfrida made her way down the hall to find Lynette.

# 7

July passed into early August. The crimson bells of Foxgloves stretched thick and tall in lush places among the green of spreading bracken. The high moors were thickly carpeted with purple and gold where heather was splashed with yellow gorse and broom. Mostly the month was fine, interspersed with thin rain and occasional thunder that left the earth smelling with a heady overpowering sweetness.

Never had the air and atmosphere of Cornwall seemed so potent to Elfrida, so heavily charged with atmosphere and passionate longing. In demanding moments Henry Ashforth was able to allay the cravings of her body, but frequently her spirit rebelled. There were times when he sensed defiance in her and quelled her mood by force. Once he remarked coldly, when despite intimacy she turned deliberately away and seated herself at the mirror, dampening her forehead with cologne and drawing the brush firmly through her tumbled hair, 'Don't play with me, madam, and don't imagine now you've had your way you're mistress of this place able to take what you want and say what you choose. I'm master and you'd better see you don't forget it. What I say goes. A little show of affection on your part wouldn't be amiss — even if it's pretence.'

When she didn't reply he moved to the back of her chair swiftly, and pulling the neck of her lacy negligée by one shoulder, wrenched her head round and up to face him.

'Did you hear what I said?' he demanded.

'Yes, I heard.' She smiled with brittle false sweetness, primping her lips mockingly. 'Is this what you want, Henry?'

He slapped one cheek sharply.

'You vixen,' he said, 'that's what you are, and no mistake.'

She laughed, but without humour.

'Of course. I was born wild, on the moor, didn't you know?'

Her strange blue eyes held a fey look that disconcerted him. With her cloud of silver gold hair tumbled from her face and forehead, there was a taunting evasive quality about her that made him suddenly desire her again with an obsessive urgency, so that all memories of her past were quelled for ever, making her utterly and wholly his. He'd paid for her, by God, he thought relentlessly. Never before had he spent so much on any woman, not even his wife. Yet he sensed — he *knew* there was a part of her withheld from him — something he couldn't locate or understand. He wasn't a subtle man — he'd never in his life had to puzzle over a female as he did over this one. He'd heard whispers about her of course — noticed certain glances between servants when any allusion to her life before she arrived at Heronsmere was mentioned. Jealousy had risen in him then, because he suspected some other man — some mystery yokel who'd had her before he appeared on the scene. Maybe the child was his. Maybe that's why he had impulse to take a slipper to the little girl almost every time they faced each other. He'd no doubt at all secretly that the youngster was Elfrida's. And he resented her. He resented anything about this tantalising mistress of his that he couldn't entirely own. Well, he thought, there was an answer to that. He'd get her with child himself. When she had a son by him, the other saucy little chit could be sent off to boarding school somewhere — France maybe — some place far enough away where a suitable husband could be found for her so she never troubled Heronsmere again.

The idea so stimulated him, he momentarily forgot that morning his anger, and very firmly pulled her to her feet from the chair, and carried her again to the bed.

She gasped, as her heart started its wild pumping.

'But I thought — oh Henry — you said you had to meet someone. And we've only just—'

She broke off as his hot lips travelled her shoulders, breasts, and lips, smothering further remonstrance from her.

'Once more, darling,' he muttered thickly against her ear. 'Once more — aye — until it's all — safe and sure—'

She struggled ineffectually. '*What*—'

'A son, my sweet. A boy — *mine*.'

Faintness threatened her. She closed her eyes, wishing for the void to claim her. But there was no void — no emptiness — no escape. He was merciless in his ravishing — so arrogant, so monstrously determined, that at last she succumbed, knowing, and in throbbing terror, that he would achieve what he wished.

When half an hour later he tidied himself and left, she still lay flushed and breathing quickly on the bed. Fear encompassed her. But there was no fear in Ashforth as he strode down the path to the stables. Instinct told him he had her now, where he wanted. And one day, she'd be glad of it. Any child of his and hers would be heir to a great deal. He might even induce his wife to divorce him so he could have a ring on Elfrida's finger with everything settled legally in proper order. The one child he had up north was a girl. He'd see she was all right — with a dowry handsome enough to tempt some young buck into marrying her. As for Lucy, his wife — she'd accept things his way. She'd have to, and she was a placid enough creature to make no trouble, especially when she'd be so well provided for. In the flush of such triumphant reasoning he never paused to wonder that a wayward chit of a Cornish girl could so easily have reduced commonsense values to nought. Never before had the possibility of breaking a perfectly satisfactory marriage occurred to him. He'd had women on the side, to which his worthy spouse had turned a blind eye.

But this was different.

And so was she — his Elfrida.

He'd never let her go, even if he had to use a switch. But that wouldn't happen. She fancied him all right — always had. Her moans and kisses — her strange glances and captivating coquettish moods! God help him — he was obsessed.

Whatever his obsession was to achieve personally, in the future, that day it was effective in ensuring the continuance of Red Bell and Wheal Mary, and jobs of all miners employed there, with many others as well.

He returned to Heronsmere in a well satisfied genial mood. That night Elfrida was left at peace.

She went to bed early, and dreamed intermittently through the night, not of Henry or present circumstances, but of Ben Curran astride his horse on the edge of the moor, with his arms out, waiting to receive her.

By a strange coincidence Maria, Ben's wife, was that same night in the difficult process of giving birth to his son. The child, born late, lived. But Maria, exhausted, and in the throes of an agony too terrible to endure, succumbed and died in the early hours of the morning.

Ben, dazed and distraught, was at length led away by the doctor after the sheet was laid over his wife's head.

Lines of strain and lack of sleep made his face haggard almost old. For a whole hour while the life slowly drained from her body and her heart failed, he had sat by the bed, holding her hand.

No one could know the guilt he felt — the remorse for not having been able to love her. But later, when he managed to think at all clearly, he knew what he would do. He would build a memorial in her memory — on the moor somewhere — a sculpture of his own as tribute to a good woman who had been helpmate as well as friend, and whose only frailty had been her complete incapacity to rouse his ardour or desire.

It was autumn when he procured the site — a patch of land bordering the boundaries of Heronsmere property, half way along the ridge between his old home and that of the late Sir Geoffrey's. A neighbouring farmer sold willingly at the price offered. The half acre of scrub and moor was bleak and of little use for farming. Its rocky tump stood at the highest point for some miles around, commanding a view of distant valley on both sides, including the turrets and chimneys of Heronsmere below.

A fold of shadowed land indicated the spot where he and Elfrida had once lain together limbs passionately entwined in love. A wave of bitterness flooded him briefly as he told himself wryly, 'This new work I create will be more potent than memory; and more enduring. Long after I've gone

Maria's influence will dominate the scene — blotting out the rest, so one day perhaps even the heather will wither and die.'

In October he paid several visits to the site, constructively planning the sculpture in his mind, imagining its effect from every angle — its relationship to the surrounding rocks and terrain. He met no one, until the end of the month when a young girl appeared from behind a nearby twisted elder tree in its clump of brown furze.

He was startled. Her hair was so thick and dark and wild — her eyes so vividly blue they held the challenge of flashing swords newly polished. Her cream skin shone golden in the slanting rays of the afternoon sun, and his first thought was — a gipsy. She held sprays of berries in one hand. There was a certain boldness about her, unconscious defiance, that puzzled him, yet made him long to put her at her ease.

'Hullo,' he said, 'where do you come from?' She studied him for a moment then replied, turning her head in the direction of Elfrida's old cottage, 'There. It's where I have my treasures.'

He felt a lurch of his stomach and tensing of muscles. What was she up to? He wondered. Was this some trick to discomfort him? Until then he'd kept his eyes and mind firmly from the tumbled place that had once been Elfrida's home. The granite relic was well off his route, and he never rode that way. But something in her expression forced him to take a brief glance at the shadowed walls.

'Do you then!' he heard himself saying automatically. 'But it's no more than a ruin. A place for sheep and foxes I'd have thought, not a nice little girl.'

'I'm not a little girl. I'm eight.'

'A very great age indeed.'

'Don't laugh,' she said, with her small chin jutting out. 'There's nothing funny about it — or about me liking it. And foxes are nice; nicer than people. That's why I come.'

'People?'

She looked down. 'My Aunts. Oh well — one's all right. But that horrible man they make me call Uncle Henry—' She broke off biting a lip, then continued quickly, 'and that silly governess creature — she's got her eye on him although she must be quite ninety!' her eyes widened. 'Well, fifty at the least. But he sucks up to her you know — because of me. "Put her over your knee," he said once. And she tried, but I bit her hand. Then she screamed and he — he pulled me into his study and took a switch from the wall and beat me. If Aunt Elfrida hadn't come into the room—'

'Elfrida? Did you say Elfrida?' His pulses were hammering.

'Of course. She's the nice one. We live down there — at Heronsmere. It was all right while Sir Geoffrey was alive. But when he died — at least afterwards — he came. Mr Ashforth.'

'I see.' Ben had heard the name, reports of mines to expand, and the personal rumours, but until that moment he'd forced himself to disregard them, especially where Elfrida was concerned. In a daze he heard the childish voice continue, 'He's not always there of course. But when he is everyone's supposed to be nice to him because of the money and Red Bell, and all the debts Uncle Geoffrey left behind. But do you know — I don't really think he cares a bit about the miners or Aunt Marion, or the house. He just wants Aunt Elfrida.' Very solemnly for so young a girl she added knowingly, 'She sleeps with him, you know.'

'No, I didn't.' The words came out with a snap. His fair handsome profile was suddenly granite clear and set against the fading sky.

Lynette was puzzled, wondering what had changed him so completely from a friendly gallant stranger who'd appeared suddenly as though from nowhere, like a young king in a fairy tale — into this stern brooding man with set jaw and brows drawn fiercely over his blue eyes. She hesitated for a moment, then asked tentatively, 'What's the matter? Have I said something wrong? Do you know Aunt Elfrida?'

He looked at her then. His tones were wry when he answered, 'I thought I did, once, but it was evidently someone quite different.'

A moment or two later he'd said goodbye and was striding across the short turf to where his mount was tethered to a wind-swept thorn.

Watching him ride away Lynette was filled with a sense of deep loss. It was as though just for a brief time she'd contacted someone — a friend of her very own, who could become dear and understanding to her — and then, in a flash, it was over. He had gone. When his erect form on the grey horse had finally disappeared, she turned with a curious dejection in her, and wandered back to Heronsmere.

Elfrida, coming out of the large parlour, saw her walking up the hall softly from the kitchens, obviously not wishing to be seen. She went to meet her at the foot of the back stairs.

'Where have you been?' Elfrida asked, after a quick glance round to make sure Ashforth was nowhere about.

'Just a walk.'

'By yourself again? You know you're not supposed to.'

'Only *he* said so — that nasty man of yours — Uncle Henry.' There was scorn in the young voice. Elfrida, shocked, put a hand to her lips warningly, while the other went to the little girl's shoulder.

'Sh — sh you mustn't say such things. If he heard! Oh, Lynette, you know what would happen — and—'

'Don't care. I hate him.'

'Well I *do* care. I love you.'

'If you love me, then why don't you send him away? He doesn't like us, not Aunt Marion or me; not the miners either. He just pretends — so that you do what he says and let him kiss you in that horrible way. I can't bear it. It's sort of — of sickening. That's why I go out, so I can be with nice things away from Heronsmere—'

The words tumbled out in a flood of anguished resentment. Elfrida, at first, was too dismayed to speak. When at last she got her emotions under control, she said, almost in a whisper, 'Come along, Lynette, this isn't the place for such conversation. We'll go into the garden. I've something in the arbour you may like to see.'

Suspicion in Lynette's large blue eyes gradually changed to interest. 'What?'

'Wait until I show you.'

The two of them left the house by the front door and went

down the steps, from where they crossed by the path to the far
side of a lawn. A summer-house stood in a corner under a
large elm. In the past, before Henry Ashforth's appearance,
Lynette had often played there, but when new gardeners
were taken on to help the faithful retainer Moses Peters, who
in Sir Geoffrey's will had been left a legacy and the use of a
nearby cottage for his life time, Lynette had been forbidden
by Henry to trample over the newly laid turf, and her small
place of sanctuary had been forbidden.

The door was slightly ajar. Elfrida pushed it open quietly.
Lynette looked up enquiringly. 'What would he say?' she
enquired in hushed tones.

'It doesn't matter,' Elfrida told her firmly. 'Anyway Uncle
Henry's busy in his study, I expect. Come along—'

Almost on tiptoe, Lynette followed. There was the warm
sweetish smell inside of cedar wood dried by the sun, but the
air was moist as well, and when night came the interior would
hold the faint mist of dew from the spreading tree above.
Wooden seats and a little round table had been used in the
past for picnics, and Lynette remembered days before Sir
Geoffrey's death when he'd sat there, rug over his knees,
telling her stories. They were strange tales she didn't understand, but she'd listened, fascinated, until he fell asleep
before the end.

As Elfrida guided her to a shadowed corner there was the
chortle of a bird from somewhere, and the scamper across the
floor of a small mouse. Lynette laughed delightedly.

Elfrida glanced up to a corner. 'Look,' she said.

Lynette stared.

There in the shadows perched on a strut of wood close to
the ceiling, was something with round eyes watching.

A small brown owl.

'Moses found him weeks ago,' Elfrida explained. 'He'd a
broken leg — of course he might turn out to be a she. I don't
know—'

'Then would she be a mother owl and have eggs and hatch
them?'

'She might, if she's not disturbed too much.'

'Has it a name?'

'Moses called it Brownie, which is a good name whether it's a he or she.'

'And does it ever go out?'

'Not yet. Not until the leg's properly healed. Moses looks after it — he even fixed a kind of splint on the leg.'

'A splint?'

'A small piece of wood to help it heal. He's very clever with birds.'

'I know. I like Moses. But I don't think he does — Mr Ashforth.'

'Uncle Henry, Lynette.'

'Oh all right, Uncle Henry. Moses knows he doesn't too. He won't be ordered about or told what to do. He just glares, and goes on with what he's doing. Once I heard Henry say, "You're sacked, get out." And do you know what Moses did?'

'No.'

'He pulled himself up, and he looked so big — bigger than Mr Ashforth even, and his face was red. "Oh yes?" he said, "you tell that to another, mister. I've got my place here for good. It's in the will. So don't you come threatening me." That's what he said — or something like it. So — I don't suppose Uncle Henry will make him get rid of — of Brownie, will he?'

'I'm quite sure he won't,' Elfrida told the child comfortingly. 'Your uncle's more concerned with the mines, the property, and seeing the house and main gardens are in order, rather than bothering about one tame little owl. While Moses keeps an eye on him the bird's safe. Every evening the arbour door's shut so no fox or stranger can get in — Moses feeds him, inspects the leg, and already they're firm friends. Sometimes Brownie perches on his shoulders and goes for a little airing.'

'I wish he'd perch on mine.'

'When you know him better I'm sure he will,' Elfrida told her. 'Only you must be nicer and more obedient with Uncle Henry. If you could make him like you everything would be so much easier.'

Lynette thought for a moment. Then she said, 'All right, I'll try. For Brownie's sake.'

For a few weeks following this incident the days passed more smoothly at Heronsmere. Lynette kept out of Ashforth's way as much as possible, and made a point of being more amenable with her governess. She didn't wander away so frequently or obviously, although she often wondered about the fair-haired horseman she'd met on the moor. She said nothing to Elfrida about her brief conversation with Ben, sensing there was some mystery about him — some secret she'd one day solve for herself, and that until then it was better to keep the matter to herself.

Elfrida meanwhile did her best to concentrate on the advantages of being Henry's mistress — indulging herself in having whatever she wanted for her own adorment — making gifts of food and clothes when the occasion arose, to cottagers and estate workers, even paying visits to miners' families, who gradually started to accept her generosity without prejudice. Henry who could be close-fisted in the normal way, indulged her whims, simply because her beauty so obsessed him, and the more she depended on him for her pleasures, the more completely he felt he possessed her. Their physical life was stimulus to his pride, the sight of the mines' pumping rods working again rhythmically against the sky, gave ballast to his self confidence. The grounds of the house could now be an affront to no one. True, the expenditure was vast, but his instinct, and the assertions of engineers dealing with the futures of Red Bell and Wheal Mary, told him that in a couple of years he'd be beginning to reap considerable profit, providing another little fortune in his fist including Elfrida with the bargain. The only snags were that giant of a yokel Moses, and the defiant youngster Lynette, whom he proposed to get off his hands in a month or two by sending her to boarding school.

He'd broached the matter to Elfrida once. At first she'd said nothing, but the mounting colour in her face proved to him she wasn't pleased.

'I don't think Lynette would settle there, or anywhere from

Heronsmere,' she said at last. 'She's not like most ordinary children—'

'No. And that's what's wanted. Proper discipline. I've stood quite a good deal from that young lady—'

'Not lately. Lately she's been good.'

Ashforth threw her a wry glance, irritated by her protestations on the child's behalf.

'Only because she remembers the walloping she once got,' he said. 'As for being good — she manages to keep out of my way, that's all. In any case why are you so concerned about your — niece? Or is she really only that.'

The direct question caused a bumping of her heart, that made her for a moment feel faintly sick.

'I don't know what you're talking about. Why should I say she was if it wasn't true?'

He smiled with his lips but not his eyes, took her by both shoulders, forced her face up towards his and answered, 'Only *you* know, madam. But I'm not a fool. Remember that, and remember I'm in charge now — the only one you should be concerned with. If I ever find any other man sniffing round — I'll kill him.'

She shivered.

'Oh Henry. Please don't. When you speak like that it's—'

'Well?'

His breath was hot against her cheek.

'Horrible,' she told him, determinedly. 'Revolting.'

He let her go, and laughed.

'Words,' he said, 'merely words. Frightened, Elfrida?'

'No.' It was a lie, but convincingly spoken.

'Well you should be. But don't worry — "kill" perhaps was an exaggeration. But by God, my love, if you ever play me false you'd wish you'd never been born. And him.'

Her face whitened.

Noticing it he added, 'You should be flattered I think so much of you.'

She said nothing. They were in the library, where she'd gone to fetch a book. Henry had recently taken to using the room when he felt his study too confining.

Suddenly practical he turned to the table where some letters were lying, and continued, 'I'm getting legal things into order. Yesterday I saw my solicitor – the Penzance man. Everything will be all right.'

She stared, with a thin frown drawn between her eyes above the nose.

'What do you mean, all right?'

'Lucy. My wife. She's agreed to a divorce. We'll be married, you and I, just as soon as the whole business is through.'

'But—'

'No buts. It's what you want, isn't it? A ring on your finger, to be able to call yourself Mrs Henry Ashforth—'

'You never said anything to me. Why didn't you mention it? And what makes you so sure I'll agree. I didn't want another woman hurt – it wasn't in the bargain. You were quite content with the arrangement—'

'Aye. But things change. There's no going back to the old way now. I mean to be sure of you. As sure as any man can be under the sun.'

Her senses froze.

'I'll have to think about it. You must give me time—'

'Time?' He strode towards her again, encircling her waist and buttocks with a strong arm. 'You've had plenty of that. Don't say you haven't got a hell of a lot out of it either. You damn well have and you know it—'

She shivered, partly through fear, mingled with a dark stirring of her physical senses. She didn't love him. She never could. The strong animal coarseness of him, though challenging in one way, at times disgusted her – filling her with a slow welling up of primitive hate. Yet always, in the end, he won. And this time it was the same. She closed her eyes against the hot flame of his eyes, and after a moment he released her.

'You'll see,' he told her, 'we'll make a fine couple, and have a grand family. That's what I want – your son, and more to follow.'

She'd known it of course, and had suspected for a week or two that his wish had already taken root in her body. If so there was no escape. So perhaps after all — a little sigh escaped her.

'Well?' he said.

'As you've made up your mind what I say hardly matters does it under the circumstances?' The underlying contempt in her voice entirely escaped him.

'Exactly. The circumstances. I'm sure you'll find her ladyship approves too. She'll be able to "cock a snoot" as they say at all the malicious tongue-waggers who've spread evil about her in the past.' He grinned wrily. 'Can't say I entirely blame them. She's a sour enough spectacle these days, with her stick and limp, and mean looks. Still, witch or not, she's got background. Whereas you—'

Elfrida stiffened.

A malicious quirk of humour stirred him. 'Whose by-blow are you, Elfrida? There's a certain look about you — a gesture of the head that has a curious resemblance occasionally to Madam Marion's. Odd that. From all accounts your mother was ambitious in her day — whore or not, she aimed high—'

Elfrida's hand suddenly struck his face sharply.

He stared at her.

'Damn you, madam. For that I should beat you. But to save scandal we'll leave it — for the present, until the marriage lines are safely in my keeping.'

'I have not said I'll marry you.'

She turned from him and walked away to the door.

'You will though,' she heard him say. 'Come here, love, before I make such a scene the servants will have sufficient tittle-tattle for months to come.'

Very slowly she obeyed. All colour had drained from her cheeks and lips. Her eyes blazed.

He beckoned her close.

One hand enclosed her buttocks, the other tilted her chin upwards, while his lips drained hers desirously. The sensuous contact of her firm flesh through her thin gown inflamed him. He slapped her smartly twice, and at that moment the door opened quietly. Marion stood there, with her hand on her stick. Both turned. The older woman, outraged, was breathing heavily.

For a moment or two there was silence between them, then she said, 'I'd be obliged if you'd reserve such personal scenes for your own private premises. The library was my father's particular sanctum. Such a crude display — of — of eroticism — is extremely distasteful to me.'

She retreated again as quietly as she'd appeared. Ashforth felt his jaw tighten. Forgetting the recent challenging little interim with Elfrida, he said, 'The old harridan. Thinks she owns the place does she?'

'She does,' Elfrida pointed out flatly. 'I've always said I wanted none of it for myself. If Marion wished me to leave at any time, I'd go, and you would be left with just your two rooms.'

Inwardly she smiled. For once Ashforth was at a disadvantage. He eyed her speculatively for a second or two then remarked, 'It wouldn't be quite as easy as that. If I withdrew my capital the place would be in a sorry state.'

'Would it? But the mines are on their feet again, aren't they? Or almost. And the mines alone give Heronsmere a certain independence I'd have thought. Besides, to withdraw your shares would reduce your — your image rather badly. Cornish people might think you needed the money. And you don't, do you Henry? You're rich.'

He nodded.

'Aye. Rich enough to buy up half the county, and you with it, if I had to,' he said.

'Except the moor of course,' she told him quietly, half dreamily.

'What do you mean by that?'

'Something you'll never understand,' she replied. 'The moor has no price. It belongs to itself, its menhirs and quoits — its rocks and far-off past that no one — ever will be able to tame.' Her words had a dark sound and affected him strangely.

'I'm not concerned with the moor, except for its tin,' he stated, 'and your fancy talk's just fairy tales. So don't try it on me, Elfrida. Flesh and blood — and brass. That's what I live by. And it's what you need too.' He touched the dip above the curve of her soft breasts, where a diamond pendant glittered. 'You wouldn't want to lose all that now, girl, and well you know it.'

Yes, she did know.

It was pleasant savouring the wealth at her disposal. But when she pondered over things honestly she also recognised that she'd have sacrificed everything in the world for the touch of Ben's mouth on hers, his strong arms encircling her, for the scent of heather in her nostrils and once more having his limbs entwined with hers in love.

Oh Ben! Ben.

Fiercely she fought memory of him away. There was no point in resurrecting dead sweet things, and in all probability she might never even have to see him again.

Ironically this did not happen to be true. The following week, after her final acceptance of marriage to Henry Ashforth, she and Ben Curran met unexpectedly on the moor. Ashforth had been called away unexpectedly to the North, leaving early in the morning. Feeling free for the first time for many weeks, Elfrida had put on a cape and wandered to the ridge, in the direction of the Curran cottage.

She had no intention of calling there; it was a considerable distance from where she'd glimpsed Ben weeks ago on his horse against the horizon. But she'd heard rumours of his acquiring a patch of land nearby and curiosity mingled with a suppressed excitement drove her that day towards the site. In one hand she carried a spray of Autumn berries. Her pale hair fell loosely to her shoulders. The soft wind brushed her face gently, almost as a caress. At one point she turned her head to the left where the huddled cottage now lay as a derelict of the past, in its hollow of shadowed undergrowth. A bird, startled, rose from a clump of thorn flying with a shrill cry and flap of wings into the air. She tore her eyes from the shell of what had once been her home, and it was then she saw him. Ben, astride his grey, cantering at a leisurely pace along the narrow moorland track. Against the skyline horse and rider held at first, the imagined quality of dream assuming every second more reality. Delight rose in her. She stood quite still, waiting. He reined, and during that brief watchful interim truth registered between them in a great wave of pain and joy.

A minute passed, then he dismounted, and with the horse held by its bridle came to meet her.

Only a few feet lay between them when he said with a catch in his throat, 'Elfrida!'

Involuntarily she took a step backwards. The first rose-flush of her cheeks had died, leaving her white and trembling when she said, 'Why have you come? What do you want?' The words were all wrong, she realised it a moment later, as the swift pleasure, the expectancy, faded from his face, leaving it set and cold.

He laughed shortly. 'I've as much right as anyone here — more maybe. That piece of land—' indicating a newly fenced-off area near the menhir '—is mine. I'm surprised you haven't heard.'

She shook her head. 'I don't often come this way.'

'No? Too many memories perhaps?'

She shrugged and answered with a pretence of non-chalance, 'I never look back. What's the use?'

'Never?'

She shook her head. 'The past is over, Ben.'

'And your future's very well assured, I'm told.'

She flushed again.

'I have everything I want. I'm well provided for, and Lady Marion needs my company—'

'And him; naturally. The rich furriner who bought you.'

'He didn't buy me. He—'

'Just stepped into your life, dangled his money bags before your greedy eyes and said, "my wealth for your body, woman?" Was that it?'

More hurt than she'd ever been in her life before, she cried wildly, 'Yes — yes. Something like that — because of what you did. Your shame of me, and contempt. Your neglect, and—'

'I tried to explain, but you shut the door in my face. Why? Clear, isn't it? You'd already made other plans—'

She said nothing. Speaking more quietly he continued, 'Anyway as you said, there's no point in remembering. Not that far back. I've other memories now. Duties — to myself and — her.'

'Your wife?' She could hardly bare to speak the words.

'She died, you know.'

'Yes. I'm sorry.' How dull her tones were, how trite and meaningless.

He tore his eyes from her face. 'She was a good woman. I treated her badly. Because of you.'

'Why me?'

'I couldn't get you out of my blood. But my God, Elfrida, she was worth the two of us. That's why I've bought this land — not much, but enough to mark it as hers — a tribute to all she did for me, in help, encouragement, and in giving me the son that killed her. I'm going to put it there—' He waved an arm to the spot. 'A monument — a sculpture of a woman and child. It will be simple — I've already got the design started, and it'll be of marble — green marble with a blue-ish tinge from Connemara. The name will be inscribed — "Maria", and it'll command a view of the whole area — even the turrets of that damned doomed Heronsmere—' His breathing was quickening as he spoke, the blue light of his eyes, though warmed by passion, was condemning as it fell on her piercing her to her very soul. 'So in time maybe,' she heard him saying, 'everything else will be wiped out. When folk walk by, the rest will be nothing — no one will guess a man and woman once lay in passion down there in the dip. Long after you and I have gone, Elfrida, it will be Maria they'll see, Maria who'll be remembered and reign.'

He paused before swinging himself up and into the saddle. She watched him with the tears choking her throat.

As a parting shot he added, 'Go home, Elfrida, you don't belong here any more. And see that swaggering rich fat lover of yours keeps away. If one foot of his trespasses on my land I'll have the hide off him. And that's a promise, not a threat.'

He rode away, not looking back once.

She stood for a time, shaking, and wanting to die.

Presently, when her nerves quietened and commonsense returned, she turned and made her way down the slope. From behind a clump of brambles entangled at the base of a large boulder, the crouched dark form of an ancient woman darted with surprising speed in front of her. Her dark eyes peered bright and warningly from her brown wrinkled face. The black shawl and straggling grey locks fell grotesquely to her shoulders. She could have been some legendary troll or creature of the elements, but Elfrida recognised her as Lynette's ancient companion, the gipsy woman she'd un-expectedly met with the little girl on the day of Ashforth's return.

'There's danger, princess,' she croaked, 'unless thee take great care. All round I see it — danger, and terror and death maybe. So listen to thy heart, dordi — to the whisper when the night's dark and the owl cries. Listen, and all may be well.'

A thin brown gnarled hand was thrust out, grasping Elfrida's wrist. The wrinkled lips parted, showing two fangs of teeth in a wide smile. Then the contact was over. The old creature lifted a hand in blessing, uttering words in a foreign tongue. The next minute she had gone, disappeared through the tangled undergrowth like a wild thing fled to earth.

What had they meant, those sombre words of prophetic doom? An icy chill shivered through Elfrida's blood. Instinctively her pace quickened. When she reached Heronsmere the light had dimmed beyond a rising belt of sullen cloud.

Marion was waiting for her in the large parlour. 'I wish you wouldn't go wandering,' she complained, 'Sometimes, Elfrida, that streak in you frightens me.'

'But why?'

'Well — look at you now, with your skirt torn and hair loose. Almost as though you'd been running away.'

'If I had, I'm back now,' Elfrida answered calmly enough. 'You needn't worry, I won't leave you, Marion.'

Marion sighed.

'If you did, I'd understand. There are times when I blame myself bitterly for your plight.'

'What do you mean?'

'My dear—' Marion's voice warmed. 'It's only when he's not here — Henry Ashforth — that I realise how very brutal he can be. And lately it seems to be worse—'

Elfrida forced a smile. 'Some things are better. We must concentrate on those. Please, Marion.'

The older woman shook her head slowly.

'I suppose it's the only answer. We shall have to see.'

Her voice was quiet. Her expression enigmatic, and somehow far more chilling than any garbled prophecy from the old creature on the moor.

# 8

Following her last unhappy encounter with Ben, Elfrida deliberately avoided either walking or riding in the vicinity of the ridge at the back of Heronsmere. The meeting had been so painful, resurrecting so many hurtful passionate memories and secret longings, she felt unable to face him again.

Ashforth remained only a week up North. When he returned she made at first an outward show of affection towards him, even trying to beguile herself into believing she could eventually care for him. Passionately he was still able to arouse her, but as the days passed his lack of sensitivity and overbearing physical possessiveness turned her feelings gradually to resentment and developing aversion. His streaks of crudeness offended her. Sometimes she had to fight hard against showing dislike, keeping her lips tightly closed, and her body available for his ravishing. They had nothing in common mentally or emotionally. In the daytime his energies were mostly concentrated on Red Bell, in constant business meetings either on the site, or in Penzance where he had acquired business offices. Most nights he returned, well satisfied that his plans were going as he'd anticipated. After eating and drinking from a well prepared table, he would eye Elfrida in a half bemused, half lascivious state, and presently order her upstairs where she would steel herself for further demonstration of his sexual prowess.

Inevitably self-contempt began to burn in her, with a gathering sense of rebellion. She tried desperately to smother it, for Lynette's sake, and Marion's, more than her own. Her one consuming wish those days — almost a prayer — was for Ashforth's departure again to the North. Thank God, she thought frequently, that commitments to his Mills and his other business interests there demanded his presence from time to time. There was as well, his family. Lucy Ashforth had apparently been acquiescent about the divorce, although as Henry pointed out to Elfrida, a certain natural affection for her and their daughter remained, and would have to be observed at intervals.

'I quite understand,' Elfrida had told him. 'You've no need to explain. The situation must be very painful for her.'

'Aye.' His voice was smug. 'But she's a good woman — always ready to put my wishes before hers.' He paused before adding, 'Not like some.'

Disregarding the significance of the last sentence, Elfrida was silent.

Ashforth's colour heightened a little. 'I said not like some—' he reiterated more loudly. 'Did you hear?'

'Of course.'

'Hm. Well — I hope you remember the side your bread's buttered. Lately—' He paused.

'Yes?'

'There's been a bit of a wandering look in your eye. Or is it my fancy?'

He clutched the lace at her throat, put one finger beneath her chin, and forced her to meet his eyes.

'I asked you a question,' he said.

'What do you want me to say? What is there to say? If I like walking sometimes, or riding, surely it's natural. I hardly see anyone, I'm faithful to you—'

'Are you sure?'

She jerked herself free with a force that astonished him.

'Of course I'm sure. And so should you be by now.' Temper overcame her at last. 'I'm not your prisoner, Henry Ashforth, and I don't intend to ask your permission every time I wish to go out. Remember that.'

'And you remember, madam, that what I say goes. I've heard that young braggart — the jumped-up stonemason's been lurking round the moor—'

'That jumped-up young stonemason as you put it — is

Ben Curran the sculptor, and he's having a monument put up in memory of his wife.'

'Is he now! Is he. And how do you know about it?'

'I met him one day by chance,' she answered boldly. 'I used to know the family. The father and brothers work at Red Bell.' The moment she'd told him she knew it was a mistake.

'So they do. Hm. Well he'd better watch his step — for all their sakes, or I'll have them turned out of the cottage and without employment into the bargain.'

'You can't,' she flashed. 'The cottage is on Job Peter's property — the farmer Ben bought his patch of land from—'

'I see. So it's Ben. You're intimate, you two?'

The colour left her face quickly. 'We were children together, and if you harm the Currans in any way, Henry, I'll never forgive you, never, never—'

'I don't want your forgiveness, nor need it,' he told her brutally, 'and I shall have what workers I choose down my own mines—'

'Yours?'

'Aye. Mine now. And well you know it. Another thing — I don't like the way you spoke just now. What that brat of yours got from me once, you'll be getting with full bonus, if you go on fighting me. And don't say she's not yours. She is, isn't she?'

Elfrida bit her lip.

'Of course. And Marion's. We adopted her.'

'Very convenient I'm sure. But who's the father? That's what I'm wondering.'

Suddenly, drained of all energy, and with a feeling of approaching faintness, Elfrida's defiance collapsed. She clutched the back of a chair as darkness dimmed her eyes.

'Oh Henry. Does it matter? Why are you worrying about Lynette, when — when—' She paused momentarily before the wave of dizziness passed, then concluded, as though from a world away,' when you're going to have a child of your own?'

At first the words did not properly register with him. When they did, his anger collapsed into sudden jubilant satisfaction.

He sprang towards her again, grasping her shoulders, with his eyes blazing fiercely.

'Is it true? Repeat that, will you? It's worked then? My seed in your belly? Mine? Mine?'

She winced.

'Yes. Yours.'

He pulled her close, half suffocating her with hot animal force. Then he abruptly released her. He strode to a desk, took a Bible from it, and laid it on the table.

'Put your hand on it and swear,' he said. 'Take an oath on it, repeating what I tell you—'

In a daze, sickened with despair, she obeyed.

He stared at her afterwards with such intensity — such fanatical gratification, she had to turn away. Then his large hands were urging her to a chaise longue. He lifted her up, and laid her down, putting a cushion beneath her head.

'Rest, woman,' he said. 'You've done well after all. I believe you; it's what I wanted. A son — that's what it'll be. Something of both of us that'll make his mark on the world.'

'How do you know? It could be a girl. And making a mark as you call it isn't everything.'

'What else would you want for a child then?'

Glancing away from him she answered, 'Happiness, affection — a way of appreciating freedom and nature—'

'What do you mean by nature?'

She stared at him wonderingly. 'Sometimes you don't seem to understand me at all, Henry. You sneer when I mention the moor and the life I was brought up to — to know the ways of animals and — and—'

He shook his head, 'You've a strange one and no mistake. I've raised you up, haven't I? And I'm going as far as any man could to please you. All the way I'm going — but just to sit round watching while weeds climb over the place where there could be industry — no, I couldn't do that, Elfrida. To have a fine house and grounds kept clean and tidy — to have earth and ore under my fist, and gold and brass in my pocket — that's reality. Expansion. The reality that makes empires, and gives a proper living to working men and women. I may be a hard man in some ways, but I'm no cheat. When I strike a bargain I see my side of it's kept. And I'll go on doing it. So will you. Keep your dreams and fancies, girl, so long as they don't intrude too much. And if it's a monument you're wanting, like the one that braggart's aiming to put on the moor, you shall have one twice as big — white marble if you like, a real Diana or a Boadicea on a white horse. Aye!—' He drew a deep breath of satisfaction.' Its nostrils can have fountains of water spurting from them in a place that will shut any bit of a granite figure from view. Right at the top on Heronsmere land.' He paused before asking more quietly, 'What about that? White marble's costly — the pure sort from Greece. But price doesn't matter where you're concerned—'

All Elfrida could say was, 'Oh, Henry. I'd so much rather have a flowering cherry tree — the pink kind.'

He stared. 'You would?'

'I don't need monuments—' she said wearily. 'We have so many old ones round here, the real Celtic stones of the past—'

'Well—' his lips twisted wryly, 'you seemed intrigued enough by that mason's idea—'

'I wasn't,' she said, lying to herself as well as to him. 'It seems rather — fanatical in a way. For a child, anyway, a tree's so much nicer. Why not do that? Have a tree planted and called by the baby's name when it comes?'

He frowned.

'Maybe you're right.'

'After all,' she continued, 'to show rivalry, by placing a large figure or fountain, just to overshadow another man's effort is unnecessary, isn't it? You don't have to fight Ben Curran in such a way. There's no need.'

He smiled.

'You're a clever one, Elfrida. But quite right. What is he to me?' He gave a crack of his fingers. 'Nothing. So long as he keeps away from you.'

'He will,' Elfrida answered. 'Don't worry.' Sadness filled her with a sudden nauseous feeling of exhaustion. She closed her eyes, and felt Henry's hand pat a breast.

'That's right. You rest, my dear. From now on you'll have to take care of yourself. And after this month I'll be on the spot to see you do. I have to go away again next week, but only for a fortnight. There's a bit of trouble on at the Mills. All the fault of those new fangled trade unions. But I'll put a stop to it. 'Tisn't as though my workers don't get fair pay.' His mouth set grimly. 'No,' he continued, 'no one can say I'm not a fair man.'

She said nothing, and made no movement except to open her eyes and nod faintly before he left the room.

Until the time came for Ashforth's departure at the beginning of November, Elfrida forced herself to be outwardly compliant and agreeable, being careful not to provoke him or rouse suspicious ideas by absenting herself from the house. Never had she so longed for freedom to walk the moors, or ride her mare in her oldest, most comfortable attire with her pale hair loose on her shoulders over her dark cape.

Marion, sensing the wild mood in her, and said when he'd gone, 'There'll be some freedom for a time now, Elfrida. For all of us. You look pale, as though you needed it. Or—' she hesitated before continuing, 'Is there some other reason?'

Thinking it advisable for Lady Marion to know the full truth Elfrida told her about the coming child and of Henry's determination to marry her.

'I see.' Marion drew a long breath and sighed. 'Well — perhaps it's for the best.'

'In what way?'

'The marriage I mean. I can't speak about the baby. Do you want it, Elfrida?'

'No. One child's enough in this house. You know how Henry detests Lynette.'

'It will be different with his own. You may not find him so completely obsessed with you. I'm quite surprised though that his wife is submitting so — equally apparently — to a divorce.'

Elfrida's smile was bitter.

'During her life with him she's probably learned that what he wants he gets. She may even be relieved.'

Compassion stirred Marion briefly. 'Oh my dear! and to think I brought this on you.'

'You didn't. I went into everything with my eyes open. Although if I'd known—' She stopped abruptly in mid-sentence, stifling the words that wanted to pour out 'If I'd known Ben's wife was going to die and we'd be free to come together again nothing in the world would have induced me to have anything to do with Henry Ashforth — not even you, Marion, or the estate, or the miners — you could all have gone to Hell. Because that's what I've gone through recently, and for a long time. Plain Hell.' The impulse for such an outburst was hard to quell, but she did so, knowing that the truth would only have made things worse for all of them.

'If you'd known what, Elfrida?' she heard Marion asking quietly, after the brief pause.

'Oh nothing,' Elfrida said listlessly. 'We can't foretell the future — none of us can. Except just a few possessing the sight.'

'The gipsies, you mean?' Marion's voice held suspicion mingled with faint dread. 'They're back again I know. It would be better if they kept away.'

'Why?'

'Because Ashforth won't approve, and if he does anything to evict them there may be trouble.'

'I don't see why. They don't intrude on Heronsmere property. Their site is perfectly free.'

Marion threw a wry glance towards Elfrida. 'I'm sure you don't believe that. Not when your lover — your husband-to-be — is around. You've said as much yourself. Oh don't try and gull me, Elfrida. I know how the land lies. If Henry Ashforth considers anything or anyone an obstacle to his complete power, he'll somehow manage to get rid of it. Moses included, I'm afraid. Yes — especially him.'

Elfrida's lips tightened mutinously. 'He'll never succeed there. Moses is as much a part of Heronsmere as — as the rock it's built on. And your father thought the world of him, didn't he?'

'Yes. And you needn't any more refer to him as *my* father,

my dear. We both know the truth. It's what holds us together mostly. Moses too. I think Moses has always had more than a shrewd suspicion. He's never said anything, or hinted. Just because he happens to be loyal. But if anything threatened us I know he'd defend us to the death.'

Elfrida went suddenly cold.

'You sound so doomful. Marion dear — aren't you well?'

'I've felt tired lately,' the other woman confessed. 'My leg has pained me; but then that may be partly the weather. This time of the year always depresses me, and my headaches start then.'

Elfrida glanced towards the moor lying bleak and cold beyond the gardens. The sky had a fading greenish tone. Soon it would be twilight, when ghosts walked. Ghosts? What an absurd idea. What had put such ridiculous nonsense into her head? Just thinking of the past, she supposed — the dead, sweet, bitter memories that try as she would she could not always suppress these days.

'I wonder how the Currans are?' she said half-absently.

Marion, who was at the door preparing to go upstairs, turned sharply. 'What made you think of them?'

'Comparing our circumstances with the miners,' Elfrida answered, 'Nothing more.'

'Hm. Well, I heard a bit of news yesterday. Moses told me, when I went into the conservatory. The wife's ill. She's not expected to last the winter. Consumption they say.'

'Ben's mother?'

'Of course. He sees she has everything she wants, naturally. I've heard the cottage is quite smart now, the husband doesn't have to work any more, thanks to Ben's success. She could go to hospital, but she won't. Ridiculous, I call it.'

'I don't. I can imagine how she feels. When you're used to a place like she is to the moor, it would be frightening and upsetting to have to leave. She'd be very lonely in any kind of institution — like a — like a wild bird trapped—'

There was a long silence between them in which only the clock's ticking and the screaming of a gull from outside registered. It was broken at last by Marion enquiring, 'Are you ever lonely, Elfrida, living here away from your old home and the simple people you were used to − as a child, I mean?'

Elfrida smiled faintly; her eyes had a far away expression, when she admitted, 'Sometimes. But then loneliness is a part of life for all of us, at odd moments. It must be. Still—' she braced herself to say lightly, 'it's stupid to brood. I'm sorry about Mrs Curran. I shall go over one day and see her. Take her something pretty and cheerful, a gift. Flowers from the conservatory perhaps.'

'I shouldn't if I were you.' Marion's statement was so shrill and curt, Elfrida was startled.

'Whyever not?'

'Henry wouldn't like it. It would be dangerous.'

'Dangerous?' Elfrida laughed. 'In what way?'

Marion's eyes shone hard and fierce in her thin yellowish face when she replied, 'Mr Ashforth's a jealous man. And we mustn't get involved with Ben in any way. Surely you realise that?'

Elfrida pretended acquiescence, but inwardly resolve deepened. 'Why not?' she thought, 'Why shouldn't I visit Mrs Curran? I shall do just what I choose, and I don't care a − a damn what Marion or Henry or anyone else thinks. Even if I did happen to meet Ben − what about it?' Oh what indeed! for a moment her heart quickened and a wild restlessness seized her. On Saturday, she decided, in five days time, she'd ride over to the Curran home and see if there was anything at all she could do for the poor woman. Her gesture would be merely a kind and charitable one. No one need know, except Lynette, Marion who'd have to accept it, and Moses. There was a fair on at Braggas six miles away, and the staff had been given permission to go. Henry so far away up North, would never know of the incident, and if he did he could hardly take exception to such a natural act of compassion on her part.

And she might see Ben.

From that moment all other considerations were completely erased from her mind. She lived in a whirl of inner excitement until the time came for Moses to saddle her mare in readiness for her journey across the moor.

At three o'clock on the appointed day, Elfrida was cantering up the slope towards the ridge. The weather was mild and calm for the time of year, the moors yellowish grey under a lowering sky. The pale sun was already low in the west, hidden behind the belt of unmoving cloud. Later, perhaps, fine rain might fall, but at present the air held a hushed quality as though all nature watched and waited for some climax or rising wind from the sea to stir the elements to activity again. As the girl and horse took an easy pace along the track upwards which was a narrow one, threading between clumps of gorse and stunted dark trees, elation flooded the rider. Just for that time she was once more Elfrida of the past, at one with the giant boulders scattering the wild earth — with the ancient standing stones of years long gone, and the small wild creatures of the moor. The very idea of contacting Ben's family, of anything to do with him, excited her. In delivering flowers to his sick mother she was in some subtle way creating a new bond. They had met each other only once or twice during old Martha's lifetime, chiefly because of her grandmother's strict supervision and determination to have Susannah's child 'better herself.'

There had been, also, supervision on the Currans' part concerning the fairy-like strange young creature always so prettily dressed, who it was said by inhabitants of the local vicinity, had been taught charms and magic by her ancient guardian.

Well, all that was over now. Superstitious stories could no longer be hurled at her. She had become benefactress instead of witchling — the part owner of Heronsmere itself, and therefore someone of quality to be respected.

Respect? Elfrida smiled at the idea. She had doubts about it, although outwardly her new status generally received a show of welcome from workers and villagers to whom her patronage was important. They needed the wherewithal to live by, and she had it to give.

From Henry.

Her spine stiffened as his image briefly shadowed her mind. Then she resolutely managed to dispel it, and kicking her mount to a gallop, sped along the high ridge, with her shining loose hair a flying pennon behind her, her dark cloak thrown back over her shoulders.

When she reached the Curran cottage she dismounted, tethered her horse to a tree, pushed the gate of the small front garden open, and walked briskly up to the door, with a bunch of Christmas roses in her hand. The patch of ground was well-tended now, she noticed, the woodwork of the small building had been freshly painted in blue and instead of the cesspit which was common to most miners' homes, a new 'privy' had been built about twelve yards away, sheltered by a spreading thorn tree.

She rapped sharply and heard a woman's voice ask faintly, 'Who is it? What do you want?'

Without answering Elfrida went in. She was momentarily taken aback by the comfort — by the transformation of the small dwelling. Copper and brass shone, a fire blazed in the large fire place, the living room had been enlarged, and stairs led up now from a second door to the upper floor. At the back of the living room a partition shielded the kitchen from the front.

A comfortable rocking chair which looked new was placed between a round oak table and the fire, and facing that against the wall was a bed covered by a cheerful patchwork quilt.

Jane Curran lay there, and half raised herself as Elfrida entered.

Elfrida hurried forward. 'Please, Mrs Curran, don't disturb yourself. I've only — I—' She broke off embarrassed by the shining questioning look in the woman's dark eyes, which appeared enormous in the thin face lying against the pillows. During the second's pause Elfrida became aware of the fiery red spots on the gaunt cheeks that were otherwise so white — almost transparent, and of a certain sweet sickly smell typical of approaching death.

'I've brought you a few flowers,' Elfrida heard herself saying automatically, 'I'm — I'm Elfrida — Martha's granddaughter. Perhaps you don't remember me. But—' She swallowed hard. 'I'm so sorry you're ill. Moses — you know Moses don't you? He works for us, for Lady Marion, at Heronsmere — he told me.'

The skeletal fingers clutching the coverlet let the quilt fall, and the frail hand went out.

'I'm glad to see you, miss. To see anyone. I doan' know as I'd have recognised you — except for that hair. Lovely hair it always was—' She spoke with difficulty. 'And the flowers — nice they are. Your grandma went in for flowers — didn' she?'

Elfrida nodded. 'I wish I'd known you better then.'

Jane's eyes closed for a moment or two. Her breathing had become rapid, shallow. Elfrida waited. When the frail figure had recovered sufficiently to speak again she resumed, 'Ben always liked you. Ben's a good son, done all this, he has, sees I want for nothing. An' the other boys they're good too. Still workin' at Red Bell.'

'Yes. And your husband?'

'Oh, James is all right. Does a bit of part-time gardening. If you care to wait he should be back in an hour, but—'

Elfrida shook her head.

'I'm afraid I can't stay long, Mrs Curran. I just wanted you to know that if there was anything you wanted — anything at all, you have only to ask, and I'd see you had it—'

The frail smile was grateful, but an underlying note of pitiful independence tinged Jane's faint voice as she said, 'Thank you, miss — ma'am — but my family and Ben see to everything. I want for nuthen now. And it isn't often I'm alone at all. Oh — in my way I'm a lucky woman—' The rasping tones died off again, the eyes closed.

Elfrida left shortly afterwards, feeling guilty at the relief she felt to be away.

Sickness had always oppressed her. She could feel pity, and was expert at tending hurt animals and any defenceless wild creature. But there was always something mildly repugnant to her in having close contact with human disease. it was as though — like trespassing into a different dimension — the natural reaction of one with a healthy life ahead, rejected corruption and death.

So she rode her mare quickly back in the direction she'd come, and as she was about to take the slope down towards Heronsmere, she saw him.

Ben.

He was cutting up the moor, and would obviously have taken the turn to his right along the track leading to the cottage if he hadn't seen and recognised her.

Abruptly he changed course and galloped towards her.

Without thinking she reined, and a minute later they were face to face.

He jumped from his mount, took the bridle and stood looking up, with his other arm out ready to take her hand.

'Please, Elfrida,' he said.

Gone was all her resistance and reserve. For a brief interim time died between them. The past was forgotten, swallowed by the wonder of the present — the excitement of meeting him again. As his hand closed over hers, she could feel the blood pounding through her whole body, feel the pulse beating strong in his palm. For the first time she knew, without a shadow of doubt, that there could no longer be any evasion of truth. Although their lives had been so widely divergent, and in spite of any other commitments, they belonged and always had — to each other.

Yet at first he made no effort to embrace or kiss her. After that long look, he simply took the reins of her mare and saw both horses were loosely tethered; then he came back to her and stood staring down on the lovely ethereal face that had so long haunted and distressed him in unguarded moments — for so long hovered as an unacknowledged ghost at the back of his mind.

'Oh Elfrida,' he said again.

'I've been to see your mother,' she said with difficulty. 'I — I didn't see the harm—'

'Harm?' The light of his blue eyes was so brilliant, so magical and overpowering, she trembled. It was as though the earth beneath their feet shuddered. Then, suddenly, he had taken a step forward. His arms were round her, his lips hard yet soft and demanding upon her mouth. Half fainting

with desire and happiness she relaxed against him, feeling
presently, his fingers gently trace every line and contour of
her face. The greenish glow of the fading sky lit their figures
to clarity as a last beam of light filtered through the clouds.
Then, suddenly, reality returned. She pulled herself from
him.

'I must go, Ben — I must go—'

'Why?'

She turned away abruptly, brushing the film of tears from
her eyes. 'It's no use. You know it isn't. I — I'm—' she faced
him once more, with all the softness gone leaving only a wild
despair on her face, a desperation so fierce it chilled him.
'You must have heard,' she continued. 'I'm not free any
more—'

'You mean Ashforth?'

'Yes — yes — *yes*—' Her voice rose in a scream; she
plunged away from him, jerked the reins of her mount from
the wizened tree, and swung herself on to the saddle, crying
tauntingly, 'Don't ever speak to me again — never, never.
I'm *his* — he *bought* me — because of you. *You*, Ben, when
you married that woman.'

He made a quick violent gesture towards her, but was too
late. The next moment the mare and girl were galloping
recklessly down the hill side, regardless of tearing undergrowth, rocks, furze and the shrill crying of scared birds
rising with a whirring and fluttering of wings into the air.

# 9

From a back window of Heronsmere, Henry Ashforth, who had returned unexpectedly to find the place deserted, except for Moses, Marion and the child, watched with mounting savage rage and shock the little scene between Elfrida and Ben on the far ridge of the moor. They were mere dots of darkness on the horizon, but unmistakable to one who knew her well. His jealousy so overpowered him he could neither breathe or move properly. The wanton little bitch he'd squandered his attentions and fortune on, had deceived him after all! The whole lot of them, probably, had been smirking and conniving behind his back — including the sly Lady Marion closeted in her own apartment with the bastard brat; and that hulking brute Moses! — had *he* known from the start what was going on? Was his tale of Elfrida 'probably gone to the fair Braggas way' — just a lie too?

Well, he'd show them all. Prove what happened to those he trusted, and provided for, who deceived him.

As the dark figure with flying pale hair and dark cloak neared the house, he forced himself to move, and fetched a thin cane from the study. His hard hand gripped it fiercely till it almost cut into his own flesh. Then he went downstairs, and placed himself in a shadowed recess in the hall, to wait for her when she came through the house from the stables.

The time seemed an eternity; but it was not long.

Presently he heard the kitchen door close, followed by the light tread of her feet.

Her startled cry when he caught her, the terror glimpsed briefly in her eyes filled him with triumphant savage lust.

One hand of hers went to her throat, he slapped her sharply on both sides of her face, and when she attempted to explain, he smothered the words on her lips.

'Whore!' he muttered. 'Slut. I'll show you, begad. I warned you, didn't I? No other man I said, and you — you—' Words failed him. She struggled wildly, kicking his shins. He picked her up and smacked her face again hard. Then he half pushed, half dragged her into the library and flung her face down over a table. With one arm firmly pinning her body to the hard surface, he brought the cane smartly across her back, thrashing her mercilessly, only pausing to tear her clothes apart so her flesh could receive the full sting.

At first she fought a little, but it was no use. The punishment continued, until even her faint moans ceased. By then something of the disturbance had penetrated Marion's apartment. She reached for her stick, but Lynette was before her, racing down the stairs to the hall.

'Stop it,' she screamed, rushing into the library. 'Stop it — help — help!'

Like a young tiger she sprang at the hated 'Uncle Henry' and when he turned his attention from Elfrida to her, catching the child by the neck of her dress, she bit his hand so savagely the blood ran. Elfrida raised her head painfully. 'No—' she tried to protest, 'not the child — not Lynette.' But no sound came. Only a meaningless whisper left her lips. The room spun round her in a vortex of shuddering anguish. Her eyes closed again as a hand stretched ineffectually out, clutching only the empty air. She did not see the shadowed figure of Marion at the door, did not glimpse the set blazing face or hear the tap, tap, of her stick as she encroached stealthily upon the scene. No word passed her lips. But her automatic stance, more of a marionette's than a human being's, held a menacing deliberation beyond fear or reason. She knew what to do now. She had the weapon, and the will. He had asked for it.

Just as Ashforth was about to flay the screaming child who was now kicking on the floor, Marion's stick rattled to the ground. With both arms free she lifted them above her head purposefully. There was something clenched in her hands. For one quick second Elfrida's eyes opened. She saw the dark shining object — a heavy bronze ornament, brought crashing down on the back of the male skull.

There was a shout, a tottering of limbs as Henry, one hand grasping the table's edge lurched suddenly backwards, and fell.

For moments, following his last gurgling breath, there was complete silence. A trickle of blood from his mouth slowed and started to congeal. His eyes glazed. Lynette gave a scream and rushed from the room. Marion stood staring; stiff and rigid as an effigy, until after a timeless pause, Elfrida managed to ease herself from the table.

'Oh God!' she whispered then. 'You've killed him. He's dead — he must be — Henry Ashforth's dead.' Forgetting her own smarting agony, she bent down, felt for a heart-beat, and in spite of her revulsion drew a hand across his forehead. It was already cooling; there was no sign of life at all.

She looked up into Marion's stony face. 'He's dead — do you understand?' she repeated. 'Henry's dead.'

Then Marion spoke, without feeling or regret, quite emotionlessly.

'Good riddance,' she said in cold practical tones. 'He's out of the way now.' She stared at the bronze statue still grasped in one hand. It depicted a warrior with spear raised, astride a rearing charger. 'My father always liked his piece,' she remarked, 'he admired bravery you know. I'm sure he'd have approved of me now.' A little smile tilted her lips.

'Oh, Marion.' Elfrida wanted to comfort the other woman who she realised was suffering from severe shock. But every movement caused her pain, and she was forced to drag herself to a chair.

'Well, now,' she heard Marion say briefly. 'How are we going to get rid of this — thing?' Her good foot gave a con-temptuous push at the lifeless figure. 'What do you think,

Elfrida? Shall we bury him in the garden or push him into the pond? On the other hand—' She paused and took a deep breath, 'if we could get him to the moor, that old shaft's always waiting—'

'Don't – don't—' Elfrida put both hands to her ears. She was by then shuddering violently. 'How *could* we? And he'd be found—'

'Yes. You're right. Well, there's only one thing to do. Moses. Moses will help.'

Without waiting to hear Elfrida's reaction Marion turned, reached for her stick and left the room, leaving by a side door for the stables.

Minutes passed – a drawn out period in which Elfrida sat with her head bowed, eyes closed, trying to disregard the dead man near her feet. How long it was before Moses and Marion returned she had no way of knowing. Moses was the first to arrive. He made a brief examination of what had once been his enemy, the tyrant Henry Ashforth, poking and prodding and lifting the eyelids above the sightless orbs.

'He's dead all right,' he announced. 'And the better for all of us too.'

'But what are we going to say to the servants when they get here? From the fair – and the – the police?' For the first time since the beating Elfrida found herself able to face practical issues.

'You leave that to me, missis,' Moses answered. 'I'll get him down to the stables and saddle him on that demon stallion Blackfire. Thwarted and ugly he is at the moment lusting for a mate. With a flick of the whip, he'll be hell bent for freedom and mark my words when he's thrown Lord-Tom-Noddy here and dragged him by the stirrups for a yard or two, there'll be no need of an inquest. No talk, no enquiries, just—' his voice deepened, 'a kind of satisfaction you could say. 'Cos no one likes him, rich as he is. Now don't you go worryin', ladies. This is my affair, and, believe me, my pleasure. But I must get going. No time to be wasted. You two – if you're capable – get down to clearing the mess up here – not too bad, all things considered. Then ma'am—' with a meaningful look towards Elfrida, 'it might be best for all concerned if you got to bed and was found there lookin' comfortable and sleeping when the servants is back.'

In a daze both women watched the burly figure of Moses take Ashforth by the heels, and drag him into the hall. Except for furtive bumpings, and a thudding as the dead man's head hit the floor, there was little sound of the proceedings.

Five minutes later the stable doors were open, and Blackfire, with its helpless rider, was speeding as though all hell was after them across the drive and crashing through the fence towards the moor. A liberal amount of whisky had been poured over Henry's chin. No one would question that he had been drunk in attempting to ride the brute.

It was only when Moses returned to relate that everything had gone to plan — and to remind Elfrida and Marion they must know nothing, for only *he* had seen Ashforth set off, and that he had been blind drunk, must've been to imagine he could master such an animal — that Elfrida remembered Lynette.

Where was she? Had she seen anything? And if she could, would she be silenced?

There was no need to worry about the latter.

Lynette was found later hiding terrified in a boxroom. If she had wanted to speak she could not. Neither did she cry, but remained mute and shocked for weeks following the postmortem and funeral of 'Uncle Henry'. None could get anything out of her. She ate mechanically, and did what she was told with an acquiescence that was in itself frightening.

When Elfrida and Marion had recovered from the strain Marion did her best to comfort her half sister. 'Perhaps it's as well,' she said. 'Just for the present. I'm sure she didn't see what happened — it was the shock of you being beaten before her eyes — and sheer terror for herself — that was too much for her. She'll never know the real truth, Elfrida. It may even be that when she comes to herself again the whole incident will be blotted from her mind. There has to be escape in some way, for a child, from such horror.'

Lynette's 'escape' however, was to be very different from what either woman imagined, and occurred soon after that brief conversation between her mother and Lady Marion.

# 10

Christmas came and went — a brief period in which Marion and Elfrida put on a superficial show of festivity. Large log fires burned in most of the downstairs rooms — holly and mistletoe decorated the frames of portraits; round doors and windows, and in the great hall. There was a choice of duck or roast beef for the main meal, with a plum pudding set alight by brandy. Punch was served from a large bowl on the side board in the dining room, and on Christmas day presents waited at the foot of Lynette's bed. Later, in the evening, servants assembled to receive their gifts. Everything was done in an attempt to stir Lynette from her apathy. She smiled occasionally, complacently accepting what was offered. Outwardly her appearance had not changed. Her vivid looks were emphasised by the pink muslin dress she wore and the slender gold necklace given to her by Marion. It was studded with diamonds, and flashed gaily in the lamplight. A slight twist of the child's red lips indicated she was pleased. That was all. No word came, no young feet tripped or danced when Moses played the flute. He had been invited specially on Lynette's behalf to do so. But she merely stared with an uncomprehending look on her face, and presently Moses left, saying, 'Tedn' no good. The maid's still 'frit' — leave her be, till her mind wants to come back again.'

His words frightened both Elfrida and Marion.

'Suppose she's always like this?' Elfrida said. 'Dumb and — and kind of strange?'

Marion tried her best to allay such fears.

'The doctor didn't seem worried when last he saw her,' she answered, 'remember what he told us? Shock could do funny things. Henry's sudden death could account for the withdrawal into herself — even loss of memory for a time—'

'But supposing when she *does* remember — if it ever happens — and she starts talking—'

'She won't talk,' Marion said firmly. 'She didn't see the — the act — *mine*. What I did. Please don't fret so much of wild unnecessary eventualities. Ashforth's dead and buried. So is the past. No one — certainly not Lynette, is going to resurrect it. If she did — a drunken scene that sent Henry staggering to the stables to saddle Blackfire is our explanation, *that* — and only that, just as we said. No one questioned it then, and no one in the future will. So for my sake, Elfrida, if not your own, please try and view things rationally. It hasn't been easy for me either, you know.'

With a stab of conscience Elfrida noted the dark rings shadowing Marion's eyes, the drawn set mouth, and slight twitch at her temple where a nerve throbbed. Her figure too — so bent and thin — so unlike the young woman of a few years ago, who in spite of her limp had been gracious looking and comely in a classic way.

'I'm sorry,' Elfrida remarked. 'Here I am worrying you, when I should really thank you, I suppose.'

'For murdering Henry Ashforth?' Marion's voice was biting, hard.

'Murder? Don't be ridiculous.'

'Of course it was murder. It happened. But I'm not afraid. I'd do it again. And my father approves. I'm sure of it.' The emotionless statement was unnerving.

A new fear — fear of the unknown, sent a shudder down Elfrida's spine —

'But—'

'Oh yes, he knows.' Marion said flatly. 'He's here — everywhere. Can't you feel it? "Good girl," he's saying, "Heronsmere's yours once more. In the family. See that it remains so."'

When Elfrida made no reply Marion continued in more normal tones, 'I expect you think me a little mad. But I'm not, my dear. Possibly it's just Heronsmere itself whispering. Walls can retain secrets and impressions from the past; that I do believe. You though — you're too young and innocent to

hear — and too remote, half of you — from family tradition—' her voice wavered and died.

'Yes,' Elfrida agreed. 'I accept that.'

Moments later she went up to her room, leaving Marion
alone, a dark figure hunched by the blazing fire.


Winter passed gradually into an early spring. The first
celandines and daisies appeared in lush ditches and fields,
followed by primroses and pink thrift starring the headlands,
and rocks about Hook's Cove. After wandering further than
she should one late February day, Elfrida tripped on a rock
and fell. She lay in pain for an hour, somehow managed to
get to her feet again and make her way back to the house.
Once in the hall she collapsed and when a servant discovered
the unconscious figure lying on the cold flags, little could be
done for her but to get her to bed and call upon the Apothecary. He administered a potion, saw she was as comfortable
as possible and before he left gave her laudanum to ease her
agony.

By then it was too late to save the unborn child.

When evening came she was feeling better, but did not
have to be told she had lost the baby.

'I know,' she said. 'It doesn't matter. Please Marion, bring
Lynette to me.'

Marion did as she asked. The child, however still did not
speak, and after a few moments turned away — without a
smile or gesture towards her mother, and slowly walked from
the room.

'She doesn't need me,' Elfrida remarked lifelessly, 'I don't
even know if she knew who I was.'

'Children don't like sickness, my dear,' Marion reminded
her. 'They don't understand it. When she recovers I'm sure
she'll respond and you'll mean more to each other than ever
before.'

Staring unseeingly over Marion's shoulder to the window
and a belt of clouds beyond, Elfrida replied, 'I should have told
her the truth about her father — as my daughter I owed her
that; then things might have been different.'

'There was no need.' Marion's lips darkened. 'She's had a happy life so far. Everything she wanted; except—

For Henry,' Elfrida finished for her. Her face paled from distaste and renewed shock. Marion patted her hand lightly.

'You must try and forget Henry. So must I.'

'I shall never forget. Never.'

'You must put him into perspective then — for the sake of yourself and Lynette. And me. Do you hear — *me?*'

Brought suddenly back to brief reality — remembering what Marion had done in defence of Lynette and herself, faint colour stained Elfrida's cheeks in a wave of remorse.

'All right, Marion — of course; I *will* try.'

This she did to the best of her ability. But events had left her feeling so drained of energy that for a week she never left her room. When at last she managed to drag herself downstairs, even the spring sunshine failed to penetrate her melancholy mood.

Daffodils were already speared buds of gold in the garden — the first blossom frothed against clear paper-pale skies, and pale green feathered the networked branches of the trees. The distant sea glistened in a silver film beyond the cliffs. Gorse flamed along the moors, and the morning air held the dewy tang of heather and fresh thrusting undergrowth. Elfrida sensed and saw it all, but it was like staring at a picture, or something seen through a mirror that held no reality.

Then, one afternoon, Lynette disappeared.

She could not be found for her tea, although all the house, and grounds were thoroughly searched. At first it was believed she might have merely gone for a walk, and wandered further than she'd meant to. But when, after two hours, no sign was found of her, Marion felt it her duty to tell Elfrida.

'I think we should get Moses to make a tour of the moor,' she said. 'The child could have fallen and sprained an ankle, or—' she paused meaningfully, while the possibility of far worse things — a yawning mine shaft, or bog, penetrated Elfrida's tired mind. Wild fear flooded the lovely eyes. All apathy was shattered to sudden alert activity. She jumped up.

'Yes, tell Moses. And I shall go myself—'

'Nonsense. You'll stay here, Elfrida. And if Moses isn't successful the police must act. Now be reasonable.'

Eventually Elfrida agreed. Moses set off wishing his old dog Beth could have been with him. But Beth had broken a leg the week before and was still being treated by the vet. He combed the moor as thoroughly as possible round every place known to be dangerous, calling the child's name constantly. There was no response. No clue or indication that the little girl had been there.

Near the ruined cottage he met the old man Dan who no longer worked as a shepherd, but lived in his remote hand-built shack half a mile away.

Moses questioned him. The ancient head moved in a gesture of negation.

'Why shud a young critter from down theer wanter cum this way?' he queried bringing his shaggy brows together in a frown. 'Me an my ole goat doan' need compn'y. You go look for them theer tinkers. Moved off they did this afternoon.' His watery eyes held a knowing glint.

'Which way?' Moses demanded, grasping a bony shoulder. 'You tell me the route they took, or I'll ring your neck like a scrany hen, you old scoundrel—'

Dan flinched, tried to free himself, failed, then thrust his narrow lined face forward. He cocked a thumb downwards to the right, beyond Heronsmere. His lips widened in a snarl, showing two fangs of yellowed teeth.

'That way—' he answered, 'an' good riddance. Quick they was travelling. Penwilly way, or mebbe Thark. Thark I shud think — cos there's a fair on—'

Moses stared hard a moment into the watery eyes, then released the bent old figure and cut back towards Herons-mere. Dan could be right, he knew, and the girl might easily have been prevailed on to accompany the tinkers. Penwilly was the nearest village, and the route more accessible. The gippos might be staying there for the night, before cutting inland, or have gone in the opposite direction to Thark. The hamlet lay in a wild spot near the coast where there was a large copper mine working, and mining families always ready for a little sport in their leisure moments. A fair was on, Dan had said; but there was also a festival of some kind due, which would gather crowds from a wider district. He decided to try Penwilly first. Conjurers and fortune-tellers were always welcome at such an event, and the gippos were well versed in displays of that kind. If Penwilly failed he'd have to retrace the route, and travel northwards to Thark. For that rough journey a speedy and amenable horse would be needed. He'd take the gelding. Since Blackfire's macabre gallop with his dead rider, the animal had been lent to a nearby farmer for breeding. In any case Moses didn't fancy the great brute, and had decided privately that it might be better for the female owners of Heronsmere to sell. A woman like Lady Marion didn't want any reminder left of the dark events leading to Ashforth's death.

Elfrida had her eyes strained to the hillside as Moses eventually appeared nearing the dip of the moor. From quite a distance away he noted the pale blur of her face against the glass. What he didn't know, was that old Dan, too, stood by a thorn bush above, also watching. When at last Moses disappeared through the gates of the paddock, a smug smile creased the ancient's wizened face. He turned, and with head thrust forward, hand on a stick made his way along the narrow overgrown track to the deserted relic of Elfrida's cottage.

The door, half draped with brambles, was ajar. Dan put a fist to his mouth, made a quivering bird-like whistle, and croaked, 'Tes all right, midear, he'm bin' an' gone. You'm safe with ole Dan, an I've a tatie in me pocket, with a bit of rabbit. Come down chile, we'm friends you'n me. All ready to beat the enemy, eh?' He gave a rasping laugh, stared upwards at the ricketty steps leading to an upstairs portion of the building, and after a few moments Lynette appeared. Her large eyes, wide and startled, blazed from her face in a tangled mass of dark hair. She wore a thin black lace shawl round her shoulders, which over her blue dress merged into the shadows eerily, giving the fleeting impression of a ghost risen from the ruins.

Dan beckoned.

'Here, chile — tek this.'

Cautiously Lynette approached. She paused at the door, and glanced at the food in the old man's hand. She was tired and hungry, and when he made no attempt to touch her, she grabbed it and clutched it to her breast, then took a bite.

Dan nodded.

'Tha's right, girl. What's your name eh? You tell ole Dan. Critters of the moor we be, you'n me. Come from down theer, doan' ee?' And he cocked a thumb towards Heronsmere.

Lynette nodded.

He turned and spat in the direction of the big house. 'So we'm together an' that's f'r sure. What's your name, girl?'

Lynette kept her lips closed, while she studied him carefully letting suspicion give way gradually to a grudging instinctive trust. Dan waited. Hermit, and a bit of a scamp he might be now. But he knew wild things, and had a way with all frightened creatures.

Suddenly Lynette spoke.

'Lynette,' she said, and her tones were light and clear. 'That's what they call me — Lynette.'

Once more he glanced to Heronsmere.

'Them? Down theer?'

She nodded.

'There was a horrible man there. Uncle Henry they made me call him. He hated me and hurt things. Then there was a fight. He rode away on the stallion, the biggest horse in the stables — and got killed. I was glad.'

Old Dan nodded approval.

'That was right, midear. Them as hurts frit creatures shud be hung higher'n any scrawny crow.' A bony finger touched her shoulder tentatively. 'You bide here, chile, ole Dan'll care for 'ee. Got me own place, sure nuff, but I'll see 'ee doan' starve.'

Now Lynette had at last spoken, the words tumbled out of her in a torrent like a stream dammed, broken free. She told the old man about days before Sir Geoffrey's death when she'd been happy at Heronsmere. 'He was nice to me,' she explained. 'We had tea in his room sometimes, and he gave me the top of his egg. We laughed together — about Paulie — she's my governess, so silly, and always curtseying and bobbing. Of course it was only our own joke. Uncle Geoffrey's and mine I mean. No one else knew. The aunts — Aunt Marion, and Elfrida kept out of the way a lot. I've wondered if they were plotting to get that beastly Mr Ashforth in, and didn't want Uncle Geoffrey to know. It could have been. But Aunt Elfrida's nice really. No, I don't think she meant him to spoil everything—'

'Y' never do know,' Dan muttered. 'Y' c'n never tell with a couple o' witches like them two.' He pulled his grizzled beard thoughtfully.

'Witches?' Lynette gasped. 'But they weren't. Witches wear black hats and cloaks and ride broomsticks. That's what the fairy books say. And Aunt Elfrida's pretty — like a princess.' She sighed, continuing, 'Oh yes, it was all right, everything was all right at Heronsmere until that hateful man came. Then there was nothing nice at all, except Moses.'

'Ha!' the old man snorted. 'Think so, do ee? — threatening and bullyin' kind o' creature if you ask me. He'd of had 'ee back in that theer place in no time if I hadn' sent him away with a flea in his ear—'

'A flea?'

'Big as a bullet,' Dan commented wickedly.

Lynette frowned. 'I don't believe you — quite. Not about the flea, or Moses being a bully. He never was. He used to take me to see Brownie sometimes.'

'Brownie?'

'Brownie was an owl, quite a little one. He had a nest in the summerhouse. It was our secret — mine and Moses'. We had to be careful so that Uncle Henry never knew.'

'An' he'll never know you're here now, neither, will he?' Old Dan croaked, 'No one will, 'cos you'll live in this eer place all quiet an' hidden, with jus me an' them others.'

'What others?'

'Go back inside, midear,' Dan said, 'an' I'll show 'ee.'

He took her hand in his own which had the crackling feel of

dried twigs creaking. Lynette agreed grudgingly. For a time she'd wanted just the touch of the spring air on her face, and to draw the dewy sweetness of evening into her lungs. Still munching the potato — a large one that had been baked in its jacket, she trailed after Dan into the deserted cottage. There were cobwebs everywhere, draped curtain-like across corners and ceiling, over the ancient oak furniture, and Martha's spinning wheel. A stream of damp trickled down one wall from a hole in the roof. Moss and fine grass grew among the flagstones. In parts the rugs had half rotted away. And yet — somehow, Lynette thought, it was still a home. A secret place, where she could hide until the man with the shining hair — the one she'd talked with on the moor, would come back one day, and rescue her like a knight in a fairy tale.

She had told nothing of the encounter to Dan, sensing in a deep intuitive way, that he might resent anyone else at all knowing where she was. But she had already made a plan. From the broken window of the cottage, upstairs where she'd first hidden before the old man found her, she could watch the moor until the figure on the horse appeared. She was sure he'd come one day soon. Then he could take her away — far far away from Heronsmere, so she could forget the terrible things that had happened — somehow erase from her mind the picture of Elfrida screaming as the lash of the cane struck her, with Uncle Henry's teeth gleaming in his snarling red face.

Just for a second or two she started trembling again, and only came to herself as Dan said, 'C'mon, chile. Doan' 'ee lag. Didn' 'ee hear what I said? — Somethin' to show 'ee in this corner.'

Lynette jerked herself to attention, pushed a cobweb from her eyes, and crossed cautiously across the room. The old man bent down, gave a whistle, and something came scurrying to his hand.

The little girl stared. The creature was plump with a shining grey coat, long tail, whiskers, pointed nose, and very bright eyes.

A mouse.

She gave a long 'ooh' of astonishment, adding, 'A real one. And how fat. Like a — like a—'

Dan chuckled.

'A mother one, that's what, midear. An' well fed, 'cos I sees to it, as well as her.' He brought a few crumbs from his pocket, fed the tiny animal, then parted a piece of sacking and a few dried leaves to reveal a carefully made nest where a number of half-blind almost bald babies nuzzled and squirmed together.

Lynette bent down, placing the tip of a finger towards one minute nose. It was not afraid, but the mother went scampering back quickly, making a series of squeaks until she'd settled down again with her brood.

Dan got up, looked down on Lynette, and said, 'So you'm not alone, midear, even here. Them stuck-up gentry doan' know first thing 'bout livin', that's what I do say. Livin's here — on th' moor, with all wild things — big an' small — fox an' badger, an' bird an' mouse; so should he be — that theer Brownie critter you tole me of. Better to be on th' moor wi' you'n me — not cooped up in that theer prison place, 'Eronsmere.'

'Don't you ever go anywhere?' Lynette asked, tearing her eyes away from the nest.

'Where would I go? An' for what?'

'What do you think about all day then?'

The old man turned away, scowling. 'I doan' think. 'Cept what to eat, an' studyin' the clouds mebbe, an' how to kip away from them theer below. Once that theer Moses of yours came along wi' a gun. 'Ef you do shoot one o' my rabbits' I sez to meself, "I'll throw a rock at 'ee sure 'nuff." An so I would've too.'

Lynette shivered suddenly and turned away.

'I'm going now,' she said.

'Where?'

She indicated the ladder.' There. Upstairs. I've got to make my bed.'

Dan grunted. 'You'm got that sackin' I brought,' he remarked. 'Well then you jus' be sure you do cover yourself proper so no peepin' Tom, Dick, or Harry, or that skulkin' Moses can find 'ee.'

When the old man had left, Lynette waited, watching, until his bent brown figure had disappeared into the deeper brown shadows of the darkening moor. Like a gnome, she thought, he's just like a gnome, only a kind of nice one. But of course gnomes didn't really exist, she knew that. They just came out of books and fairy tales. Still, fairy tales could seem very real sometimes — especially when twilight was deepening, and everywhere was so hushed and silent.

She sighed and suddenly made a quick move to the ladder. It was very ricketty. Several rungs had gone; it shook as she climbed gingerly upwards, and when she reached the top she stood for a moment or two, noticing what she had not before — the large gap in the ceiling, the holes in the wooden floor, the dust and cracks everywhere, and the trickling damp stream from where a chimney had been. The rafters too were crumbling in places, and when she moved to her corner not far from the broken window facing the ridge, something scuttled across her feet and disappeared behind a tumbled brick. Another mouse? Or a rat?'

She wasn't at all sure she'd like a rat near her, although it was better than having to live with anyone like Uncle Henry.

Presently, with her cloak round her, because the air was rapidly chilling, she made the sacking into as comfortable a pillow as possible. But it was rough, and the smell was musty. So she collected twigs and leaves that had gathered and used the sacking as a pillow.

Night came, and gradually, as exhaustion claimed her, she drifted into sleep, dreaming intermittently of a rider on a pale horse, looking like a young king on his way to rescue her.

Soon the moor was in complete darkness, with only one star penetrating the clouds and thickening mist.

# 11

When Moses, following his unsuccessful search, set off for Penwilly, Elfrida was not long in deciding what to do.

Marion, completely exhausted had gone to her bed, and taken a potion to ensure sleep. The servants were occupied in the kitchens; only the boy was about when Elfrida quietly let herself out by a side door and made her way to the stables.

'Stable Diamond, please Joe,' she told the youth abruptly. 'And reach me that old pair of breeches from the peg.'

Joe, who was on the simple side, eyed her suspiciously for a moment, then obeyed.

'What you want them for, missis — ma'am?' he enquired as he handed her the garment. 'Them's old — belonged to the boy as wus here before I come. A thin little feller 'ee wus, not like me,' he grinned and thumped his chest in self-admiration.

'I'm sure he wasn't,' Elfrida agreed cryptically. 'But you heard what I said, get the saddle on that horse as quickly as possible — I'm riding her.'

The boy gaped. 'Mr Ashforth — he said as no one — no one wus to tek—'

'Diamond's my mare,' Elfrida stated coldly, 'and Mr Ashforth's dead. Do as you're told Joe, or you'll have no pay this week.'

The threat startled him to action. Elfrida went into the groom's kitchen, removed her skirts and struggled into the breeches. They were shabby and worn, and had a mouldy smell, but nothing seemed to matter except to find Lynette, her daughter — Ben's child — and bring her back safely so they could meet as father and daughter, with no more secrets between the three of them.

The clouds had lifted a little as they set off; a rim of misted silver over the distant line of cliffs and sea, denoted a watery moon rising. She knew her journey to Tharke would be hazardous. Some kind of light was essential if she was to make the difficult journey without mishap. The winding road crossing the valley to the opposite ridge would take her many miles out of her way and an hour of precious time would be wasted. Once in the region of Carn Kessay, the lonely landmark above Devil's Pool reputed to be haunted by a demon water-horseman — she would have to cut down again towards the sea by a threadwork of misleading tracks. The main road to Tharke was from the opposite direction, so all she could do was to risk following an overgrown coast path skirting bog and dank deserted shafts in order to overtake the itinerants.

At first Diamond was amenable, and the going was not too difficult. As she'd thought, the moon soon pierced the clouds, spreading its pale light over rocks, brambles, clutching bushes of gorse and heather, and glistening black pools of hungry bog. Standing stones and dolmens were washed at moments to clarity against the wild landscape. Once, passing a remote kiddleywink hunched in a dip above the glassy sea, a drunken figure swayed from the door yelling obscenities at the flying figures of horse and girl. Diamond reared for a second, then plunged ahead recklessly, only calming to a canter when the ribald singing from the dramhouse had faded, torn away by a rising wind.

On and on they went, pausing intermittently for Elfrida to assess her bearings. At periods when the moon's full brilliance flooded the scene, lean dark shadows struck upwards in wild shapes clawing like hungry ghosts to the stark silhouettes of mine-workers and occasional twisted trees. Seawards giant tongues of rocks jutted to the angry rising tide. Diamond, alert now to the elements and lurking danger of the treacherous terrain, became uneasy, transmitting instinctive fear to Elfrida. Were they lost? They should by then be nearing Tharke; yet so far no sign of clustered cottages was visible, no twinkling glimpse of fair-lights or faint tinkle of distant music and merrymaking. She stopped by a boulder, and reined, scanning the night scene in all directions.

Then suddenly, she glimpsed a faint rosy glow beyond the distant headland, and it seemed to her, optimistically, that mingled with the scent of brine, heather, and damp earth, was the faint drift of woodsmoke.

The gipsies, she thought. Perhaps they'd pitched camp there, or perhaps it was Tharke itself.

She kicked Diamond to a canter, and then to a swifter gallop, forgetting caution briefly, taking lumps of rock, brambled hole and sudden thrust of undergrowth in ever increasing speed.

At what point she fell, she never knew. There was a sudden swirling blackness round her as the mare stumbled, pitching her forward into a mesh of soggy earth and weed. Luckily her feet were freed of stirrups. As unconsciousness claimed Elfrida, Diamond stood for a second snorting, then raced ahead towards a huddled thicket of small twisted trees.

It was dawn before Elfrida opened her eyes, and at first nothing registered except a dim memory of racing through the air followed by a black void lit briefly by flashing pin points of fire — a vortex of terror into which she was thrown and lost. Then, gradually, she remembered.

Tharke! the Fair — and Lynette.

She got up abruptly, wincing in pain as she tried to move her legs. One was all right. But the other sent such a searing agony through her whole body, she collapsed helplessly drenched in sweat. The boy's breeches, she found, had been removed carefully, replaced by a woollen skirt.

A brown wrinkled face peered down on her from a tangle of grey hair. 'Rest, dordi,' an ancient voice said. 'Rest, princess. The leg will heal, so will thy spirit in its own good time—'

Elfrida knew the voice, and when her sight cleared again she recognised Lynette's acquaintance, the old gipsy woman who'd wandered so frequently on the outskirts of Heronsmere. 'The chavi will be safe—' the cracked dry tones continued.

'Thy daughter will find what is right for her. Fear not Rawni—'

'But where *is* she?' Elfrida raised herself again on one elbow. 'And where am I? Where are we going?'

The old woman shook her head. 'Inland now. Tharke's no good to such as we. Bible thumpers be there, and gavvers on the watch. So we'm packin' up. The vardos is ready, an' you'll travel with us, dordi, till the leg's healed. Eh?'

'But I can't—' Elfrida gasped. 'I have to find my little girl.'

'No. It's she who'll do the seeking. An' time's passin' Delmar's gettin' the horses ready now—' Her words trailed off as Elfrida's glance pierced the dark branches of the thicket. Only a short distance away she could distinguish vans and figures moving, silently and purposeful. 'We couldn't leave you here all helpless an' hurt ready for the first mochard mumper to fall on thee, now, could we?'

'I must get back,' Elfrida reiterated. 'I've got to. My leg's not broken. I—' she winced, glancing through the gap of the tent at the interlaced branches of the trees. 'If I rest for a time I shall be able to find my own way—'

'Without a hoss? Walkin'? like a lame fox? An what if harm comes to thee, an' the gavvers learn we'm bin about? Oh no, rackli. The way's too far. You'm comin' with us, an' Delmar an' Rosa. An when we reaches Truro or Redruth or some place where we c'n leave thee with a doctor or apothecary of sorts, they'll get 'ee back to th' big house. An' mebbe then, princess, the child will be back too.'

Elfrida had to give in, and presently, when the three vans and cart were packed, the small company of travellers set off by the most secluded route possible leading through hidden lush valleys north west.

For three nights and days Lynette, with the aid of old Dan managed to secrete herself in the cottage, spending much of her time at the window watching for a sign of Ben. Occasionally a stranger crossed the moor riding in the direction of the patch of land bordering Heronsmere. But the man was broad and dark haired holding no flash of brightness in the sunlight, and bore no resemblance to her friend — the knight of her imagination — come to rescue her from the terror of her experience at Heronsmere.

Sometimes, when the air was misty, providing protection from being discovered by anyone searching for her she wandered about the back of the cottage, and on the third morning she discovered a hole covered by a round half rotted piece of wood. She thought at first it might be a well, but when she'd pushed the brambles away she found there were rough steps carved into the rock and earth, leading downwards into a narrow dank passage. The air was cold, but from the distance somewhere she seemed to hear a thudding that could have been the echo of waves breaking or someone working with a large spade or hammer.

Very cautiously she walked a few steps, with a hand pressed against the dripping wall for support. Her heart thumped. What was this place? Where did it lead to? She glanced upwards. The beam of pale daylight still penetrated the grey shadows. She had an impulse to clamber back, but her natural curiosity drove her on and ahead again. A few yards beyond the bottom of the steps, there was a curve and the passage widened. By then her eyes were becoming accustomed to the eerie green glow, the shining surface of dark granite, slimy in parts, at others dripping with strange straggling weeds, encrusted with snails, and other crawling subterranean creatures.

Once she trod on something soft that squelched when her foot touched it. At another time she dimly glimpsed a black hunched shape, squatting in a recess of rock. A murmur of fear half choked her throat, but when she forced herself to pass she saw it was only a tub like thing or barrel, broken and propped on its side. How funny, she thought, there should be a barrel in this dark place. But perhaps there had been smugglers there once. Perhaps this was one of the hiding places used by 'wreckers' — cruel natives who'd plundered ships and stolen cargos — or by adventurous characters she'd read of in books — men who traded illegally in bringing brandy and lace, and other forbidden goods from France?

Fear was forgotten in her excitement. She went on more quickly; how far she had no way of knowing. The passage occasionally took abrupt turns, narrowed, then widened again. Gradually the stuffy damp air freshened. The booming sound was suddenly accentuated, and a salty odour was driven inwards on a strong waft of wind.

The dim light lifted to a quivering brightness. She ran ahead, and then, to her amazement, found herself near an opening in the rock. It was almost round in formation; but beyond she could see the white glistening spray of foam breaking on pale sand and boulders.

Spindrift.

Oh lovely place. Relief and release from the frightening journey made her breathless for a few moments. She waited, staring out across the expanse of breaking sea which was bound on each side by arms of granite — black, dark green, washed silver-white and gold from the lifting sun.

Her dark curls were blown back by the wind, the sting of brine was sharp and sweet on her lips and the lashes of her brilliant blue eyes.

Instinctively and unknowingly, she lifted her arms wide, as two gulls rose from a nearby boulder, their white wings bright against the sky. Then she stepped out on to the narrow ridge of pale sand. Her cape swirled from her shoulders, revealing beneath the torn dress the strong but exquisite lines of her virginal form. She could have been some legendary young Aphrodite risen from the waves.

For a time no sound stirred the air but the sighing of wind, and lapping and breaking of the tide on the shore. When thought registered she realised that somehow, miraculously, she must be in Hook's Cove — the place that had always been forbidden to her by Aunt Marion and her governess at Heronsmere. But it was lovely there — lovely. All around her small pools glittered luminously between shining rocks. Tiny pale fish darted among the weeds, and a crab scuttled by close to her toes. There were round glistening pebbles too, glinting with all the colours of the rainbow. She pushed a stray lock of damp hair from her forehead and then she heard it — a voice.

'Hullo there—?'

She turned quickly, poised ready for flight. But there was no need.

Approaching her on her right from behind a jutting crag of granite was a figure she recognised and seemed to have known all her life — the one person who just then symbolised comfort, security, and an answer to all the aching longing of her child's heart. His hair shone bright in the early mist, his mouth and blue eyes were smiling.

He came towards her, and she ran. Ran straight into his arms. In those few enlightened moments, the truth registered. The flame of recognition conveyed itself miraculously between man and child. The features were Elfrida's. But the blue eyes were his. There was no spoken proof. But none was needed. Oh God, he thought. Why hadn't he discovered her before?

When he'd heard her story, Ben was silent for a time, then he said, with an arm still round her, 'Yes, this is a nice place, safe and hidden, but more than that — much more. It was here I first dreamed of what I'd do one day—'

'You? What do you do?' she queried solemnly looking up at him.

He indicated a nearby rock, still wet, but shivering with light from sun and sea. 'I carve things — try to make something similar to these great stones — but things with a meaning, that folks can understand. Others just for myself.'

'Statues?'

'Some.' He smiled reminiscently. 'Trouble is — Nature always goes one better.'

'How do you mean?'

He tried to explain, and in a dim way she sensed the urge that drove him.

'But why do you have to carve big things?' she enquired, 'when all these small ones are so lovely? They are, aren't they? All the different colours shining?' She bent down, scooped a pebble up, and showed him. It was some kind of quartz, reflecting a medley of changing colours and fragile cobwebbed lines. 'So smooth and wet,' she continued. 'Can you make anything so lovely as that?'

'I don't try to. Just perpetuation.'

'What's that?'

'Well—' He paused before continuing, 'When the tide goes out this pebble may be taken with it, and never be seen any more. So I do my best, with tools and ideas to create textures from memory. That's not always possible. But shapes can be revived, and new ones. Large images—' He broke off, and smiled down at her. 'Now I'm talking in riddles. Silly of me—'

She shook her head.

'No, no. I understand now; I really do. It's funny isn't it? How we can think alike?'

'Not really, Lynette.' His voice had dropped instinctively. 'Look at me; straight into my face.'

She did so, wonderingly. 'What is it? Tell me.'

'I think you're my daughter,' he told her then. 'And if you are, Elfrida's your mother.'

She didn't speak, just stared, believing him, yet unable to comprehend. The sun brightened and cast a spreading glow of magic around them. For a brief interim even the wind seemed to hold its breath. Then, after the long pause Ben heard Lynette's child voice saying, 'I wish we'd known before. If we had, none of those awful things couldn't have happened. Why didn't you come before?'

'That's a long story, longer than yours, and mostly my fault. Later, quite soon, when we've returned to Herons-mere, we'll have a talk and—'

She pulled her hand abruptly away from his.

'No. I can't go back there. I won't—'

'With me you can,' he said firmly, but with extreme gentleness. 'There's no need to be afraid of the bad things any more, love. They're gone. And I'll see nothing – no shadow of them ever returns to haunt you.'

But how could he? he thought, after the pledge was made – how could anyone – most of all a blunderer like himself hope to allay the shadow of cruelty from a child's mind – even a ourageous one such as herself — the one he believed — *new* — to be of his own flesh?

He took her hand again. 'Come along,' he urged. 'Surely ou can trust me?'

When she looked up once more, the light in her eyes half linded him.

'All right; I'll come,' and as they turned to make their way long the beach towards a bend of rock bordering the cove, vhere his horse was tethered, she added thoughtfully, 'I'll be ble to see Brownie anyway. He's a little owl. His leg was roken, but Moses mended it and put him in the summer ouse. If he hadn't I expect Uncle Henry would have killed im.'

'Sh!' Ben told her. 'Forget Uncle Henry. He was never your ncle, and he's gone for ever, thank God.'

'I wonder if God really did it?' Lynette said pensively. 'Kill Uncle Henry I mean? I don't think so, because God doesn't kill anything does He? No — I don't think He could actually. *P*'raps He just whispered in the stallion's ear. I expect that vas it.'

'It could be,' Ben agreed, not knowing what else to say.

Together, as the sun's brilliance broke completely clear of ny remaining vestige of mist, man and child made their way ack to Heronsmere.

Marion was in the large parlour, staring out of the window vhen Ben and his daughter arrived. She was seated in a high arved chair, a rigid figure wearing a severe black dress, with er stick leaning against one knee. From their attitudes — omething confident and serene — a certain indefinable ntimacy in the way they walked, hand in hand, from the tables evidently, up the side drive — she sensed they knew; ad discovered the bond which for so long she'd tried to reject nd hide.

Her parchment pale features were set and emotionless vhen at last they entered the room, her voice cool and con- rolled as she said in dry tones, 'I'm glad to see you, Lynette. Where have you been?' There was obviously no point in

scolding, with the child's champion there to defend her. I
any case personal feeling for anyone — even for Ben
seemed to have dried and withered in her since Elfrida's reck
less disappearance on Diamond.

'Where's Elfrida?' Ben demanded, forgetting in those firs
moments even to enquire about Marion's health or offer
polite 'good morning'.

'You know as much as me,' Marion answered shortly. 'Sh
left days ago.'

'What do you mean?'

Glancing towards Lynette, this woman who in so man
different ways, good and bad, had played such a crucial pa
in her destiny, said almost accusingly, 'Perhaps we shoul
discuss things without a child's presence.' She touched a bell
and a maid appeared.

Ben grudgingly persuaded Lynette to accompany the gir
to the kitchens for a few minutes while he had a talk with he
aunt.

'All right, just for a little,' Lynette said. 'Perhaps Mose
will take me to see Brownie.'

'Brownie?'

'A brown owl in the summer house,' Ben explained t
Marion. 'But perhaps you didn't know?'

A niggle of hurt that she could have been kept in ignoranc
forced Marion to say sharply, 'People very seldom think fit t
confide in me. Especially those I've cherished. Well — hurr
up then, child. I'm sure Moses will be glad to see you. Bu
don't be too long. That dress is a disgrace. You must b
washed and changed as soon as possible.'

When the door had closed and the patter of Lynette's foot
steps had died down the hall Marion beckoned Ben to a chai
facing her.

'You may as well sit,' she said. 'Having to look up from her
is not only tiring, but rather humiliating. These last few day
haven't improved my — infirmity.'

'I'm sorry — I—'

She waved a hand imperiously. 'I don't need your pity, o
your regard — or even your affection any more, Ben Curran

For years and years there was nothing in the world I wanted so much as your presence from time to time, even a little love. Now I know what a fool I was. And, why — this is the first time I've properly realised it — you're nothing at all to me now. I don't even like you very much.'

Except for a deepening of colour in his face Ben showed no reaction.

'*Elfrida!*' he persisted. 'I apologise for lack of courtesy. I'm sorry you're not well. But—' automatically the fingers of both hands tightened against his palms, 'for God's sake tell me about Elfrida. Where the hell is she?'

Marion smiled mirthlessly.

'Don't bring God into it if you please,' the relentless icy voice continued. 'You and I, I think, have too long lived apart from the Deity to concern Him with our affairs. We're both ruthless people. I, because I lied to Elfrida about our — yours and mine — passion for each other—'

'Passion?'

'Oh yes. If she hadn't thought — if I hadn't made her believe we'd been lovers, you would never have been sent away from Heronsmere that day you called so many many years ago. I was responsible, I did it, because I thought you owed me something. Consideration at least, and an answer to those letters.' Her lips curled in self contempt, 'Such pitiful, ridiculous naive letters. But they were genuine. And you scorned me.'

With a sudden violent gesture she reached for her stick and struggled to her feet. Her eyes when they stared at him were narrowed an cold — ice-cold in her plain face. 'Blame me if you like, hate me — strike me down. I don't care. Do you understand? I just — *don't care!*—' The rage died in her as quickly as it had risen. She eased herself wearily back into the chair.

There was a long pause before Ben said slowly, 'I see. But then I knew part of it. All my life apparently, I've been the tool of scheming women.'

'I didn't mean to scheme. In the beginning, when you were a little boy and I was only — what was it, seventeen? — it was your talent I admired. From the first I recognised genius, and then — but what does it matter? Nothing can change things and now that you've found your daughter—' She hesitated before continuing, 'When I watched you walking up the drive I knew you knew; realised absolutely, that what I'd guessed at the time was the truth. Elfrida had never openly told me. She was very — loyal.' Again that short bitter laugh. 'If she had it would have made no difference. I was and still am fond of her in a way. I suppose you know she was my father's bastard?'

The word, though ironically spoken, held no contempt.

'No, I didn't know,' Ben answered. 'Gossip? Yes. But such stories never interested me. It was the girl herself.'

'Ah yes — the lovely nymph — the vision of perfection, with no scar or limp, or blemish to mar her. I know. I know. No one could compete with her, nothing; no fortune, or even your wife. And it will always be the same.' The mechnical smile returned to Marion's face. She looked remote, half-dead, a figure carved from stone.

'Marion,' Ben said, with an urgency that did not escape her. 'Please tell me where she is. I gather she's left Heronsmere?'

'Yes. She went looking for Lynette.'

'Where?'

'Now that I cannot say, except to find the gipsies. I've no notion where. Moses searched the moors, Penwilly too, and Tharke. There was no sign of them, nor of Elfrida.'

The desperation — the wild longing in his eyes drove her to add with a faint hint of feeling, 'They could be anywhere. Sometimes when they're afraid, nomads of that kind 'go to earth' like animals looking for safety. So you could try southwards through the wooded areas, or take a valley route to Truro. You should know those lanes by now.'

'Thanks. I'll be off then.'

'What about Lynette?'

He turned at the door and said sharply, 'I'll be back for her as soon as possible. When I've located her mother.'

'*No.*' The one word was a command, so emphatic it halted him.

'Take her now; first,' Marion said, 'get her from this damned doomed house as soon as possible.' She got to her feet again, and something in her face frightened him. 'There are too many ghosts here. Heronsmere itself's become a victim of all the evil that's happened. I shall stay, because it's my home — my responsibility. But if you value the child's sanity and your own future with Elfrida — go, *go*. Before it's too late. You have a horse, you can ride. Then put her on it and be off—' She broke off, breathless, but for a few seconds managed to pull herself erect. Then, as without another word, he strode out, slamming the door behind him, she crumpled suddenly, and with one hand on her stick, the other outstretched like that of a blind thing, took a few tottering steps to her chair. She sat there rigidly, unheeding of voices in the hall where Ben was presently rejoined by Lynette for their journey cross-country back to Gwynck.

Except for the clop-clop of the horse's hooves and whining of the wind, they rode silently, she seated before him, cheek pressed against his coat. Miss Paul had insisted on swathing her in a cape with a hood. But in the first hour the hood had fallen back, leaving her curls free, lit to glossy brightness from dew and sun. When they had set off the morning had been free of cloud, but gradually the weather was changing, and by the time they passed Redruth, the landscape was once more silvered by mist. Stones, bushes and moorland furze loomed intermittently in macabre shapes — eerie forms that held a threatening intensity every time Lynette looked up. She was remembering again; recalling Uncle Henry's thin cane, and its ugly swish against Elfrida's body. The clawing branches of the briars were ugly too. She would never forget, *never*. She must have shuddered. Ben touched her cheek. 'All right, love?'

She swallowed hard, and managed to smile. 'Yes — with you.'

And this was true. Whatever bad things were in the world she knew that with her father — this wonderful fair-haired gentleman, she was safe.

Ben might have smiled grimly to himself had he guessed

the depth of her trust. The fact was that during those miles of travel his inmost feelings had little gentleness in them. All his instincts told him to turn back — search wildly every nook, and cranny of the coast — every kiddleywink, wood, and hidden lane — until he found her, his love, Elfrida.

But Lynette was his also. A duty he could no longer shirk nor would he wish to.

At last they reached Gwynck.

His new housekeeper, a middle-aged, kindly practical woman stared in astonishment as the wind-blown child and man arrived at the kitchen door while Willie led the tired animal to the stable.

'Whatever's happened?' she demanded, 'an' who, for mercy's sake, is this young thing?'

'My daughter,' Ben answered abruptly. 'And I want you to look after her, Mrs Breame, while I take off again to find her mother—'

'Your daughter? And her mother — but—'

'No questions please,' Ben remarked shortly, 'not now. When she's been fed let her see her baby brother. The sooner they're acquainted the better.'

Lynette, by then too tired to fully comprehend the news, and only concerned not to lose her father again, resisted at first. But Ben managed to calm her.

'Now be good, love,' he said, 'and do what kind Mrs Breame says. The sooner I go, the sooner I shall be back. Understand?'

Her large eyes blinked stared straight into his head, then she shook her head slowly. 'No.'

'Well — don't try then. When we're altogether again you can ask any questions you like, and Elfrida and I will answer them.'

Reluctantly, because she was too tired to make a scene, Lynette agreed. And presently Ben, mounted on Willie's black horse, set off on his random search again.

He decided to scour the peninsula first, taking in the towns and larger villages — Perranporth, Perranzabulo, wild St Agnes on the coast, Redruth, Camborne, Hayle, Ludgvan nd down to Helston, then west once more towards Penjust. omewhere the gipsies must have camped. Maybe in the nining localities where both honest and dishonest gains ould be taken. He'd locate every small, dubious inn and kiddleywink where a landlord or customer might be bribed to whisper a clue, however small, that could give guidance. ilver or gold might not even be necessary. The 'gippos' were requently resented, and regarded by many as thieves and agagonds who'd get away with poaching, even sheep steal-ng, given half a chance. On the other hand they had friends n certain areas — cunning natives always ready to make a enny on the sly, given the necessary information by any ravellers passing by.

For the rest of the day, until nightfall approached, and the ky darkened behind the western moors, Ben searched the andscape relentlessly, stopping any pedlar or journey-man e met, calling en route at each possible dram-shop or aucous tavern. Occasionally a look was passed, an eyebrow aised, followed by shrugs and negative shaking of heads. The answer, in essence, was always the same.

'No, none's passed this way that we do know of. Try the Fairs, mister. Conjurers and gippos gen'lly end up theer.'

He did this as much as possible. The Fairs, again, provided no useful clue.

Then, when darkness fell, to be lightened later by a pale noon flooding the sky, Ben had his first stroke of luck.

On a road cutting again inland towards St Kerryak, he saw a waggon approaching, driven by a man in a decidedly dis-orderly state. A lantern showed a red scar running from forehead to temple, his neckcloth was awry, and one sleeve of his brown coat was ripped from shoulder to cuff.

He stopped the horse as Ben's figure darted in front with a hand up. 'Git out o' me way mister,' the man ordered strongly, 'or I'll run 'ee down. Gone through more'n enough I have this day, what with them preachin' folk, merrymakers and gippos—'

'Gipsies?' Ben shouted, 'did you say gipsies?'

'What's that to do with 'ee? Git out o' th' road I say—'

Ben searching frenziedly in his pocket found a couple o
coins and thrust them forward. Through the moonlight an
lantern's glow they flashed temptingly. A tongue moistene
the rough lips, the man quietened the restless anima
reached for the gold, and mollified, asked grudgingly, 'Wha
d'ye wanter know, mister?'

'Where are they? Tell me exactly, and there's another coi
for your pocket.'

The man cocked a thumb behind his shoulder in a west
ward direction.

'I know where they *waz*! — two miles or so theer — o
Tregale Hill wi' the rest. There wuz a meetin called wher
them teetotalars had their gatherin' last year. Different thi
time though. "Enemies o' temperance" they called theirselve
this lot — whole bag o' tricks theer — lots o' liquor an
wrestlin', booths, an' dancin', that made mock o' the prayin
— a few fights, an donkey races. Ah. A real riotous night
Some of 'em 've bin took, so I drives off an' gets away.'

'What do you mean, took?'

The driver grinned with more than a touch of maliciou
amusement. 'The law, mister. An' if you's anything' to do w
gipsies, then best kip away, that's what I do say — them p'lic
doan' like gippos.'

Ben flung the man the money, and without another word
kicked his mount, and was away at a wild speed along a
narrow heather-bound track in the direction of Tregale. The
wind sang in his ears his pulses raced wildly as the horse
reared, recovered, and plunged ahead again over the rough
entangled surface of the moor. Twice he reined and listened
as the unmistakable sound of merrymaking and drunken dis
sension echoed faintly from the rising rocky terrain ahead.

Tregale was a landmark of that particular area; its tump
rose in primitive monolithic shape above the furze and
tumbled boulders at its base.

A few waggons and vehicles were still huddled in the
nearby lane when Ben arrived. Banners were strewn about
and from the ragged rocky tip of the hill a flag had hal
broken from its post. The singing, which from the distance

had echoed with raucous intensity had now died into an occasional drunken murmuring. Stragglers, one by one, were making their way tipsily from the scene. Booths, from the rubble of past rejoicings and broken glass, were being packed up. Some remained as mere wreckage, while reeling owners took a last swig from a bottle. There was the neighing of animals, intermittently pierced by the shrill high crying of gulls as they dipped as scavengers, from the moonlit sky.

But there was no sign of the gipsies.

Ben enquired from one of the quieter booth tenders, who told him the whole lot of them had been taken off by the law.

'But where?' Ben demanded. 'Tell me, man, for God's sake?' Would it ever end, he wondered, would the time ever come when there was no need for that desperate question.

'T' the clink I s'pose, Redcross,' was the answer. 'You try theer first, mister. Maybe they'll be took further later — Bodmin, for th' next assizes. I dunno.'

Automatically Ben gave a nod, untethered his tired mount, and rode away.

He rode cross-country to Redcross, and when he reached the prison there at last, he was forbidden entrance after being told that indeed a company of itinerants had been brought in that same night, and would possibly face the magistrates the following day. In the meantime no contact was allowed.

Ben demanded to see the governor. Again he met with blunt refusal. But when the jailer or officer in charge — whoever it might be — was informed that Ben believed they had with them a lady of quality and close relative of Lady Marion Penherrion, the expression on the official's face underwent a subtle change. He stroked his grizzled chin thoughtfully.

'Have you any credentials, surr? Can you prove that's so?'

'Only when I see her,' Ben answered curtly. 'But I can assure you I speak the truth, and if I'm denied access there'll be trouble later. My name is Curran, Ben Curran the sculptor. You may have heard of me, you may not. However, I happen to be an intimate friend of the Penherrion family, and would be obliged if you'd conduct me to the lady without delay.'

After a little more humming and haaing, and without the governor being aroused at such a late hour, Ben was conducted to the cells at the back of the building. The larger one, dank and dark, with a treadmill for grinding corn, stood in the shadows. There was only one small window, which was barred, and few miserable looking individuals were huddled in corners on sacking, or on the floor. The stench was offensive, the air thick and cloying.

With a jangle of his keys as the warder closed the iron door behind him, the portly figure strode forward.

'Which one is it?' he enquired of Ben, and to the huddled group, 'Anyone here name of Penherrion?'

'Elfrida Penherrion?' Ben said clearly over the man's shoulder. Then, suddenly, he pushed the heavy figure aside and went boldly ahead. There, lying flat on the floor was a woman covered by a filthy piece of blanket. Stupefied for a second or two Ben stared. But only for a moment. The next instant he was bending down, removing a dark shawl from a white face that had been almost completely hidden. A shivering spread of silver gold, lit to brightness from a pale beam of moonlight filtering through the narrow window, caused a gasp of astonishment from the warder. An old woman's voice croaked — 'That's her — the princess. Tek her away man — tek her, she's nought to do with us—'

Ben, kneeling down, raised Elfrida's head up, and held it tenderly to his breast.

'My love, my darling — my—'

'Sh sh—' her blue eyes were clouded by tears. 'Don't talk — just—' Her voice faltered. 'Oh Ben — you've come. You've really come—'

The prison officer coughed.

'Best come with me, surr,' he said in conciliatory tones. 'And the lady with you—'

Elfrida struggled to her feet, wincing as the sprain caught her in a stab of sharp pain. Ben lifted her in his arms. He was already following the warder to the door when Elfrida jerked her head up and cried sharply. 'Not without them. They've done nothing — *nothing* — except tend me when I fell.

They're no criminals or trouble-makers—' Her voice dropped to gentler tones, 'Please, officer. There was no stealing done by them — Tregale was in an uproar when we got there, and that business of thieving — of the black cockerel, had nothing to do with them. I'll swear in court if necessary—' Breathless with exhaustion the words faded. Stroking her hair, smoothing it from her damp forehead, Ben, looking like the sturdy young Viking of his ancestry, regarded the other man steadfastly for a brief pause, then said in hard ice-bitter tones, 'Well, what about it?'

The man shrugged. 'They were brought in by the law, and I'm merely a servant of the authorities—'

'Then prove yourself master for once, or I'll see you in chains myself.'

Abruptly the man's mood changed.

He inserted the key in the lock, opened the door, allowing Ben still holding Elfrida, to pass through, followed by the pushing, gasping group of travellers.

'And see you don't come back again—' he shouted, 'Go on, quick, skit. Out of my sight and make sharp about it.' The gipsies needed no command. Like a company of scared wild creatures they scattered up the street towards the darkening shadows. Once the old woman turned and held a hand up, obviously in some sort of blessing. The words were in Romany, and Elfrida understood nothing except 'Princess' and something about 'thee and thine'.

Then they were gone.

Ben stared down on the lovely flower-like creature in his arms. She smiled. His pressure increased for a moment, but he did not speak. There was nothing to say beyond the expression in his own eyes which held all the fire, desire and ardent longing of youth, lit to the sudden glory of love's over-powering compassion and understanding.

He took her first to a small inn in the main street a reputable place used mostly for gentry on their travels. There the filth was cleaned from her face and body, and the gipsy attire removed by the Hosteler's kindly wife who provided a fresh smelling cotton gown and a cloak of her own.

Ben paid liberally, although the woman appeared at first loth to take anything.

'Tch!' she said shrugging, "tis only a spare dress got ready for a new servant; as for the cloak — I c'n make another myself when I want. Still—' she smiled broadly at Ben's persistence, 'none such as us can properly afford to turn away a pretty penny, I s'pose. Thank you, surr. An' now when you an' your lady's ready, there's a meal waitin'. Only simple fare at this time o' night I'm afraid. But with a taste of hot toddy it'll put a bit of heart into you.'

Ben and Elfrida warmed by the rekindled fire in the small parlour, ate and drank gladly, wasting no words at that point, simply relaxing in a great tide of relief, following a growing sleepiness which threatened to overcome them both. Ben jerked himself abruptly to life and action.

'We must be going, my love,' he said. 'Come now.' He put the clean cape round her shoulders, and pulled the hood over her hair. 'Both of us have had more than a fair share of travelling. It's time we were home—'

'Home?' she murmured, 'where? Where's home now?'

'A simple place with no ghosts in it,' came the answer, 'no fine grounds or rich estate — just an ordinary house in a quiet village street, with a yard where I do my work. Oh — and someone else — someone very important — a little girl called Lynette who's waiting for her mother, in the capable care of my housekeeper Mrs Breame — and — and another. A baby boy — my son.'

At first the import of the message did not clearly register in Elfrida's mind. Only the one name — Lynette. For a fleeting instant a soft rose glow tinted the pale face. In the lamplight Elfrida's eyes widened to radiant joy.

'Lynette? — Have you found her — *really*?'

'Oh yes. A very real young girl indeed,' Ben emphasised, 'and in full possession of her senses — that one, as my housekeeper will no doubt discover for herself. A true little adventuress, our daughter is, you mark my words.'

'But—' remembering the Lynette of the past weeks following Henry Ashforth's death, Elfrida hesitated.

'Yes?'

'Did she say anything? Did she speak?'

In spite of his tiredness, Ben smiled.

'My love, except for during the ride, she hardly stopped.'
He sighed. 'I wish you'd let me know about her before,
Elfrida. Still there's no point in talk now. Come.'

Presently, after bidding the Innkeeper and his wife fare-
well, they were making their way on Willie's horse, along the
main street towards the moors.

It was early morning before they reached Gwynck, and the
vague rim of light beyond the eastern horizon predicted a
clear day ahead.

Ben did not wait for Mrs Breame to conduct a very tired
Elfrida to the room she'd prepared for her. Ben insisted on
carrying her there, and removing the cloak and cotton dress
himself. Then he lifted her very gently on to the bed, and
before touching her lips with his, stared down — almost
reverently — at the slim and lovely creature lying so defence-
lessly before him. Memories swept through him of another
day long long before, when they'd lain together with the scent
of heather sweet in their nostrils. But on this occasion there
was no need for ravishing, neither was it the time. The
delicate subtle awareness of body and spirit flowered to his,
beyond the realms of physical compulsion.

He lifted her hand to his lips.

'My Elfrida,' he murmured. And those two words held the
wonder of all the days and years ahead that he was determined should work out for them now, whatever problems
had to be solved — whatever reaction followed, and however
deeply the bitter experiences of the past had eaten into
Elfrida's personality. He'd have to go carefully, and he knew
it. Something of the same quality that had stirred him as a
young child to sense the moods, hidden impulses, and instinctive delights and hurts of small animals and wild
creatures — his inborn ability to mould and carve them —
was now concentrated in restoring Elfrida's trust in life
again — and in him. It would not be easy. Physical restraint,

to a man of his calibre would demand the utmost self-control.

When she lay in his arms, despite the anguish, his body had still leaped at the contact. Lying on the bed with her pale gold hair loose about the pillow, he had had to fight the impulse to draw her close and possess her. The hunger of the years was like a hot white flame, searing him.

Staring into the bewildered tired-blue eyes had been a momentary drowning in a pool of forgetfulness, in which nothing else mattered or had substance. The memories of Maria — his ruthless dominance — the son she'd borne him — and even of Lynette — had held no reality. Conscience and remorse had died, swept away as ghostly reflections of some far-off mirage.

His lips had touched a cheek, then travelled gently to a shoulder. He'd trembled as a finger traced the delicate curve of neck and one white breast.

Then he'd managed to pull himself together, stand stiffly erect, and brush the hair from his forehead. Her eyes had already closed again. As he went to his room, fatigue for the first time overcame him.

For an hour or two he slept heavily.

When he woke — still clothed and badly needing a wash and food, he could hear from the distance unmistakable sounds of Willie and the boy working in the yard.

He got up, mechanically performed the necessary ablutions, redressed, and went downstairs. Mrs Breame, who had kept something hot for him in the kitchen, told him Elfrida was still sleeping, the baby, Edward Saul, had been fed, and that the little girl was with the daily 'nurse' upstairs.

'She's a strong child, that one,' Mrs Breame said with grudging admiration, 'and quite a beauty.' She did not ask, 'What are you going to do with her? What place does she have here?' although it was on the tip of her tongue to do so.

Sensing her thoughts Ben decided honesty was the best policy.

'Lynette is my daughter,' he stated bluntly, 'and in future will be known as such. Her name at present happens to be

Penherrion, but as soon as possible I mean to have it legally changed to Curran.'

After the first shock the housekeeper gained composure. 'I thought that might be it,' she said. 'It's your affair of course. But there's bound to be gossip.'

'Gossip wears out,' Ben said. 'And if it doesn't I can shoulder it.'

'An' what about her — the "lady"—' slight hesitation on 'lady' — 'You brought back with you?'

'I hope to marry her in all good time.' Ben answered.

'I see.'

'I'm quite sure you don't; in any case there's no need for you to worry. Your position at Jacobs' is assured as long as you want it.'

He turned and was about to leave the kitchen, when he was reminded sharply that he hadn't eaten. He went back to the table, had a slice of ham, eggs, and hot coffee, then, with only a short thanks, went out through the back to the yard.

Willie was working on a memorial plaque. He had become an expert in lettering and finer script writing, which had proved of invaluable assistance to Ben. At the end of the yard was the great slab of greenish blue Connemare marble which was partially carved in the first primitive stages, depicting a woman and child — the proposed memorial to Maria.

Ben stared at it thoughtfully for a few moments, then marched straight past it to his office at the side.

He went to the table, studied the designs, and with a stab of discomforting truth recognised the stupidity — the ineffectual achievement such a project would be — simply a personal vain effort to erase past mistakes and his own conscience. At the time it had seemed right. But he had been wrong. Nothing could do that — nothing in the world. Neither did he need to; life was for the living and not the dead. The living! Preservation of Nature's domain and wild life of the moor! — this could be done.

In time he could acquire sufficient means to purchase more land above and joining Heronsmere estate, so that a domain could be established free of covetous men like that brute Henry Ashforth utilising it for his own gains. There could be a clear pool perhaps — a bird sanctuary! — once more his imagination was alight. He braced himself, left his shed, took Willie by the arm and led him to the great slab of blue marble.

'It's over, Willie,' he said.

'Over? What, surr? What, Mister Curran.'

'The statue. I've changed my mind. Break it up — smash it. And if you need help I'll give a hand. No wait! I'll have the first crack myself.'

The man gaped.

'Smash it? That — that fine stone—

Ben, if he heard, took no notice, but in a spurt of terrific energy set about the destruction of his own creation.

When, with the sweat streaming from his brow he felt satisfied, he threw tools and hammers down, and told Willie coolly, 'Get on with it now. Hack the rest into small pieces.'

'But Mr Curran, this is fine marble!'

'And it'll be put to good use. No arguing now. I know what I'm doing. You'll find out yourself later.'

'Hm!' obviously Willie considered the young master was demented, but the blue fiery light of Ben's eyes — the thrust of jaw and savage stance compelled him to obey, and Ben, satisfied, but with a perceptible ache in his muscles from the effort on top of his long gallop returned to the house.

His thoughts that day were mostly concerned in making plans for the future. Once an idea had taken root in his mind he was always impatient to put it into action. Willie's reference to waste of good marble was very far from the truth. Already he envisaged a whole new collection of smaller things — birds and mammals of the countryside carved by his own masterly hand — fox, badger, mouse, hedgehog, fish, heron — simple in design and line needing no embellishment or intricate detail, but contrived to reflect the shining quality of marble and stone and any material he worked with. As a child such subjects had been his inspiration. Now, with fame to back him, they could be masterpieces — Ben Curran's personal collections for galleries, and for dealers willing to

sell them. 'Curran's Curios'. Each one would be a work of art
— pricey, but not too dear for an enthusiast with reasonable
means to purchase. One day, when further fame had been
ensured through occasional larger commissions — every
small sculpture and minute carving might be regarded as a
treasure. But whatever their future in the annals of sculpture
— they would provide, surely, sufficient income for the
upkeep of his moorland reservation.

A dream?

Perhaps.

But without dreams his life would be a wasteland, with
nothing to give Elfrida. And he wanted everything of her and
for her now — her presence, her beauty and body, her trust,
and for her to see with his eyes as well as her own — as the
child did; her child and his, Lynette.

With a tiny niggle of guilt he remembered Edward Saul.

'How are they all?' he asked the housekeeper brusquely,
'Miss Penherrion? The baby? And young Lynette?'

'Miss Penherrion'll be down soon,' the woman told him.
'The baby's being fed, and the child Lynette—'

'I'm here,' a young voice cried.

She bounced into the room, with shining eyes, her dark
curls flying. Quite close to him she stood staring up into his
face.

'Hullo,' she said. 'Aren't you going to kiss me?'

He swept her into his arms, did as she asked and put her
down again.

'Have you seen your brother?'

'Oh yes. He's so tiny, isn't he? He pulled a face at me, and
he screamed.'

'I expect he'll pull many faces at you before long.' Ben told
her wryly. 'You'll have to help take care of him and teach him
to smile.'

She shrugged. 'I'll try. But he doesn't look the smiling kind
of baby.'

'He will, in time,' Ben answered. 'Now—' he paused before
continuing, 'you be good, I'll be back presently after I've seen
your mother—'

'You mean Aunt Elfrida!'

'Your *mother*,' Ben said sternly, 'so just remember that in future.'

Lynette pouted. 'All right, so long as you don't go all horrid, like — like—'

A sudden memory of Uncle Henry swept over her. Ben sensed it and took her hand. 'I'll never be horrid to you, pet, you're my own daughter and from now on I'm going to care for you like a proper father. But just be patient for a little, and when I come back I'll take you to my workshop and the yard, where I do my sculpture.'

Her face brightened. He patted her head, left the kitchens, and went upstairs to see Elfrida.

She was standing by the long mirror, putting the final pins into the coils of pale hair swept to the top of her head. She was wearing something blue and soft that emphasised the delicate complexion and slim yet luscious outlines of her figure.

He closed the door, and strode towards her, sweeping her up into his arms.

'I've wanted you so much—' he murmured gruffly, holding her close. 'For so many years. How many, Elfrida? Dreamed of you, longed for you, yet tried to get you out of my heart and blood. There were times even when a kind of hatred filled me because of the loss! — the waste of passion and love — the hours we would have had—' he broke off, to press his lips against her cheek. 'Do you understand?'

'Of course.'

'Life can be so irrational — and in the end, so short. If I'd not found you—'

'But you have. And we're here—' Through her tears she smiled.

He took her hand, gripping it so hard she winced.

'We'll be married just as soon as it can be arranged,' he said. 'I shall see about the licence today—'

'So soon?'

'The sooner the better. I'm not having you slip away again.'

'Me? but it was *you*. You, with your lofty ideas and statues — your tremendous ambitions—'

'Well, my love, those ambitions, as you call them, have provided the collateral to keep you here under lock and key if I have to — safe in your own home — at Jacobs'.'

'Safe?' She smiled. 'But are we the safe kind, Ben? Can you see us tied to this very respectable nice house and yard forever?' Her expression became enigmatic, far away.

His arm tightened round her waist, the ardent gaze of his eyes deepened with the bright sparkle of one setting out on an unknown exhilarating adventure when he answered, 'No, Elfrida — no, no, no. You're right. We'll start here, where the spreading roots are. But there'll be surprises all the way. I'll show you places you've never dreamed of — through the whole world — far-off spots with the name Ben Curran carved for all to see. You've set me alight again — understand? There's nothing we can't achieve together.'

'No, Ben. Nothing.' Her voice was hushed, the fey blue eyes filled with wonderment. 'And in the end we'll return. That will always be the same, won't it? Cornwall waiting, with the moor, and the children — ours!'

He murmured acquiescence, but said nothing at that point concerning his plans for the reserve and Curran Curios. Such things were for later. At the moment he was content to lose himself in the sweetness and beauty of her — the enchantment and allure that had been there from the very beginning — from the first moment he'd seen her, as a young boy, standing on the cliffs alone Hook's Cove, with her pale hair driven in a golden cloud by the wind, and the gorse flaming bright around her.

## 12

Elfrida and Ben were married quietly at Gwynck, on an
April day when warm sunlight spilled a film of gold over
Church and village. Willie was best man wearing a cut-
away black tailcoat, white waistcoat, neckcloth, and
drainpipe trousers — all hired from a male store in Truro.
His broad form and ruddy complexion retained their rustic
air, although everyone agreed he looked 'truly magnificent.'

Lynette, the one bridesmaid, appeared a striking young
figure in primrose yellow, with a wreath of flowers circling
her glossy dark curls.

The bride and groom of course were the centre of attention, and even the gossipmongers agreed that Martha Crane's
granddaughter had done well for herself, in spite of the past,
and had become a 'real beauty'.

Her dress was simple. White silk with a fitted bodice drawn
into a tiny waist. Her veil of white net, crowned by the traditional sprays of orange blossom, drifted gently in the wind
as she walked from the church to the carriage following the
ceremony, on her husband's arm.

Ben, smart, but quietly attired in black and grey, out of
respect partly, to the memory of Maria, was nevertheless a
striking looking young giant of a groom.

'Of course — 'tis rather early after his first wife's death to
be mated again,' one housewife whispered to another. 'Still
say what you like, there's sumthen' about a weddin' that lifts
the heart. An' after all — Ben Curran's a famous man now.
Different to the rest of us.'

And so it was.

When the small reception at the house was over, the sun,

though lower in the sky, was still bright and warm, and what wind there'd been had died.

In the bedroom, after holding his wife close for a few passionate moments, Ben said, 'Put on your cloak, my love, we've a tryst to keep.'

Wondering what he was up to, what new bewildering idea had suddenly seized him, Elfrida, after removing the wreath and veil did as he'd said.

A minute or two later, seated before him on his grey, they rode through the gates of the yard at the back, and took a moorland route past the outskirts of Truro, cutting from there to the right seawards, in the direction of the distant hills above Heronsmere. Not far from the patch of land acquired by Ben, they took a gentle curve downwards. The earth, pale green from springing young bracken was spattered with clumps of flaming gold gorse, and patches of thrusting blue-bells. Mingled with the scent of growing things was the faint tang of brine and heather.

When they reached a certain dip in the moor, Ben reined, lifted his bride from the horse, and tethered his mount to a sturdy blossoming May tree. Smiling, he strode back to Elfrida, and took her hands.

'It had to be here,' he said. 'Most folk will be expecting us to be on our way to some smart hotel with fine sheets, soft carpets and maids and waiters fussing round — gold taps and scented baths — wining and dining, and off every day to see the sights—'

He broke off, lifted his fine head to the dying sun, then laughed — not for fun, but for the sheer joy of being alive and having this lovely woman — his wife, beside him.

'Come, Elfrida,' he said. She reached out to him willingly. He removed her cape, then gently, with her help, unfastened the white dress and petticoats beneath.

When both were ready he eased her down into Nature's bed — the bed where they had first lain so many years ago. The heather and young ferns were sweet about them as he took her, in passion to his own wild heart. Did a lark or black-bird sing when her body flowered and opened to receive him? — Or was it only the murmur of a nearby brook, rippling over the stones? To Elfrida and Ben it was as though in that moment of culmination — of complete union — the whole earth and heavens rang with the glory of the ancient gods — of man's commitment to woman from earliest times.

Later, when they'd lain for a brief spell in peace, forgetful of past, present, or even the future ahead, they got up, dressed, and remounted the mare.

Below them — far below, it seemed — the dark shape of Heronsmere faded and was taken into a shroud of rising mist.

Marion had not attended the wedding, but both knew they had to return one day soon — not for their own pleasure, but as a gesture of reconciliation which might be effective eventually in removing any lingering bitterness and anguish of the past.

She sat waiting. A dark figure in a high backed chair of the front parlour, watching a brougham take a turn in the drive and draw up below the steps of the front entrance. The afternoon was grey, but pale watery beams of sunlight intermittently streaked the sky, fighting the thin features to brief clarity. The brown eyes were enigmatic, the once soft lips networked by tiny lines of strain. Yet her figure, from the slim waist, was held deliberately erect; her chin above the high neck of her black gown proudly set. The knuckles of the thin hand resting on the gold knobbed stick shone pale as pearl under the stretched skin. No one could have guessed what she was thinking, as the man, woman and child, dismounted from the carriage and climbed the steps; her attitude was motionless betraying no flicker of feeling.

Moments ticked by. There was the sound of footsteps and voices in the hall, followed by a light tap on the parlour door.

Marion's head turned slightly. 'Show them in, Jane,' she said. The maid left. A second later, Lynette, wearing a rose coloured muslin dress moved tentatively ahead of the others, stood for a second before the static form, smiled, then with a little rush went forward and planted a kiss on the woman's face.

'Hullo, Aunt Marion,' she said. 'We've come to see you —
all the way from — from—' She tore her gaze momentarily
from the tired face staring round the room she had once
known — the room which had seen so much happiness once,
then tragedy, fear and despair. She hadn't really wished to
accompany Ben and Elfrida when they suggested the visit.
But now, suddenly she was glad. This strange 'aunt' of hers
had been kind to her, although she'd always seemed old. And
in the end she'd been brave in sending 'Uncle Henry' away.
She'd been nice about Brownie too.

Brownie.

'Is he still there?' she asked in a sudden burst of expectancy.

Marion's expression momentarily darkened.

'Who, dear?'

Elfrida and Ben glanced at each other. Oh surely — surely
— the memory of Henry Ashforth wasn't going to rise again
and spoil things?

'Brownie,' the child said, 'the owl Moses looked after in the
summer house.'

Marion allowed a faint smile to curve her lips.

'I believe so,' she said, 'and I believe, too, there are others.
Brownie, you see, turned out to be a "she".'

Delight, like sunshine transfigured Lynette's whole being.
Any slight doubt there'd been in her mind concerning the
dark past was suddenly swept away. 'May I go and see them?'
She said breathlessly. 'I can, can't I? Moses will be there—?'

Marion nodded her head. 'I should think so. Yes — he's
somewhere in the garden. You run away and find him, and if
he's not about ask the boy. We've got a new one now, his
name's Pete. Say I sent you.'

Lynette skipped out. Ben and Elfrida went forward. And
after the first greeting, a silence which could have meant anything — happiness, relief, resentment, or mere surprise —
possessed the three of them.

Then Marion spoke.

'Bring your chairs up, both of you. My hearing isn't so
good these days, and I suppose you've come to — talk —
among other things.'

Seating herself beside her half sister, Elfrida replied quietly, 'Mostly those other things. Talking isn't always important. It's feelings that count in the end. And we — we both care about you—'

'Me?' An uncomely dry-as-dust spinster? — now!' lifting a hand, 'don't deny it, don't flatter and puff me up. I know what I am, and what I'll be in the future — an eccentric recluse living in this great lonely place until I die. It doesn't worry me at all, so please don't pity me. I've all I want, the mines are thriving. Families are employed again, so the upkeep of Heronsmere as it once was is no problem. However—' Her gaze strayed to Ben meaningfully. 'When that times comes, which I hardly think will be far ahead, you'll find I have left Heronsmere and the whole estate to you, Ben, since you, Elfrida legally renounced your share recently.'

'But—' Ben looked uncomfortable.

'Sh sh! no buts. There's a proviso. When I go, I wish the house to be demolished. In fact such is my strict command. It's a white — or perhaps one should say —a dark elephant that has outstayed its purpose, and left too many distasteful ghosts for anyone to inherit. The land though is good. Use it for any purpose you wish, Ben. Pasture — a Nature reserve — even for building again if you wish, but constructively to give pleasure and sanctuary for any who need it. Do you understand?'

Under her direct gaze, Ben could not hedge from the truth. 'Yes, and I'm grateful, although I didn't expect it.'

'No, I believe you. Why should you? Things didn't work out the way I meant. But then perhaps in most human lives they seldom do. The important thing now is your future and Elfrida's. I think I always knew you were meant for each other.' She sighed. 'I have of course, made certain personal bequests to the child and yourself, Elfrida. And there's a clause in my will to provide for Moses for the rest of his life. My treasures—' She eased herself up painfully with the aid of her stick, and shaking Ben's arm aside limped to a corner cupboard at the end of the room. She took out a sandalwood box engraved in mother-o'-pearl, carried it to the table, unlocked and opened it.

One by one she lifted a number of figurines and small carved animals out. Ben stared; they were so tiny — almost minute.

She held up the smallest of all — an applewood mouse with pointed nose raised enquiringly.

'For you, Ben,' she said. 'These were among the very first you made. I purchased them when you were a tiny boy if you remember. They should be of great value now. Take them. Before anything happens—'

'What should happen?' Elfrida interrupted sharply.

Marion regarded her quizzically.

'Life and death are unpredictable my dear, and one never knows what surprises are in store—' the statement held faint irony.

Ben in a burst of gratitude and feeling, was about to give her a dutiful peck on the cheek, when she straightened suddenly, briefly, and turned her face away.

'No caresses please,' she said shortly. 'Such kisses were never the kind I wanted from you, Ben. And now I want none at all. However — I am glad to feel you're happy, which is quite obvious. And now shall we all try and relax — with a sherry perhaps? And you can tell me all your plans.'

In relief Ben agreed.

The rest of the hour they spent together was spent mostly in a discussion of his career — the plans for establishing 'Curran Curios', and an important commission he'd recently been offered for a large sculptured figure at the entrance of an official building in Austria.

Marion professed interest, but by the time they left appeared to have become gradually more withdrawn and remote from human ties. A month later she died.

No tears were shed, no true regret felt, except by Moses who feared the end of an era had come. After the funeral, however, when the terms of the will were read, gratitude, with a flood of ambition, slowly spread through his burly frame and heart.

'I c'n still help you, Mr Curran surr,' he said after Ben's plans for the estate had been expressed. 'A keeper! that's

what I c'd be − kind of agent or general manager for this
here magnificent piece o' Cornish land − that is, if you want
me and feel I've the ability. It's what I believe in. Growing
things, and tending 'em. Animals. Hosses too. Maybe we c'ld
do a bit o' breedin'—'

He paused then added, 'I do b'lieve it's what she'd've had a
fancy for − Lady Marion − if anyone could've properly got
through to what lay inside her.'

'I'm sure of it,' Ben agreed.


Time passed. At the end of July, 1837, Ben was invited to
Belfield in Yorkshire, to discuss a monumental design
honouring Britain's recently crowned queen the young
Victoria. The statue was to be erected at the opening of a new
workhouse for the poor − a tribute from the city donated by
its Lord Mayor, Arthur Baltham.

The Baltham family were prominent mill-owners of great
wealth originally, self-made but now firmly established in
most governing bodies of the district, wielding considerable
influence in local affairs.

Arthur, as head of the clan, was openly but warily benevol-
ent, always ambitious, with an eye to further acclaim and
increasing power ahead. He was a portly pink-cheeked genial
figure, with a shrewd calculating mind behind the small
bright blue eyes. His mansion, situated on the moors, high
above the city, was large, square and granite-faced, the
exterior opulent with red plush, thick carpets, glass, silver
and all the ornamental trappings of the era.

His wife was set in the same sturdy mould. They had two
daughters, Carrie and Frances, both at an expensive finish-
ing school, and three sons, all of whom were destined to carry
on the family business.

The invitation to Ben and 'his lady' therefore was not to be
dismissed lightly. It would mean further recognition and
could be a challenge, because Ben guessed his own idea for
such a commission might deviate considerably from what
Arthur Baltham had in mind.

'Will you go?' Elfrida asked after studying the letter which was headed 'Grey Friars, Belfield', on ostentious gilt edged paper.

'*We*,' Ben reminded her, 'You're included,' He paused, throwing her a wry, slightly mischievous glance. 'I'm sure your presence would be quite — sensational. It might be worth it, even for that.'

'Be serious,' Elfrida told him. 'It's a good opportunity I suppose. For your work I mean. More fame.'

Ben's smile faded.

'It could be; if I do what I'm told and produce some vulgar sentimental edifice to suit Councillor Baltham's requirements.'

'It needn't be that. You don't *know*.'

'I can guess, I've met his type before.'

'You're very sure of yourself, Ben Curran.'

'Of course. Otherwise I wouldn't be where I am today.'

He made a sudden gesture, and drew her into his arms.

'Well, Elfrida? What do you say?'

Her delicate eyebrows rose in surprise.

'*Me?*'

He released her and shrugged. 'For once it's your choice. If you're against the idea say so, and to hell with ambition.'

She paused a moment before answering.

'Very well, let's take the trip. Probably I'll hate the place and the people will be rich bores. But there's just the chance I could be wrong. And if we refused I'd feel guilty — about holding you back.'

Ben's relief showed.

'Elfrida, I do love you.'

Her grey blue eyes, greenish in the mellow light of the sun, shone.

'You don't have to tell me, about Lynette though — she won't like it.'

'Then she'll have to learn to toe the line won't she? In any case I don't think you need worry. She's completely obsessed with young Edward Saul at the moment. He'll be shocked one day to find he's got such a bossy little madam of a sister.' Despite the light criticism, Ben's voice was warm, admiring.

A momentary shadow crossed Elfrida's face. 'He's such a *tiny* baby, Ben. We'll have to do all we can to see he develops in his own mould — his own personality I mean. I'm sure he'll be sensitive, and probably clever. But Lynette!' she sighed. 'We had tussles you know, it was never easygoing. She's a handful, Mrs Breame had to be very stern with her the other day. Oh I know you like to spoil her. But you mustn't — not too much. She's—'

'A chip off the old block, with a lot of you in it,' Ben interrupted. 'A free soul, and thank God for it.'

Elfrida didn't reply. In the pause following she thought, 'Yes. And a lot I wish wasn't there — memories of cruelty and terror, and dark bewilderment when I had to lie to her about that dreadful man — the man Marion killed. Because I was a bought woman. *Me* — her own mother.'

Involuntarily she must have shuddered, from a miasma of tormenting emotions, she tore herself to reality as Ben asked with a hint of anxiety, 'What's the matter? — Elfrida?' His voice sharpened.

She forced a smile, light, false, that didn't deceive him for a moment.

'Nothing. Except — I was just thinking back, you know — old ghosts.'

Deciding there would be no point in showing excessive affection just then, Ben replied a trifle brusquely. 'There mustn't be any from now on. Anyway—' more lightly, 'You'll find no "ghosts" in the Baltham menage. Of that I can assure you. I'm quite familiar with the breed. So cheer up my love, think of new clothes and frillies, and large meals of Yorkshire roast beef, steamed puddings and "by gum tha knows".'

'What do you want me to wear?' Elfrida asked pointedly.

'It doesn't matter to me. As little as possible I'd say, to ensure Baltham senior into accepting what I have to offer.'

She stared in astonishment.

'What do you mean?'

He laughed.

'All except *you*, naturally. If he attempted to put one

finger on your pretty shoulder, I'd knock him flat. I was talking about the monument.

'As you pointed out, it's a pretty important commission to aim for. But if I get to it will be on *my* terms. Understand? I'm not prepared to kow-tow to the ornate flowery sentimentality that already seems to herald the new age.'

'What do you mean? How do you know it will be like that?'

'Instinct,' Ben replied, 'a feeling, and the influence of that group in Rome — the German Nazarenes. It's getting a subtle hold here already, but with a difference — Michelangelo's genius won't hold sway forever. A new fashion's bound to get its grip on things and it'll probably mean a deterioration in art for a time—' He broke off, with his brow furrowed, his jaw set challengingly.'

Elfrida laughed. 'I don't know anything about groups and movements — only Curran curios and the things you do yourself — your own work. The living character of your animals and figures. They're enough for me. Well — I'm sure you're right, Ben, and I'll behave as elegantly as I can for the Yorkshire week-end. I shall be glad when it's over though. I'm not exactly adaptable by nature.'

'No.' He regarded her pointedly for a few moments, noticing once again the startling quality of her beauty emphasised so acutely by the dark blueish green dress she wore. Her silver-gold hair fell from a centre parting in soft curls to her shoulders. Though she was no slave to fashion — indeed had little knowledge of current styles — the effect was extremely up-to-date and similar to many depicted in the Bertarelle collection, Milan, including a portrait of the Archduchess Sophia.

A lump of emotion rendered him temporarily speechless.

'Well?' she queried, 'what's the matter? what are you staring at?'

'You.'

'Oh!' She glanced ruefully at the skirt of her simply-cut but charming gown. 'Don't worry, Ben dear, I'll do my best not to let you down — to look smart, I mean, and sophisticated. Maybe I'd better set a new hat — not too big though — one of those bonnet affairs can be pushed to the back comfortably, with not too many ribbons—?' she broke off questioningly.

'If you like,' Ben answered, 'Spend what you want, within reason. Whatever you wear you'll look — ravishing.'

'Thank you. But don't worry, I've got one dress stored away — for evenings — that should surprise you. And I shall travel in the velvet cloak.' She broke off suddenly, and in a spurt of emotion added, 'Oh Ben, how vain it all sounds. I'll do my best, honestly I will. But I'll be so glad when it's over.'

This was true; and when at the appointed time they set off by steam-train for the long and tedious two-day journey North, Elfrida was secretly envisaging their return. She had never travelled further afield than Exeter, and even there she'd felt an alien in a strange land. However, in her carefully selected attire, and with a growing sense of the importance of the event, excitement rose in her. She was, after all, not only a lovely woman, but the wife of an important and already famous sculptor. Who could be anything but impressed by their appearance? Ben looked so imposing in his waisted thigh length frac and embroidered silk waistcoat which was buttoned to the top, and had large lapels. His long trousers fitting at the ankles, covered the heels of his shoes held by straps, and to complete the effect he wore a tall silk hat.

It was late evening when they reached Belfield. Summer dusk had already deepened to night, and Elfrida, suddenly tired, was bewildered by the crowds of scurrying porters and passengers — by the shadows, curling smoke of the trains, and lights streaming through blurred steam and fog.

The Baltham tandem was waiting for them outside the station. Through a kind of dream the clip-clop of horses' hooves echoed in her ears as the carriage passed down streets of darkly silhouetted buildings, where other vehicles crawled cautiously round misted corners, eventually leaving the crowds of pedestrians and cabs behind. The fog had lifted considerably when they reached the outskirts of the city, and a watery moon was already rising behind the film of cloud. Relaxing more comfortably, Elfrida saw that they were gradually climbing towards a darkened stretch of hills. Hills that could have been Cornwall in the distance, but with a subtle difference. There was no scent or suggestion of sea in the air, only a chill dampness that increased the higher they went and a grim occasional glance of isolated industrial buildings. Her first impression was of hostility. Ben sensed it, and squeezed her hand under the rug. 'Cheer up,' he said. Once you get a good look in daylight I expect you'll like it. And don't have nerves about the Balthams. What I said about them may not be at all true. Yorkshire people are supposed to be kindly – especially the women. A race on their own, in a way – warm-hearted but filled with guts and determination.' He paused, then whispered, 'You'll be a match for any one of them.'

Ben's prophecy concerning Matilda Baltham proved to be apt. Her stoutish well-corseted figure exuded warmth, and everything possible was done to make the travellers fell at ease and comfortable.

The bedroom was immense, with a large fire glowing in the grate. Solid mahogany furniture was given an air of elegance by the massive canopied bed and satin drapes. Lamplight glittered on silver toilet accessories put ready for use, and extra candles flickered on either side of the dressing table.

The gold and pink wall-paper gave an effect of thickly entwined roses. Red velvet curtains had been pulled over the blinds of the two large bay windows so no chill breath of night air penetrated the warmth. Elfrida found the heat at first overwhelming, and the scent of flowers from a crystal vase slightly sickening. But when she'd washed, changed her travelling clothes, and could relax before going down to a late dinner, her natural radiance returned.

She smiled brightly at Ben. 'I shall just wear my simple grey dress tonight,' she said brightly, 'with that new shawl you gave me. Tomorrow I'll surprise them – and you.'

Once again Ben marvelled at her good taste.

As he'd predicted, the meal was lavish and sumptuously served. But there was no remonstrance on Matilda's part when Elfrida asked for only small portions of fish, duck, and fruit pie.

'I understand, my dear,' she said, with her ringlets of dar
curls bobbing under her lace cap. 'We northerners have bi
appetites — bred to them I suppose, through climbing a
these great hills. I s'pose it's different in Cornwall.'

Elfrida smiled. 'Oh we have hills there too. But no moun
tains really. Just one — Brown Willy.'

'Brown Willy?' The plump bosom heaved, a deep rumbl
of amusement shook the stretched purple bodice. 'I like th
name, original; jolly somehow, like my Arthur.' He
travelling dark eyes strayed benevolently to the shrewd smal
blue ones of her spouse.

Elfrida smiled. The smile could have meant anything, bu
Matilda took it as agreement. Inwardly Elfrida was picturin
the rugged lump of Bodmin moor — its aloof wilderness o
shadows and mystery, and further south, of the gaunt coast
line beyone Heronsmere and certain things she wanted t
forget.

She managed quickly to dispel her brief retrospection a
the meal was concluded on a wave of conviviality.

That night, as Elfrida lay in Ben's arms following a passion
ate yet gentle coming-together, he whispered, 'You wer
wonderful darling.'

'What at? Socialising? Or — this?' Her voice was tranqui
but teasing.

'Both. But this most of all. This — and this — and this!'

His lips travelled ardently from hers, down her rounded
soft throat and one shoulder, kissing both breasts in turn.

She snuggled closer. Easing himself up slightly, he saw tha
she was on the verge of sleep. Very quietly he lay back, and
minutes later only the ticking of the clock, the intermitten
calling of an owl from outside and the rhthmic sound of thei
own breathing could be heard.

The next morning Matilda took Elfrida on a tour by carriage
of the adjoining countryside which appeared quite magnifi
cent in the light of an unclouded summer day. The hills,
though bleak, were tipped with gold. From a wooded valley
the towers of an ancient Abbey rose majestically beside the

glitter of a winding river. To the North the smoke of mills and the thriving city shadowed stark realism to clouded grey.

'That's the busy part,' Matilda told Matilda proudly. 'My Arthur's responsible for a deal of Belfield's prosperity.' She did not add — perhaps she didn't even know — that the so-called prosperity was largely due to small wages paid to mill workers who had to slave for six days a week at looms, very often under strict discipline for sixteen or eighteen hours a day, whistling or singing during working time was banned, and punishable by fines. Women and children were employed at even lower payment. Conditions of unemployment were often hot and unhealthy, causing sickness through lack of light and good air. Yet Matilda only envisaged her spouse as benefactor to the town and his own workers.

She expressed her confidence more than once to Elfrida, and later, following the short drive when she showed her guest over the austere and well kept gardens, confessed that if anyone in the district deserved royal acclaim and a knight-hood, it was her husband, Arthur Baltham.

'And it's a grand idea,' she said, 'that when the time comes you good men will have pride in it too. Aye. That's a gradely thought — to have the Curran name included. Do you realise, lass, what an honour Arthur's giving him in letting him do the monument?'

Elfrida smiled.

'We don't *know* do we?'

'Know what, love?' Matilda sounded faintly shocked.

'Whether your husband — Mr Baltham, will like Ben's ideas of design. Ben's an original. I mean — he's got strong ideas about art; there's nothing traditional about him.'

'Hm. Tradition's only made in the present,' Matilda retorted with surprising acumen. 'The work of today's the fruit of tomorrow, that's what I reckon. And my Arthur and your Ben are two of a kind, or you and him wouldn't have been asked here in t'first place. Understand?'

'Yes, of course,' Elfrida answered passively, yet inwardly extremely doubtful of the two men ever coming to agreement.

In the meantime, while Matilda and Elfrida idly inspected
terraces, rose gardens and a number of greenhouses and a
vast conservatory, Ben was being escorted first round the
Baltham Mills, which he found a depressing business, then
taken to the site of the new Work House which was to be
named the 'Baltham Refuge for the Poor'.

There were yet no 'residents' installed, but his natural
insight and sensitivity to the feelings of the defenceless,
already clouded his mind with a picture of hopeless servitude
– of humanity's victims dragging out their lives scrubbing
the sterile corridors to give an impression of cleanliness and
well-being to any influential visitors – of children being
dragged up without food, and stern guardianship of bodies
and spirit so no individual thought or complaint could reach
the ears of 'the Board'.

Board meetings would be hypocritical affairs of mutual
admiration and 'back-slapping', of praise for the worthy
work done.

Ben's emotions churned. How could he design a sculpture
for such a place? Mastering the dictates of his own imagination however, he remained silent and outwardly unmoved.

'Well?' Baltham enquired, when the inspection was concluded, 'you know now the size of the place; it's been a grand
undertaking, and it needs a fine statue to show the stuff Belfield's made of. Aye. And under my name, so the Baltham
family will be remembered and respected in years to come.
There are many masons who'd give all they've got to be in your
shoes, young man. But I don't want a mason – I want a sculptor. *You*. Think you can do it? Later this year, or next, our new
young queen may come and admire. That'll be a fine occasion.
My Matilda's already looking forward to it.' He paused, continuing after a moment or two, '—come on lad, out with it.'

'I must consider,' Ben said cautiously.

'No games now. The price I'm willing to pay is surely
generous. I shouldn't have thought a young man starting on a
brilliant career like you could afford to ignore the chance—'
he broke off, frowning, 'What's the matter? Isn't the brass
enough?'

Good heavens, Ben told himself inwardly, it was more than he'd dreamed of when the project was first suggested, and a year ago he'd not have hesitated. Above everything else he'd envisaged power in his fist — power and wealth to put his stamp on the world. Now he was changed. Fame itself was not sufficient. A sense of values had deepened and spread in him. And there was Elfrida. Elfrida justified not only the assurance of his name and body, but the whole of himself — the heart.

Still, in the end everything depended on whether Arthur Baltham accepted the designs he'd brought with him.

He did not.

That same day, following a lavish lunch, the two men returned to the library, where, over vintage brandy and cigars, Ben opened his portfolio containing primary sketches for the sculpture.

They were stark in simplicity, without sentiment or glorification of current society. They represented in fact, a challenge to life that left Baltham aghast with indignation.

'*Those?*' he said, inevitably throwing each one down, 'But they're — they're ugly, degrading—'

'So is poverty,' Ben said cuttingly. 'Shouldn't that be the aim? Realism — to give the truth?' The narrowed ice-blue eyes, the sardonic tones, sent a wave of hot blood coursing through the other man's veins. His cheeks seemed briefly to swell.

'I don't know what you think you're doing,' Baltham answered, 'nor why you've come in the first place if this sort of stuff — muck — is all you've got to offer. *Why?* damn you. What's the idea? To insult me?'

'Certainly not, sir. I've no grudge against you, I don't really know you, nor you me. You asked me to your home for a discussion about your — product. We don't agree, that's all. I don't believe in idealising sickness and poverty, or placing pretty posies at the feet of despair for the sake of power. About your aims — your own personal ambitions, I may be wrong. If so, my apologies. But I'm seldom wrong in my own creations. I fail sometimes, we all do. But that edifice of a workhouse! — I couldn't glorify it in *your* way. I really couldn't.'

The explosion that followed was inevitable, with the result that Ben and Elfrida left shortly afterwards for Belfield Station and the train for the beginning of their journey back to Cornwall.

'And I never even wore my new dress,' Elfrida said, with a sigh, as they steamed out of the station. 'I so wanted to stagger you.' She leaned her head on his shoulder, continuing after a pause. 'Not that I mind. It will do for later. Anyway — I'm glad, no — *relieved* — to be leaving. I'm sorry — for you, about the fame, and the money. It would have been a lot, wouldn't it?'

'Yes.'

She glanced up. 'And you don't really mind?'

'I'm not the kind of man to like throwing any good chance away. But this one was just the sort of thing I couldn't stomach. Anyway my intuition was proved right. And I've a hunch Arthur Baltham will find his "yes man" pretty easily — someone who'll give him the push necessary for the knighthood he's aiming for.'

'Knighthood? Is that the idea?'

'Of course. Something not too difficult to obtain, with sufficient "brass" as they call it — to squander on good deeds and publicity.'

Elfrida sighed. 'Sometimes you do sound rather cynical, Ben.'

'No, realistic, that's all. Except when I look at you of course. Then the rest of the world can go hang.'

'That's another thing.' Her brief smile died.

'What?'

'The way you can charm, and turn on the flattery just when you feel like it.'

His whole face suddenly softened.

'I never have to with you, Elfrida. To me you hold the wonder of everything, and always will.'

Through the train's misted smoke and flickering light, her face seemed to radiate all the meaning, beauty, and promise of what he'd sought for since early youth — the shining elusive quality of pools and sea-washed pebbles under the morning sky — the haunting beauty of Cornish headlands rising mist-wreathed from the water, and wide stretches of heathered moors fading rosy pink under the setting sun. Above the mechanical motion of rattling wheels, he could hear, in imagination, the cry of gulls and curlew, knowing with certainty that whatever shocks, triumph and failures lay ahead — the best was always there, waiting. Achievement might not always come, but there need be no end in aiming for it. This was what mattered. Values.

Unconsciously whispered words left his lips — words he'd learned from an old book in early youth — a book lent to him by Marion.

'This above all: to thine own self be true. Thou canst not then be false to any man—'

'What did you say?' Elfrida enquired quietly.

He smiled reminiscently.

'Oh — just something written long ago by a very good poet,' he answered. 'Simple, like most good things, but so true.'

Her sleepy eyes looked a trifle bewildered. He slipped an arm round her shoulders. 'Try and doze, love,' he told her. 'We've a devil of a long journey ahead.'

A moment later he saw with relief that her eyes had closed, and presently he too was drifting into periods of intermittent sleep.

# Epilogue

Lynette stood on the high ridge of moor near the carn. A fresh wind was blowing, spreading her dark curls wild in the Autumn sunlight. To her right, and at intervals over the valley, smoke of mines working merged into the rhythmic motion of pumping rods against the sky. But near and round her the smell of crisp brown heather, tumbled blackberries and leaves was rich and strong in her nostrils, pungent with the season's change, sending a wild delight through her veins.

She lifted her arms wide, while her heart cried, 'I want everything there is in the world to feel and hold and love — everything, *everything*. I want to race, and run, and sing and jump — and — and have adventures, knowing the real things — the sea and the clouds and what the wind calls through the heather. And people too, and strange lands far away — but most of all to be myself — *me*! Lynette Curran.'

She paused a moment caught up by the first true awareness of life and the mysterious exhilaration of the unknown future.

Then, suddenly, she started running. Not to Heronsmere the dead deserted relic down the slope — but along the rim of the moor, to a secret shining pool where she'd first seen an otter by a nearby stream. Perhaps it would be there today. Perhaps. And like Brownie's owlets there might be others. Young wild things thriving in this lovely remote land she loved so much.

Sure enough the otter was there when she arrived, sleek and shining with nose and paws up. Watching.

'Wait—' she cried. 'Please wait a moment. It's me — Lynette.'

But the otter, whiskers quivering, made a sleek dive into the pool spreading a rim of shining bubbles all around.

Lynette laughed.

'All right. I don't care,I'm like you too. Free — free.'

She turned and ran back, full of delight, towards the Curran cottage, where Ben and Elfrida waited with her grandfather, before making their way back to Gwynck.

*You'll never feel closer to your dreams*

a ravishing new novel by

# Caroline Gray

Orphaned, penniless, destitute, Wilhelmina Doberley arrives in New York armed only with an aching ambition to make her dreams come true.

Dreams that seem a million miles away when she starts work as a lowly chambermaid in the spell-bindingly glamorous Hotel Superb. There she discovers a world of champagne and oysters, ease and elegance – a far cry from her own life of drudge and poverty.

But Wilhelmina is determined to succeed. And when the outrageously attractive heir to the Superb begins to fall for her beauty, she knows where her destiny lies . . .

**GENERAL FICTION    0 7221 41041    £2.95**

*Also by Caroline Gray in Sphere Books: FIRST CLASS*

# A selection of bestsellers from SPHERE

## FICTION

| | | |
|---|---|---|
| HUSBANDS AND LOVERS | Ruth Harris | £2.95 ☐ |
| SWITCH | William Bayer | £2.50 ☐ |
| VITAL SIGNS | Barbara Wood | £2.95 ☐ |
| THE ZURICH NUMBERS | Bill Granger | £2.75 ☐ |

## FILM & TV TIE-INS

| | | |
|---|---|---|
| BOON | Anthony Masters | £2.50 ☐ |
| LADY JANE | Anthony Smith | £1.95 ☐ |

## NON-FICTION

| | | |
|---|---|---|
| LET'S FACE IT | Christine Piff | £2.50 ☐ |
| A QUIET YEAR | Derek Tangye | £2.50 ☐ |
| THE 1986 FAMILY WELCOME GUIDE | | |
| | Jill Foster & Malcolm Hamer | £4.95 ☐ |
| THE ABSOLUTELY ESSENTIAL | | |
| GUIDE TO LONDON | David Benedictus | £4.95 ☐ |

*All Sphere books are available at your local bookshop or newsagent, or can be ordered direct from the publisher. Just tick the titles you want and fill in the form below.*

Name _____

Address _____

_____

Write to Sphere Books, Cash Sales Department, P.O. Box 11, Falmouth, Cornwall TR10 9EN

Please enclose a cheque or postal order to the value of the cover price plus:

UK: 55p for the first book, 22p for the second book and 14p for each additional book ordered to a maximum charge of £1.75.

OVERSEAS: £1.00 for the first book plus 25p per copy for each additional book.

BFPO & EIRE: 55p for the first book, 22p for the second book plus 14p per copy for the next 7 books, thereafter 8p per book.

*Sphere Books reserve the right to show new retail prices on covers which may differ from those previously advertised in the text or elsewhere, and to increase postal rates in accordance with the PO.*